Cares of a Wandering Boy

Cares of a Wandering Boy

Will Lupens

EVIL UNCLE PRESS • SOMERVILLE, MASSACHUSETTS

© 2018 by Will Lupens
All rights reserved

This is a work of fiction. Names, characters, places and incidents are the product of the author's imagination or are used ficticiously. Any similarity to actual persons, living or dead, business establishments, events or locales is entirely coincidental.

Cover photo © John Chervinsky

Designed & set in Fournier at Evil Uncle Press
Printed & bound by Country Press, Lakeville, Massachusetts

ISBN: 978-0-692-06260-9

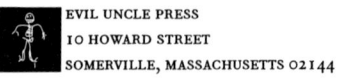
EVIL UNCLE PRESS
10 HOWARD STREET
SOMERVILLE, MASSACHUSETTS 02144

for Judi Rae Breuner

The heart needs a kindred, familiar heart, like a little clearing in the forest, a place to rest and lie down and chat.
—*Robert Walser*

The Plan

It's funny sometimes, the difference between what we *should* do and what we actually do. Like when I finally found Gordon, wandering beneath the blazing afternoon sun, pushing a wobbly shopping cart through the crowded parking lot. Instead of going to his aid right away, as I should have, I stood a short distance off and watched him, lurching from car to car, muttering to himself as he pressed his face against the rolled-up windows, scanning the empty interiors in search of God-knows-what.

The most troubling thing about these increasingly frequent episodes of his is the fact that I have no idea what he's thinking, what he's feeling, whether, at such moments, he is even *him*. As hard as it is for me to witness his distress, my upbringing compels me to reason my way through it, to try and understand the thing hijacking his brain, the thing that allows him to superimpose his increasingly broken inner world over the one we've always shared.

Gordon himself taught me that understanding begins with observation. So I observed, collecting data when I probably should have been helping. Instead of feeling guilty as I watched him, though, I felt calm and detached, almost scientific. What did I learn? The subject of my gaze was more than a little confused. He appeared to be hallucinating. Nothing I didn't already know. What was new was the unshakable feeling that this person, interrogating parked cars, waylaying the bewildered people who occasionally walked past him, was simultaneously my father *and* someone else. Some other thing, almost, something completely alien.

I continued to follow this wayward Gordon around the parking lot, careful to stay just out of his line of sight. He was growing increasingly agitated, distraught almost. With each empty vehicle his muttering grew louder, his hands balling into fists and shaking at his sides. I could see sweat glistening on the nape of his neck, trickling down the side of his face and disappearing into his beard. The fringes of his shaggy salt-and-pepper hair were damp, his shirt stuck to his skin.

I was sweating too. It was hot outside, ninety at least, and there wasn't a cloud in the sky. I knew the combination of heat and time of day were not exactly ideal for Gordon's state of mind, but still I watched. I wiped away a bead of sweat snaking its way into my eye, even as Gordon made a sudden beeline for a car pulling into a spot about twenty yards away from him.

I should have set off on an immediate intercept course, but for some reason I just stood there, watching. By the time I finally reacted and moved to intervene, he had already corralled the driver, a middle-aged woman with fluffy, pinkish hair, as she climbed out of her seat. Strategically wedging his shopping cart between the open door and the side of the car, Gordon prevented the woman from getting past him or retreating to the safety of the car's interior. In her initial alarm, she actually smiled at him, which seemed strange. Gordon's shaking fists were now turning tight circles in the air in front of him, and the woman pulled as far back from him as she could, drawing in a deep breath as she did so. Certain that she was about to yell for help, I readied myself for the uncomfortable scene that was sure to follow, for the effort that would be required to extricate Gordon from it and get him to our van, parked on the other side of the lot. I prayed (nothing spiritual, just a simple acknowledgment of my helplessness) that we would be able to get out of there before the incident turned into actual trouble.

By the time I got within fifteen feet of them, however, something had changed. I slowed to a walk and then stopped, as I saw the expression on her face pass from a kind of fearful giddiness to something that was almost motherly. Although it was clear she still had no idea what was going on, she now seemed to believe that she was not in any real danger. Her head tilted a little to one side and her face assumed a concerned expression, her eyes betraying an unmistakable look of sympathy. She pushed the cart gently aside and straightened from the awkward crouch Gordon's maneuver had forced her into. I was not surprised to see her reach out and put her hand on his forearm, as if to reassure him.

From these signs I knew that he was speaking to her. There is nothing quite like Gordon's voice. Soft and low, like the buzzing of a beehive, it's remarkable enough for its sound alone. But there's more to it than that. The words articulated in this voice are well chosen and precise, rational without being sterile, delivered in a steady but unhurried stream. The overall effect is kind of hypnotic. I wouldn't be surprised to discover that a person's heart rate lowers when listening to him. Thanks to its soothing quality, as well as its stark contrast to his slightly intimidating physical appearance, Gordon's voice has a strangely mollifying effect on people, disarming them, causing them to drop, or at least suspend, their natural inclination to prejudice. Using his voice alone, he is able to get people to do something they rarely do: listen.

If the change in the woman's body language was not evidence enough, I knew for certain he was speaking to her when I saw him lower his chin toward his chest, it being important to Gordon to look directly into the eyes of his companion. When that person happened to be shorter he would tilt his head forward and down until their eyes were level. Apart from simply establishing a kind of visual common ground, this bowing of the head also made him seem reverent, almost holy.

It's one of the most surprising parts about this whole thing: the fact that Gordon can still give off an air of dignity, even when he's temporarily out of his mind. When he's alone—that is, when he's just with me—whether having a bad dream in the middle of the night or hallucinating on a street corner in broad daylight, his voice often becomes imprecise and threatening, as it had been moments before, when he was finding only empty cars. In the presence of strangers, however, he somehow manages to marshal some portion of his true self. It's almost like there's a connection between his innate sense of manners and the gentle qualities of his voice.

The hot summer air was still, the usual sounds of mid-day conspicuously absent. Sure enough, as I made my way slowly toward Gordon and his prisoner, I could hear the sound of his voice. I picked up not only the usual deep hum, but also the hint of something else. A new tone, mixed in with the familiar: something plaintive, almost desperate. I was glad to be standing behind him, and so prevented from seeing his face and the expression of utter confusion I knew to be etched on it.

I stopped again as I made out his words.

"Where is my son?" he all but moaned. "Where is Kai? What have you done with him, you people? It's not safe here, dammit! It's not safe for him, he'll be lost without me! Where have you put him? Where is Kai?!"

I stood there, slightly off balance, while Gordon repeated

his questions. Finally, I came to my senses and intervened, taking him by the shoulders, apologizing profusely to the woman as I did so. She didn't say anything. She just flashed a nervous, uncertain smile. She felt bad for Gordon, that much was clear, but I could also tell she was profoundly relieved to be delivered from her strange situation.

I pointed Gordon in the direction of our van, herding him along as gently as I could. He twisted his head around in a series of short, artificial jerks, as if his neck worked by way of poorly matched cogwheels. He looked at me from miles away, a confused frown on his face. Part of him seemed to recognize me, even as the rest clearly wondered who this person was who dared to interrupt his search for his son. He became more docile as we marched along however, and by the time I helped him into the passenger seat, placing my hand on top of his head to keep him from bumping it on the doorframe, he was practically inert. He sat meekly in his seat, unblinking, staring straight ahead into nothing, as I pulled his belt across his chest and fastened it.

I started up the van and drove across the parking lot toward the exit. Once there, we sat with the engine idling for what seemed an eternity, since I couldn't make up my mind which way to go. Nudged into action by the angry honking of the car behind us, I stepped on the gas, cranking the steering wheel to the right and jerking the van out onto the boulevard. I drove around without the slightest idea of where I was going, wondering if maybe the whole situation was already beyond my ability to control, and trying not to think about the fact that Kai is not my name.

My name is Samuel P. Furlong. I am fourteen years old. I have read somewhere in the neighborhood of five hundred books. I use words like *pathology* and *incongruous* and *mollify*. I am opinionated, but not dogmatic. I drive a van.

I know. It sounds farfetched: a well-read fourteen-year-old with a healthy vocabulary. But who's to say what a fourteen-year-old human being is capable of, what that human can and cannot do? Think of Avicenna. By the time he was fourteen, he had committed the whole of Aristotle's *Metaphysics* to memory. Or Albrecht Dürer, who was already a master draftsman at fourteen. Bobby Fisher was Chess Champion of the United States. Norbert Wiener, the father of cybernetics, was a graduate student at Harvard.

I'm not claiming to be some sort of prodigy, like Avicenna or Fisher. I'm not even claiming to be anything special. Far from it. To myself I seem pretty much normal (and really, how could it be otherwise?). I am what I am, I know what I know. "A regular Joe," as Gordon says. My point is simply that there's no reason to put limits on what we think a person is capable of just because they happen to be fourteen. If we can accept the idea of a fourteen-year-old Norbert Wiener sitting in a graduate seminar at Harvard (and we have to, because it actually happened), then certainly we can accept the possibility of a fourteen-year-old who thinks the occasional big thought driving around in a Volkswagen Vanagon and narrating his own story.

I am what I am and I know what I know. A pretty inane statement, when you think about it. At the very least, it begs the question: How did I get to *be* what I am, how have I come to *know* what I know?

My first thought is to explain myself by way of the nature/nurture dichotomy and say that I am a combination of the two, a peculiar mix of chromosomes and circumstance. But this would be problematic for a couple of reasons. First of all, since the same thing could be said about anyone, it doesn't actually say anything about me. Second, I'm not sure I believe it. The nature versus nurture thing, I mean. Gordon, of course, would point out that since there's no way to "maintain a rigorous distinction" between the two, they can't really be used to understand something, especially something as complicated as a person. "Just another unnecessary semantic division, preventing us from seeing the bigger picture." That's what he'd say. And then there's the fact that I don't know nearly enough about chromosomes to be tossing them about in casual conversation. I know that human beings have forty-six of them (ideally) in every cell, that each chromosome contains thousands of genes, and that each gene is made up of tens or hundreds of thousands of nucleotide base pairs. That's it. That's all I know on the subject. And it's not really knowledge, since I have no idea what it actually means. I just read it in a book. Anyway, if you wanted to truly explain someone based on *nature*, you would need accurate descriptions of a hundred thousand different genes. As for *nurture*, if you take that to mean the sum total of all the environmental variables a person has experienced since they were born, well, good luck with that.

In a lot of ways I'm a copy of Gordon. We see things the same way, we react to things in the same way, we understand each other. We're both right handed. We have the same prominent ears, the same small mouth, the same natural right-side part to our hair (though obviously I don't have any gray yet). We have the same slow, wandering gait, a style of walking Gordon calls "non-linear." We display a lot of the same mannerisms and use the same figures of speech. The fact is, I'm not just a physical copy of Gordon; I also *copy* Gordon. What can I say? For as long as I can remember, I have found him fascinating. Endlessly fascinating. To look at, to listen to, to (attempt to) fathom. He has a pretty unique take on life and how to live it. As the person solely responsible for my upbringing, it's only natural that his way of life, the way he goes about it, should become my own.

So. I'm a copy that also copies. Which is another way of saying "combination of nature and nurture." But while that might account for certain physical characteristics and gestures, it doesn't explain the way I think, the way I speak, the stream of words running endlessly through my brain, my *non-adolescent* diction. Mostly, I think, it's just a question of aptitude. Everyone has an aptitude for something, something they're naturally good at. Some people can draw, some people are athletic, some people are good at working with their hands. I seem to have an aptitude for language, especially where the written word is concerned.

I can't remember ever being unable to read. Gordon says I started reading at the age of three, which seems early to me. I just picked up a book and started reading, without any guidance or instruction (though here, too, I was probably just emulating something I had seen Gordon do a hundred times). More importantly, I can't remember ever having trouble understanding what I read. That's the key thing. According to Gordon, I have "a knack for context."

Context, as everyone knows, refers to the way the words of a sentence inform each other, how they work together to generate that sentence's meaning. It's also one of the primary means of acquiring vocabulary. When you come across a word you've never seen before, you can usually figure out what it means just by the context given to it by the words around it (so long as you also know what they mean). In this way, using the words you already know to decipher new ones, and so on, it's possible to build a pretty decent vocabulary, without ever using a dictionary or asking someone for help.

Of course, having a *knack* doesn't mean I always get things right, especially when it comes to pronunciation. Like the time I pronounced the word "chaos" in a way that rhymed with "house." For some reason, Gordon, who often lets me screw things up for a while before correcting me, derived particular enjoyment from that one. I can't tell you how long he let me walk around, spouting off about how order slowly emerged from the surrounding "chowse" that existed at the beginning of the universe. And he almost wet himself the first time I dropped the word "menopause" in conversation, mistaking it for a form of genuflection.

A knack for context, then. What else? Well, I would also seem to be a natural mimic of accents. Not verbal accents (that would be Gordon, who can imitate pretty much any voice), but what you might call *written accents*. Context aside, there's usually a dozen different ways to say the same thing. Different people, by which I mean different writers, each have their own way of expressing things. Writing styles, basically. I tend to be easily influenced by writing styles. Over time, I have come to incorporate them into my own way of thinking and speaking.

By "easily influenced," what I really mean is obsessively influenced. When I was little, before I had absorbed enough to create my own personal catchall style, I pretty much walked around parroting whatever I happened to be reading at the time. Gordon endured a lot in those early days. My Fenimore Cooper jag, for example. And my Dickens jag. And, especially, my Tolkien jag (the only time he ever betrayed the slightest impulse to throttle me was near the end of that two-month period). However much my behavior sometimes irked him, Gordon always allowed me to follow my inclinations, to say and think what I liked, to be myself. To him, it's only natural that a person should "speak his mind." By which he means not so much that you should say whatever you want, as that the way you speak should echo the way you think. In this regard, it also helps that I have no peers around to speak of, no other kids to make fun of me for "talking funny," to force me over to the dark side of language, to the tedious realm of lazy contractions and affected indifference and never speaking your mind.

Of course, a knack for context and the ability to mimic writing styles would not count for much in the absence of books. It turns out that my own aptitude could only have become apparent through reading. When you read, and your mind is open to what you read, you learn. What you learn can be applied to further reading and so on, in an ever-expanding way. Since this process—which I think nicely describes my inner development, requires books—you could rightly say that I would not be the person I am, were it not for books.

Which brings us to what you might call the fortunate and primary accident of my environment: I have grown up in libraries.

When I say that I have grown up in libraries, I don't mean it metaphorically, as in, "I've spent a lot of time in libraries." I mean it quite literally.

In the same way that other people grow up in houses and neighborhoods and schools, I have grown up in libraries. To be sure, I have also spent plenty of time in motels and vans, but that's pretty much just for sleeping and getting around. I have spent a greater portion of my life in libraries than anywhere else. Libraries are my home: small town libraries, big city libraries, university libraries, bookstores new and used, flea market bookstalls. To Gordon and me, they are all manifestations of home, of what we like to call *the library*, which exists wherever you find a shelf of books. My home then, is sort of an idea, like the idea of the library in those Borges stories Gordon used to read to me.

An endless home, when you think about it. Infinite, like the sea. And just like a fish in the sea, I am at one with the library. The shelves are my water, the books my plankton. This at-homeness in the library is partly due to the fact that, just as

I can't remember a time before I could walk, or read, I can't remember not understanding the Dewey Decimal System. Not the inner logic of its categories, of course; just the function of it, the nature of its arrangement. Armed only with my index fingers, I can stroll up to the card catalogue (or microfiche reader or computer) of any library and walk away minutes later with the information necessary to retrieve a whole day's worth of books. Unlike the uniform watery world of dolphins and fishes and crustaceans, thanks to Dewey my ocean home has streets and neighborhoods, with parks and cathedrals and sports arenas and schools, all mapped out in the most orderly way and laid at my fingertips.

As for schools, I should acknowledge here and now that I don't go to one. Truth be told, I've never set foot in a classroom. Which is not to say that I'm home-schooled. At least, not in the way people normally think of it. Gordon has never sat down with me in a structured sort of way, teaching me according to some standard curriculum, keeping me up to grade level along the way. He *has* taught me, of course, in his own unique manner, and it is mostly thanks to this "teaching" that I can claim to possess what you might call a *general knowledge* of the world.

Gordon's approach is based on understanding and expectation. He calls it "aleatory learning" or "purposeful meandering." Taking into account my native abilities, especially my knack for understanding a lot of what I read, he simply makes what you might call *recommendations*. For example, one time when we were out hiking, talking about things in general, I stumbled onto the notion that it didn't seem fair that good people sometimes suffered while bad people often seemed to live a charmed life. "Ah," Gordon said, quickening his pace. "Theodicy."

"Thee-odd-a-what?" I asked, scurrying along the trail in an effort to keep up with him.

"*Theodicy.* The philosophical or theological examination of the problem of evil. Part of a centuries-old debate in the history of religion and philosophy. Leibniz devoted a whole book to it."

That was all he would say on the matter. And, as I'm sure he knew, it was all he *needed* to say on the matter.

The next day, I sat down with one of Leibniz's books (which I was only able to find after a good twenty minutes of futilely indexing under Li- and Ly-). Needless to say, five pages into the twenty-five page preface and the water was already way over my head. I backtracked from the original material to some reference stuff. An afternoon spent bouncing around encyclopedias and various histories of philosophy left me with a slightly better understanding of the subject. Good enough, anyway, to know that there were basically two main ways of answering the question of the existence of evil. One version, put forth sixteen-hundred years ago by a guy named St. Augustine of Hippo, said that evil was brought into the world through the original sin of Adam and Eve, and that humans basically get what they deserve. The other was developed two-hundred years earlier, by this other guy named St. Irenaeus. In his version, evil exists so that man can know hardship and suffering, and thereby slowly improve his imperfect nature. Leibniz, who came along during the Enlightenment (apparently an era of giant wigs), was basically in the same camp as Irenaeus, with the exception that whatever we take to be imperfect in the world is only apparent. Meaning it's not really imperfect, it just seems that way to us. Since God created the world, he said, it is the best of all possible worlds. Around the same time, a Frenchman named Voltaire (sporting a wig almost as splendid as Leibniz's) made fun of Leibniz in a book that showed just how crappy the world really is, his hero encountering nothing but hardship and suffering wherever he went. In any case, it was clear to me that the question of evil was basically a religious one, concerned more with preserving the perfection of God (who, as Gordon consistently pointed out, "very likely does not exist") than with figuring out in any meaningful way why people are evil to each other. My conclusion then, was that the question, as it is traditionally understood and discussed, is pretty much a useless one.

Understanding that I will do such legwork on my own, Gordon also expects that I will come to him and discuss the results of my labor, whether it be comprehension or confusion. In the case of theodicy, this discussion took the form of me casually mentioning, on another walk about a week later, my personal opinion that, to the extent it was a religious problem, the problem of evil wasn't a real one. Gordon's arched eyebrow was enough to tell me that I had passed the course.

For the most part, Gordon's teaching method consists of making seemingly random statements, such as, "I've always been fascinated by Galileo's sunspot observations" or, "Pretty interesting deal, the evolution of cetaceans from artiodactyls." I'm a type of bloodhound, basically, and he knows he only has to give me a scent and I'll be off, tracking down and devouring whatever information I can find on the subject in question. Sometimes, he will simply leave a book he thinks I should read out in plain sight, knowing I won't be able to resist.

In the process of following Gordon's bread crumbs and my own natural curiosity, I have gained a decent understanding of a wide variety of subjects: earth science, mythology, history, warfare, religion. I don't always fully understand what I read on these topics. Sometimes, I don't understand even part of it. Still, I'd like to think that my cursory knowledge of the world I live in is something to be proud of. According to Gordon, just knowing the names Descartes and Boethius and Cervantes probably gives me a leg up on most people my age.

Anyway, instead of spending my childhood seated at a desk in a classroom, listening to a teacher explain how to fill in blanks, getting hit in the back of the head with spit wads, or running around on a playground, swinging on monkey bars and playing dodge ball and arguing over the rules of this or that game, I have spent it roaming the stacks, gathering whatever books catch my interest, then settling in some snug and remote corner of the library and losing myself in worlds made of words. Thucydides and Carl Sagan have been my teachers, Gilgamesh and Odysseus, my uncles. I count Tin Tin and Tom Sawyer among my playmates, Beowulf and Doc Savage among my comrades-in-arms.

I once asked Gordon, I think I was five or six at the time, if we were homeless. I had seen a billboard about homeless children earlier that day. It showed a pair of kids sleeping in the back of a station wagon. Coincidentally enough, that night we happened to be sleeping in our van.

Gordon was lost in his thoughts and heard me without really hearing me. "Pardon?" he asked absently.

"Are we homeless?"

Now I had his attention.

"No," he replied, after the briefest of hesitations.

"Do we have a home?"

"No."

I frowned, not because I was confused by his illogical answer—it was typical Gordon—but simply to let him know I would need a moment or two to work it out. He stroked his beard slowly, regarding me intently while I processed. Even though I knew his two negative responses were not as contradictory or absurd as they sounded, it wasn't immediately obvious what he wanted me to understand by them. Eventually, an association stepped forward from the gray tangle of my thoughts and offered itself. I recalled the words of Odradek, one of my favorite characters from the bedtime stories Gordon read to me.

I pictured the strange spindly spool in my mind, his cautiously formal conversation with the story's narrator, who I always imagined as looking exactly like Gordon.

"No fixed abode," I recited, nodding my head knowingly and trying my best to sound like rustling leaves.

Gordon smiled, seemingly pleased with the connection I had made. He nodded in kind, then returned to his thoughts without saying a word. Apparently, I had gotten the point.

No fixed abode. But not homeless. That's us.

Not that I mind. Far from it. It's always seemed to me that I have it pretty good. I've never lacked for clothing, square meals, a warm bed, the time and freedom to explore the stacks. I've always had a father around to provide for me, to teach me new things and to clarify things I don't fully understand. Honestly, what is there to complain about?

I suppose it's one of the benefits of having Kafka and Melville and the Grimms for bedtime stories: no matter what ill might befall you, some minor clerk or hedgehog or hapless wood cutter always had it worse. It gives you perspective.

One of the things I admire most about Gordon is the fact that he has his own ethical system. Like most things Gordon, this system is based on a simple and succinct principle. He calls it, "Doing the harder thing."

I know. It sounds more like a form of punishment or the rule of some order of ascetic monks than a system of proper conduct. But it's not just a simple slogan, like the "trite Puritan bon mots" Gordon likes to mock: *A penny saved is a penny earned ... Well done is well said ... Do not confuse motion for action*, all that stuff. I can honestly say, having seen it in action, that doing the harder thing is indeed an ethics.

The system is not a grand one; it's not based on some universal theory that binds people without their knowing it. Gordon calls it *local*, by which he means personal. Doing the harder thing is just his personal way of being in the world, and he's not the least bit concerned with pushing it on anyone else (except for me, of course). So, what is the harder thing? What makes the harder thing better, morally speaking, than the easy thing? What does it mean to *do* the harder thing?

Before I answer, I should say something about manners. Gordon believes strongly in the importance of good manners. I don't mean fancy etiquette or table manners or anything like that. Nothing could matter less to Gordon than the placement of silverware, or knowing which utensil goes with which part of the meal. As far as he's concerned, there's no reason for the existence of any utensils beyond the butter knife and the spork. By *manners* I mean all the socially agreed-upon niceties that make it possible for people in the modern world, complete strangers for the most part, to peacefully coexist with each other. Rules have been established for the polite interaction of fellow citizens—like sticking to the right when walking down the sidewalk, say, or holding the door open for the person behind you—and there's really no reason for anyone not to play by those rules. Not so difficult. For the most part, employing good manners is a question of inserting the right stock phrase into the corresponding situational slot: *Good morning; Please* and *Thank you; Yes Ma'am; No Ma'am; Pardon me, Sir; Have a nice day.*

Observing good manners "signifies an individual's tacit acknowledgment of the social contract." In other words, manners are a person's way of saying to other people, "Hey, it's not all about me, I acknowledge that you exist too, even if I don't have the slightest idea who you are."

The thing about manners is that their true purpose is actually to make things easier. "Manners," says Gordon, "are simply a means of greasing the social rails. Why generate friction when you don't have to?" With the proper training, employing good manners is practically effortless. You end up doing it naturally, without thinking about it, like breathing. Equipping me with a proper set of manners has been an important aspect of my schooling. Gordon and I are generally very polite, and not just to strangers. We're polite to each other, too, and I have to say, it does make things easier.

In some cases, the harder thing is practically indistinguishable from good manners. Holding a door open for someone, for example. Obviously, it's harder to patiently hold a door open than it is to walk through that same door being held open by someone else. But there's nothing moral about it. In contrast to good manners, doing the harder thing can never become rote. That's the point. It's harder because it's not automatic.

I'll start with a basic example: litter. Let's say you're walking down the street, chewing a piece of gum. Whatever juicy flavor the gum once had has disappeared and you're not really enjoying it anymore. You could swallow it, but supposedly it takes seven years for gum to digest, so you decide against it. You could just spit it out, but you prefer not to litter (already the harder thing). You decide to keep chewing on the unwanted gum until you find a trashcan to throw it in (even harder). When you eventually come across such a trashcan, you take the piece of gum from your mouth and throw it toward the opening of the can. Unfortunately, your aim is poor and the gum lands on the ground in front of the can. You're a decent person, so your first thought is to stop, pick up the gum, and put it in the can. But thanks to the action of some strange force ("Newton's First Law of Motion," according to Gordon) you find it's easier to just keep walking and leave it there. Let's say you also happen to notice that the ground at the bottom of the trashcan is already peppered with litter, including other pieces of gum. It's not like you're the first one to miss the mark. What harm is there in your piece of gum lying there along side the others? The right thing, the *harder* thing, is to fix your mistake, to assert the superiority of your free will over the physical laws of the universe. Stop, turn around, walk over to the gum, stoop down, pick it up and put it in the trashcan. Better yet, and harder still, pick up the rest of the litter while you're at it.

I understand this is a trivial example. The point is, even in such a basic case, things end up better for you having done the harder thing. There's no more litter around the trashcan, so things just look better, and you can walk on with a clear conscience, free of psychic litter.

Of course, doing the harder thing wouldn't be much of an ethical system if it only applied to littering. It doesn't. It applies to everything, especially people. Someone needs your help. You can help or not. Easier to not help, to pass that person by, just like walking past a piece of gum on the ground; harder to stop, to be of assistance, to lend yourself to someone else. Even when it means changing a car wheel in the dead of night, in the pouring rain, for someone who is a total stranger, when you would rather just be getting back to your own place of rest. I have seen Gordon do this type of thing more often than I can count. To him, almost everything we do presents us with a choice on how to do it: the easy way or the harder way. In many cases, this choice is simply one of doing something or not.

As Gordon sees it, there are two things that make doing the harder thing ethical. The first is basically an accident of time and space. "In this world," he says, "in the here and now, it just so happens that the harder thing is almost always the right thing." The second is a little more complicated. Inside each of us, according to Gordon, there lurks a creature. Shortsighted, impulsive, selfish, mean-spirited. Our animal nature, basically. It's a big part of what we are, there's no denying it. But it's not *who* we are, and that's the important thing. Animal is *what we are*; human is *who we are*. "Our capacity for rational thought is what makes us human, our ability to pause and reflect, to choose." How many times have I heard him say that? Rational thought allows us to hold our creaturely impulses in front of us, to consider them, to decide whether to act on them or not. As a general rule, the creaturely thing is the easier thing, the human thing the harder one. Doing the harder thing helps us to overcome the creature inside of us, to act according to a higher purpose. And that's what makes it ethical. I guess it's one of the things that makes what's happening to Gordon kind of scary, the fact that during his episodes, he seems to be completely at the mercy of his creature.

In the end, I think what I admire about Gordon is not so much this system of his (though I'm mostly in agreement with it and try to practice it myself), but the fact that he sticks to it. I can't remember ever seeing him take the easy way out. The fact is, he makes the harder thing seem easy. He's a good person according to any system, about as good as you can get in this world, if you ask me.

I spent my eighth birthday holed up in the Kinder Korner of a small suburban public library. I don't remember which town it was, exactly, San Something-or-other. Then again, it *was* almost half a lifetime ago, so I guess not remembering's only to be expected. The room was empty and quiet. I turned off the fluorescent ceiling lights, giving the space back to the soft, muted light of the overcast day outside. Armed with a stack of mythology books, I commandeered a red vinyl beanbag chair from a pile in the corner and dragged it across the prickly blue carpet to a window wall at the edge of the room. I set the books on the floor next to the chair and plopped onto it, twisting my butt from side to side until I had wedged myself into a comfortable position. With my back turned to the room full of primary colors and miniature tables and chairs in various geometric shapes, I looked out onto the shaded interior courtyard beyond the large pane of glass.

For a while I just sat there, staring out at the cool stillness, the leaves of the trees planted in a ring at the center of the courtyard rustling in the gentle breeze that passed through it every so often, like the breath of a peacefully sleeping giant. I let out a contented sigh and grabbed the book sitting on top of the stack, a battered old volume of Norse mythology with a brown linen cover and heavy yellow pages filled with black and white illustrations of warlike gods and goddesses in capes and breastplates and conical helmets, armed with swords and hammers and round Viking shields. I devoured the tales, already familiar to me, of Odin and Thor, of Freyja and Loki, Yggdrasil the World Tree and the realms of Asgard and Jotunheim and Niflheim, the feasts of Valhalla, Ragnarok and the end of the world. Halfway through the book I came across the story of Kvasir, which was new to me.

The Æsir and Vanir, the two main groups of Norse gods, were locked in a seemingly endless war, in which neither side was able to gain the upper hand. Realizing that no one was going to win, they decided to stop fighting and join forces. As a sign of their truce, the gods all spat into a jar. Later, they used this spit to make a man, Kvasir. Being made from the stuff of every god, Kvasir turned out to be the wisest of all beings, steeped in the mysteries of the nine worlds. A perpetual wanderer, wherever he went news of his coming preceded him. All work in a village would come to a halt at the news of his approach. The villagers would crowd eagerly around Kvasir, asking him questions and telling him their problems. While listening to them, Kvasir would bow his head and close his eyes, indicating that he was giving them his full attention. Simple questions he would answer with simple truths, while more complex questions would be answered with further questions, Kvasir slowly guiding his listeners to the solution of their problem. He was calm and kindly, wore simple and slightly shabby clothing, and, thanks to his great wisdom, was at peace with himself and the world. Of course, being a mythological human, things were not destined to end well for him. His trusting openness was used against him, and he was murdered by two greedy dwarfs, who mixed his blood with honey and created the mead of poetry, which they stored in jars so they would have his knowledge all to themselves. Odin stole the mead from the dwarfs, carrying it off to Asgard in his mouth, bringing gods and men the gift of poetry.

I imagined Kvasir as a kind of mix between Socrates and Obi-Wan Kenobi, and that's how I see Gordon. He is calm, centered, focused, generous, wise. He even looks the part, with his shaggy hair and beard. If Odin ever needed to brew up a new batch of the mead of poetry, Gordon would make a fine starter.

That's Gordon, then. A modern day Kvasir. The correspondence between my father and the Viking myth went straight to my brain and stuck there. And it has continued to stick. Even now, as the resemblance wavers a little more each day, and the nimble-minded, wandering wise man crumbles before my eyes.

A couple years ago, I got it into my head that I was going to be a novelist. Not right away, of course. At some point down the road, when I grew up. I know that probably sounds pompous, or even ridiculous, sort of like a kid who proclaims he's going to be President some day, or an astronaut. But if you consider how much of my life I've spent with my nose stuck in a book, you can understand why the idea of writing one seemed natural to me. Setting aside the question of how realistic my dream was, I was inspired enough at the time to risk asking Gordon for advice on how to proceed.

We sat at either end of a short wooden table in a sunny alcove of the Orinda Public Library. Gordon's end was fortified with the usual array of books and note pads and different colored pens, while mine, apart from my interlocked hands, was empty. Without taking his eyes from the giant, dusty tome splayed open in front of him, Gordon said, "Writing is a tricky business, Sam. Harder than you can imagine. You will never truly capture the thing you set out to write. You might get part of it, and the part you get might turn out to be acceptable, decent even—you might even get something you're not ashamed of—but you'll never get the whole thing. Not the part you want, anyway. It will always evade you, slip right out of your hand, no matter how tightly you clutch after it."

I don't know what I was expecting him to say, but it wasn't that. To be honest, I didn't have the slightest idea what he was talking about.

Gordon sat in silence for so long I was beginning to think that was all he was going to say on the matter. Then, finally looking up from his book, he narrowed his eyes at me and warned, "To write is to commit yourself to failure, Sam. Day after day. It's the only way, the best you can hope for. Limiting the failure. Don't expect anything more from it."

I opened my mouth to respond, but nothing came out. Really, what was I supposed to say? Instead, I simply swallowed once and nodded, to show him I was undaunted.

Gordon nodded in turn and then went on. "Many famous authors, and even some good ones, were keepers of journals. That's where I'd start." He reached down to the floor beside his chair, into his backpack, and pulled out one of his unused notebooks. He clipped a pen to the cover and slid it across the table. By way of advice, he said, "You might want to keep what you write to yourself for a while."

The next day, in an-out-of-the-way corner of the library, I sat down to launch my career as a writer. I opened the notebook and clicked the pen on. In a careful hand, conscious of the need to be legible for posterity, I dated the top of the page. And then ... nothing. Apart from the date, I did not manage to make a single mark for the rest of the day. I stared at the page with its grid of light blue lines, a matrix of infinite possibility, the pen immobile in my hand, my mind suddenly as empty as each of those little squares. My thoughts, nimble and boisterous only moments before, crashing chaotically into each other in their desire to be written first, turned into a sludge of nothingness. I tried again on each of the next five days, always with the same result. It took less than a week before I was forced to admit that I was not the journal-writing type, and therefore not the novel-writing type either.

Embarrassed at the swiftness of my defeat, I made a show of scribbling in my notebook, always where Gordon could see me, trying to give off the impression that the whole thing was going great guns. In reality, I was literally scribbling, tracing geometric shapes onto the grid, filling entire pages with black and white checkerboards, fields of five-pointed stars and hollow cubes of various sizes. My handiwork gradually evolved from aimless doodles to crude line drawings of imaginary World War II battles, filled with bombers and tanks and bayonetted infantrymen, and from there to miniature celestial tableaux, fanciful arrangements of comets and ringed planets and bubbling nebulae and pebbly Oort clouds.

Eventually, I stumbled on an application for the notebook that involved the use of actual words. For a long time now, I've tried to keep a running list of words whose meaning I didn't know in my head as I read, so I could look them up later and add them to my working vocabulary. I have a decent enough memory, but I often found myself struggling to remember words I intended to look up. I solved this problem by keeping the journal ready to hand as I read, jotting down the unknown words as I encountered them, compiling daily lists of words to be mastered and looking them up later. This led to me compiling lists on any old subject, sometimes just to kill time but also, I think, as a way of classifying my experiences, of making sense of my inner world. What better use for my journal, I realized, than as a home for my lists, a kind of archive the future me could use to get inside the head of the past me?

The journal became home to lists on every possible subject:

my favorite books and characters; my favorite heroes from Greek mythology; cool pen names for the author I'd never be; comprehensive inventories of items in the van; birds I know by sight and call; the world's top cities; Gordon's favorite songs and my own; what I'd want to have with me on a desert island; my mother's first and maiden names; the things I imagined to be in Gordon's backpack.

Like so many other things over the past year, the nature of the lists has changed, from imaginary catalogues to practical to-dos and bleak reminders, things necessary to get us from the beginning of one day to its end: grocery lists; ideas for activities to keep Gordon focused and happy; calculations of expenditure; lists of possible cities and towns to visit; possible versions of his PIN number; maladies I've read about that might apply to Gordon.

When I first started writing down my lists they were pretty long, as my goal was to try to exhaust a given category. Over time, I decided that shorter lists would be more meaningful, and started limiting entries to ten. Of all the lists I've made, there's only one with less than ten items. It has only two, and is entitled, *People to turn to.*

Something is wrong with Gordon. Seriously wrong. Has been for almost a year now. It started innocently enough, nagging headaches that mostly just made him irritable and slightly more withdrawn than usual. Taciturn as opposed to just quiet. The headaches got gradually worse, sometimes lasting for days. Next came the restless nights filled with bad dreams. The bad dreams turned into conversations, conducted out loud while sound asleep. Troubled conversations with people who weren't there. Phantoms, like Kai. Even then things didn't seem so bad. It was only about two months ago, when these nighttime troubles spilled into his waking life, that I understood something was seriously wrong.

 If Gordon knows what's happening, he's keeping that knowledge to himself. Not surprising, really. For my part, I don't have the slightest idea what's wrong. At first, I thought maybe he was just working though some sort of inner struggle or self-imposed ordeal, like Odysseus shrugging off some bewitchment or other, or Jesus dueling with the devil during his ordeal in the wilderness. What can I say? I'm a bookworm, not a doctor. Whatever his adversary, I told myself, Gordon would defeat it, emerging from his own forty days victorious, new and improved. My role was simply to give him a wide berth until his troubles, whatever they were, went away. For however long it took him to get things sorted, I would act as a kind of Regent, keeping the little kingdom of our life in working order, keep doing things as close to the way Gordon does them as I could until he was ready to take over his kingly duties again.

But his troubles didn't go away. They got worse. Things got worse, and keep getting worse. Gordon is now himself only half the time, maybe less. The days are no longer leisurely, calm, under control. Gordon used to have each day in the palm of his hand, doling our life out according to his own measure. Now there's no telling what will happen, what will go wrong. Night brings no relief. If anything, it's worse. Sleep is no longer restful, and Gordon's dreams seem to bring him nothing but pain and confusion.

It was only couple of weeks ago when I finally accepted the fact that it was going to take more to survive our situation than me holding onto the wheel while Gordon took a breather from reality. We need help, which means turning to other people. And that, for us, is easier said than done.

Everything I know about life I've learned as part of a two-person nomadic tribe. For as long as I can remember, it's just been Gordon and me. Nobody else. No family, no friends, no acquaintances. I'm sure I have family out there somewhere—grandparents, aunts, uncles, cousins—but I've never met them, and it's likely I never will. I have no idea who they are or where they live. You'd think it would be important for me to know them, to be part of a bigger family, and it is. Or it was. I long ago gave up pestering Gordon, always fruitlessly, for even the smallest piece of information. The point is, since it's always been just the two of us, it's not obvious how to go about getting help.

Why not just go to a hospital or clinic? Why not see a doctor? Mostly, it's because the thought of going to some sort of institution plays right into my biggest fear: that other people will not understand how we do things, that if they found out about it they would decide there was something wrong with it. They would disapprove somehow, try to intervene in our way of life, force us into some sort of fixed abode. Maybe even separate us, send me off to a school or a foster home or something. It's not that I'm paranoid, I really don't think I'm paranoid; it's just that I'm not sure I'm willing, or even know how, to trust any stranger enough to risk jeopardizing what we have.

So who could I turn to for help? The first name on my list, pretty much the only name of someone I *know*, is Donald Coleman. *Uncle Don.* Don't ask me why I call him that. I'm not sure myself. He's not a *real* uncle, of course, and I haven't seen him for at least seven years; half my lifetime. I'm not even sure what the nature of his relationship to Gordon is or was, though I'm certain they were colleagues of some sort, and great friends.

What I do know, what I remember, are the times we spent at his home, a great old house with brown shingles and dark green trim and big windows, filled with books and artifacts and antique furniture. There were usually other people there, for dinner parties, with food and wine and lively conversation. I would sit right along with them at the big wooden table, forgotten but captivated, trying to make what sense I could of their deep discussions and their jokes, too, things gradually turning from serious to jovial to hilarious. Gordon would always look down at me then, drawing on his pipe and nodding in a way that indicated it was time for bed. Reluctantly—but not completely so, as I was usually barely hanging on to consciousness by then—I would let him lead me off to one of the spare rooms, where he would tuck me in and tell me a story before returning to his friends. I tried to stay awake as long as I could as I lay there, listening to the hum of enlightened conversation, with its peaks of laughter and valleys of thoughtful silence.

Although I couldn't remember any of the other people from Uncle Don's house, I remembered him clearly. More importantly, I remembered that he was a college professor, at the University of California in Riverside. With a minimum of thought, I determined that it was to Riverside and Donald Coleman that we—that *I*—would go for help.

I did some sleuthing in the Visalia library, and although I didn't manage to find a home address—there were sixteen Donald or Don or D. Colemans listed in the Riverside County directory—I did discover that there was indeed a Donald Coleman teaching at the University. Finding him, I told myself, would be a simple matter of going the campus and locating his office.

That, in a nutshell, was my plan. Leave Visalia and its cool, welcoming library, our home of the previous five days, and drive to Riverside, a city of three-hundred-thousand people, where I would locate a friend from the past and appeal to him for help. It's not really much of a plan, I admit. What makes it an actual plan, the thing about it that requires thinking and strategy and a lot of what Gordon calls *finesse*, is the fact that Gordon himself can't know about it. He can't be a partner in it, he can't help or direct me in any way. The second he found out I'd concocted some harebrained scheme to get help he'd put an end to it. And there's the rub: in order for The Plan to work, Gordon has be oblivious—and thus out of sorts—for however long it takes to get to Riverside. And so, I find myself hoping for the very thing I least want to happen. Such, I'm learning, is life.

Day one of The Plan began well enough. By which I mean Gordon's condition cooperated. He woke with a slight headache that only grew worse as the morning wore on. A wordless breakfast and a handful of Advil did nothing to slow his slide, and by noon he was in the back of the van, hiding from the world and its painful reality beneath a crypt of blankets. I decided it was best to wait until he was fully under before risking starting up the van and beginning the journey to Riverside. Too agitated to just sit in the van waiting, I got out and set off on an aimless loop through the now familiar streets of Visalia: north from our base in the Convention Center parking lot, through the bank-filled downtown to Goshen, east on Goshen to Burke, then down to Mineral King and back to the parking lot.

I completed three circuits of this loop, checking in after each one to make sure Gordon was still where he was supposed to be. By then, I had calmed down enough to accept that the time had come to set The Plan in motion. I felt resolved—it had to be done, there was no other choice—and confident, certain that I was doing the right thing. As I stepped up to the van, a slight motion to my left caught my attention. There, not more than ten feet away, hopping on the dusty strip of ground that marked the border of the parking lot, was a small rabbit. It came to a stop as I turned to look at it, sitting in profile between two prickly little shrubs. Although its fur blended in somewhat with the ground where it sat, the white of its cotton-ball tail was plain to see, and the early afternoon sun shone bright pink through its thin, erect ears.

I have seen plenty of wild animals while hiking with Gordon in the infinite parklands of California, birds and fish and chipmunks and woodchucks and coyotes and bears, in the mostly human-free environment which is their true home. I have also been to zoos, which I hate, where, despite the presence of so-called habitats, the animals are clearly not at home. The homesickness of a zoo animal has always seemed obvious enough. The sudden appearance of this rabbit, then, confused me. I didn't know what to make of it. It was clearly a wild rabbit, not somebody's lost pet. It had not escaped from a pet store or a zoo. What was it doing here, in downtown Visalia? The more I looked at it, the more I tried to understand its presence ten feet away from me, the more uneasy I felt. I had a weird feeling, I think maybe it was dread, as I realized that this parking lot, with its acres of asphalt and cars, with its islands of weeds and drought-resistant bushes, was its home.

Though I could see its small black nose and long white whiskers twitching rapidly, the rabbit hadn't moved an inch. The large black eye facing me was unblinking. I couldn't tell if it was looking at me or not, but I found myself staring into it anyway, trying to plumb the rabbit's being, to understand what it was thinking, how it *felt* about being here. Somehow, I could feel the rabbit's heart pounding away in its chest, beating so rapidly it was on the verge of exploding. It was nervous, exposed, frightened. Not by me, necessarily. By everything, by the place where it lived, by its home.

My heart was beating fast and I found that I was afraid, too. The rabbit's wary black eye was transmitting its fear to me. I could feel it happening, but still I couldn't look away. All the confidence I had felt moments before was gone, replaced by rabbity fear, by the awareness that I was about to trade in my natural environment, my home, for a kind of exile. Home, where your life takes place. Where you're comfortable, safe, where you're *at* home. My home was not the four walls of a fixed abode, it was the library, the Vanagon, the open road, being with Gordon, sharing his way. The second I started up the van, the moment I steered us in the direction of Riverside, I would be leaving the comfort of my home for the uncertainty of an unwelcoming, alien world.

I felt an urge to touch the rabbit, to hold it, so that, together, we could overcome our fear. My heart thudding away, I took a cautious step toward it. Its ears straightened and then, with a twist of its head, it bolted off, zigzagging at full speed through the artificial warren of the parking lot, leaving me alone with my suddenly overwhelming fear of the future.

I stared at the tangle of bushes where the rabbit disappeared, gradually regaining control of myself. I took a deep breath of resolve, opened the door and climbed into the driver's seat. I stuck the key in the ignition but could not summon up the effort to turn it. I threw my head back and just sat there, staring up at the roof of the van. For how long I don't know. By the time I came back to myself it was well into the afternoon. I looked at the dashboard clock: two fifty-two. I glanced over my shoulder at the bulky shape beneath the covers. It had to be done; there was no choice. I took a deep breath and started the engine. Despite the rumbling, Gordon did not stir. I threw the van into gear and pointed it south.

A light rain fell as I pulled onto Highway 99. Even if I stuck to the eminently legal speed of speed of sixty miles per hour, the two-hundred-forty-mile trip from Visalia to Riverside would only take a little over four hours. We'd be there before nightfall.

The storm clouds continued to darken, and by four thirty it seemed like night *had* fallen. The steady drizzle had turned into a downpour and the headlights of passing cars were on, their harsh glare reflecting off the slick, wet highway and through the rain-splattered windshield into my eyes.

I drive well enough, for a fourteen-year-old. But this was my first time driving in the rain, and I have to admit it was not my cup of tea. By the time we reached Bakersfield, it was coming down in buckets and I panicked a little, turning east onto Highway 58 when I should have stayed south on 99. We were forty miles off course before I realized my mistake, passing a town called Tehachapi. Instead of turning around, however, I kept driving, in the hopes of finding another highway that would take us across and down to 99. I finally gave up when we reached the outskirts of Edwards Air Force Base, sixty miles further along. The rain had stopped, but it was now pitch dark and we were basically in the middle of nowhere. Not wanting to make a bad situation worse, I turned around and drove back to Tehachapi.

It was eleven when we finally pulled into town. Gordon was still asleep in the back of the van, though his slumber was no longer restful: he twitched and moaned and mumbled, his breath passing sharply between clenched teeth.

I drove through the deserted streets looking for a suitable place to park for the night, somewhere not too isolated or conspicuous. I settled for the well-lit parking lot of the local

Safeway. I pulled the van into a spot near but not quite among the small cluster of parked cars on the edge of the floodlights' orange glow, so we wouldn't be in total darkness. I crawled into the back next to Gordon, pulling one of the blankets off him and spreading it over my exhausted frame. Gordon was now engaged in a less-than-pleasant conversation with Kai. I listened intently, trying to understand what he was saying, but fell fast asleep before I'd made out a single word.

So ended day one of The Plan.

Day two of The Plan would turn out no better than day one. For starters, there wasn't supposed to *be* a day two. Even though, in the semi-panic of the night before, I'd managed to cover half the distance to Riverside, all I'd really done was trade one small town for another. It would turn out to be a hard town to get out of, thanks in part to the incident with Gordon, the shopping cart, and the fuchsia-haired woman.

It was almost eleven when I woke. Gordon was already up, perched atop his pile of blankets in a kind of defeated lotus position, his legs loosely crossed and his hands plopped limply in his lap. He didn't look so great. His clothes were rumpled and his mouth was hanging open and his beard was dented in several places. The long sleep had pressed his mass of hair into a sort of granite obelisk. He didn't acknowledge my yawning, stretching presence or my tentative, "Good morning." He just stared vacantly at the back of the van and said nothing. Recent experience has taught me to expect him to be quiet and withdrawn after a bad day, so I let him be. He would be himself again when he was ready to be.

The truth is, I was more than happy to leave him alone, since I wanted to be alone too.

I opened the side door and slid from the stale cocoon of the van into a world of fresh air and sunshine. A couple of big, burly guys, probably from the grocery store night shift, were leaning against their pickups, talking quietly and enjoying an early-morning beer. They turned to look at me as I climbed out, their faces mildly suspicious. I nodded to them nonchalantly, trying to make my emergence seem like the most natural thing in the world, and they went back to their conversation. I closed the door softly behind me and made a show of taking stock of my surroundings.

Tehachapi was situated in a small valley, separated from the San Joaquin Valley to the north and the Mojave Desert to the east by golden brown hills and what you might call small mountains. The view to the east was remarkable for the thousands of wind turbines, covering the bumpy hills like a futuristic forest. About half of them were spinning, some slowly, some wildly, while the rest were completely still. It was a relaxing sight, the kind of scene that encouraged introspection, like the ocean, or a mountain view. The morning was bright and clear, the sky pale blue and cloudless. Though the air still remembered something of the evening's coolness, the sun was already warm on my skin, hinting at the heat to come. Apart from a few puddles, there was no evidence of the previous day's rain. Like the rain, my determination of the day before had all but evaporated. I was already thinking about giving up.

The Safeway turned out to be part of an enormous shopping complex, a vast parking lot enclosed by the basic squares and rectangles of chain stores. I set off across the asphalt desert in the vague hope that some idea of what to do next would come to me as I walked. I made it to the other side without forming a single coherent thought, my mind wandering along with my feet. The pavement was already throwing off its excess heat, so I made for the shady entranceway of a travel agency.

It took me a while to realize that I was not standing in front of a travel agency, but a library. It was an odd feeling. The Visalia library was a beautiful place, a New Deal art deco building filled with natural light and wood trim and big comfortable chairs and well-ordered stacks of books. A perfect library, in other words. The polar opposite of this, whatever *this* was. I could only wonder what the books on the other side of the tinted glass windows had done to deserve such an ignominious exile.

Still, it *was* a library, somewhere Gordon and I could hang out for the day if need be, somewhere I could regroup. It was actually a stroke of luck, I told myself, that I happened to stumble upon it. I leaned forward to check out the hours, printed on a piece of green printer paper and taped to the inside of the window:

Open: Tues, Thurs 11 A.M. to 7 P.M., Sat 9 A.M. to 5 P.M.
Closed: Sun, Mon, Wed & Fri

I stared at the paper, trying to remember what day it was. Wednesday. So much for luck. I groaned loudly, cursing whatever budget-cutting bureaucrat had decided that a public library should not only be stuck in a shopping mall, but also that it should be closed more often than it was open. I could feel the wind leaving my already slack sails. Pretty much defeated, I decided to walk along the ring of storefronts, just to kill time. I was not quite ready to return to the world of the van.

Halfway around, I came upon a boxy stucco behemoth painted in alternating waves of teal and lavender. A megamovieplex. The more I thought about it, the more the idea of a midday matinee appealed to me. A little "late capitalist mesmerism," as Gordon calls it, sounded perfect. A couple hours of not having to think about everything that was going wrong, just sitting in the cool darkness of a theater with a bucket of popcorn and a soda, feet propped up on the back of the empty chair in front of me.

A quick look at the box office marquee told me that a number of movies started at noon, which I reckoned to be about half an hour away. I hurried back to the van, where I found Gordon still pretty much as I'd left him. Though he still wasn't responding to me verbally, he seemed okay with my idea and followed me, a little more slowly than I would have liked, to the theater. He still looked a wreck, but I decided, this once, not to read anything into looks. The fact that he managed to pay for the tickets and refreshments without incident further convinced me that he was in recovery mode, that he was basically okay.

The movie was unremarkable, a by-the-numbers action flick, the kind where something important is taken from an otherwise law-abiding protagonist, forcing him to re-engage his black-ops past and embark on a deadly rampage across a continent or two in order to get it back. Action-packed, brainless, and predictable. And long. It could easily have ended three different times, but it just kept plodding on, as if the people involved in its production had been paid by the minute. Gordon did well enough for the first hour-and-a-half, but by the time the movie had sauntered past the first of its plausible endings, I could tell he was getting restless. He couldn't seem to find a comfortable position for his legs, crossing and uncrossing them constantly and rubbing at the tops of his thighs. Before long, he started making comments under his breath. I couldn't tell if it was the film itself that was irritating him, or something else. Eventually, he got up and stood against the wall in an effort, I assumed, to relieve whatever was bothering his legs. I wasn't too concerned. The movie couldn't possibly last for much longer, and it wasn't unheard of for Gordon to watch an entire movie standing up. When the film finally ended almost ten minutes later, however, he was already gone.

I hurried from the theater and began searching for him. He was not in the lobby, or either of the restrooms. I even checked the other cinemas, but he was nowhere to be seen. Already fearing the worst—that he had stumbled into traffic and been hit by a car, or had fallen and hit his head, or simply wandered off someplace I would never find him—I rushed out into the blinding afternoon heat.

It was my own fault. I'd dragged him to see some stupid movie, for no other reason than that I wanted a diversion, an escape. It would have been obvious, if I'd cared to look, that he was not in "recovery mode," that he was still very much in that other place. It was a simple question of the manner of his silence, of noting whether it was somber or stupefied. But I'd been thinking only of myself and ignored what was clear. Now I'd lost Gordon. I punched my forehead in frustration, so hard it was still throbbing as I ran outside. As much as I blamed myself, I have to admit that I blamed him too. The truth is I was angry with him, which maybe explains why, once I found him, I let him teeter along when I should have just helped.

Following our flight from the parking lot, I drove through the wide, mostly empty streets, stalling for time while I tried to form some notion of what to do next. My mind was not so much racing as trying to run away from itself. Doubts and fears came at me from all sides like a plague of harpies. I felt an irresistible urge to pull the van over, grab my backpack, and run for the far-off hills, leaving everything I'd ever known behind, including Gordon, sitting in the passenger seat with his hands tucked meekly between his thighs, staring silently out of the side window. The temptation was real enough, but it quickly petered out and I kept driving. Eventually, as if on autopilot, I returned to the parking lot, pulling into the same spot in front of the Safeway as the night before.

I turned the van off and sat there, listening to the engine ping and click as it cooled. I looked over at Gordon, who now appeared, ironically enough, to be in genuine recovery mode: he was breathing evenly, his hands were relaxed in his lap and no longer balled up into fists, his silence definitely of the somber variety. He stared out the passenger window at the sparkling sea of cars. I climbed into the back of the van and got my wallet from my backpack. I slipped outside and went into a smoothie shop next to the Safeway. With the last of my money I ordered two strawberry-banana smoothies, with a mood lifter for me and a gingko biloba booster for Gordon, and returned to the van. I put Gordon's smoothie in his cup holder, then went to the rear of the van and opened the doors. I climbed onto the back and sat with my feet propped up on the bumper, drinking my smoothie and looking out over the grocery store at the windmill-studded hills.

The boosters seemed to be doing their job. Not only did I feel calmer, after a while Gordon actually came back and sat next to me. I cast a quick glance at him as he settled in. He looked haggard and exhausted and he didn't smell so great, but at least he was *here*. His reddened eyes moved restlessly in their dark sockets, as if tracking something that appeared for an instant, only disappear and pop up somewhere else.

A small glob of smoothie sat on his beard near the chin like a drop of blood. I was debating whether or not to point it out to him when he said, his voice little more than a whisper: "The soul is therefore but an empty word, of which no one has any idea, and which an enlightened man should use only to signify the part in us that thinks."

I nodded. It was a quote from Julien Offray de La Mettrie, Gordon's favorite philosopher (someone nobody's ever heard of, naturally). The point of it, as he once patiently explained to me, is that there is no soul, that to the extent "such a thing as the soul" can be said to exist, it is only as a word, one which "ultimately referred to the shadow cast by various electrochemical activities in the brain."

The timing of it caught me be surprise. It was, in fact, a subject that had been on my mind an awful lot of late. I've always more or less agreed with Gordon on the non-existence of the soul, if only because he seemed so sure about it. So why was I suddenly so concerned about something that didn't exist? Why was I spending so much time these days worrying about Gordon's soul, about what would happen to it when he died?

Beyond the fact that his words resonated with my mood, there was something kind of alarming about Gordon's tone. It wasn't confident, or doubtful, or defiant. It was just ... nothing. Flat. Defeated. In that moment, I knew, he was lost. Lost as to where his mind had been, lost as to what was happening and what to do about it, lost as to how to continue being the man and father he had always been.

I had no response. I was lost too, in my own way. I could think of nothing better to do, in that moment, than just sit next to him in the back of the van, sucking absently on my smoothie, watching the windmills spinning in the distance and waiting for the desert night to fall, for things to cool down enough so we could sleep.

It is probably my oldest and truest memory. I was six, and Gordon and I were staying at Donald Coleman's house. It was an old house, with wood floors and high ceilings and tall windows. I was under the covers of the couch-bed in the study. The room was lined with bookshelves crammed with books and artifacts. Whatever wall space not taken up by bookshelves was hung with African masks. I suppose a lot of kids might have been afraid of being alone in a room with those leering and grimacing and wildly laughing faces, but not me. The room was like a miniature Natural History Museum. I lay there, unable to sleep, distracted by the walls of books and the sounds of conversation coming from the other room.

Gordon had put me to bed after dinner, reading to me from a book off the shelves—an old, oversized astronomy book with color pictures of galaxies and nebulas and ringed planets—before returning to the living room to talk with Uncle Don and the other dinner guests. When he came back later and found me still awake, reading from the same book, he was not the least bit upset. In fact, he seemed glad I wasn't asleep. He plopped down on the bed next to me, a big smile in his eyes. He leaned in close, saying nothing, his eyes glinting in the dim light. His breath was warm and sweet, and when he smiled his teeth were blue from the red wine he and the others had been drinking. I was unable to return his gaze and looked away for a second, which is when I noticed that he was holding something in his lap. A cigar box.

Following my glance, Gordon looked down at the box in his lap. As if suddenly remembering why he was there, he placed it on my chest and said, "This is for you. Do you know what it is?"

"A box?"

He laughed softly and smiled his blue smile. "Ha! Yes, that's correct. It's a box. But not just any box."

He stifled a small burp, then leaned in close and whispered into my ear, "It's from your mother. She told me to give it to you when I thought you were ready to have it."

It took Gordon a moment to realize that my arms were pinned beneath the covers by the weight of his body. "Oops," he said, smiling sheepishly and scooting back just enough for me to wriggle them free.

I scrambled eagerly into an upright position, my back propped against the pillows. I held the box in my lap and stared at it. It was covered in glossy black paper, edged with decorative gold tape. The lid was embossed with a ring of gold coins, inside of which was a gold emblem, encircled by writing: *Flor de Tabacos, 1845*. And in the middle, the words: *De Paratagas*. A beautiful thing. A miraculous, impossible thing. I was so wrapped up in contemplating this fabulous object that I almost forgot about the truly miraculous part: It was a gift from my mother!

Gordon, meanwhile, had slipped quietly from the bed and wandered over to one of the bookshelves, where he pretended to be interested in some title or other, leaving me to my business.

Had my mother given me nothing but an empty cigar box, it would still be my most prized possession. But it wasn't empty. A gentle shake was enough to tell me that it contained additional treasure. I opened the lid slowly, deliberately, hoping to make the thrill of opening it last forever. Inside I found a treasure trove, an Ali Baba's cave of riches: an army-issue folding compass; a pearlescent blue fountain pen; a small oak twig with three perfectly-formed acorns still attached to it; a brown snakeskin coin purse, filled with foreign coins of various shapes and sizes; a corn cob pipe that smelled like cherry tobacco; a red enamel pin in the shape of a hammer and sickle with the letters CCCP in gold; a shiny silver jack.

I was stunned. I stared into the box for a long time, trying to grasp the significance of it, but I simply couldn't. Strangely enough, of all the happy thoughts that could reasonably have gone through my head at that moment, I found myself instead assailed by a dark, ominous one. Still looking into the box, unable to pull my eyes away from my new treasure, I asked Gordon warily, "Is she dead?"

Gordon stood at the shelf with his back to me. He tilted his head, then turned around to face me. "No," he replied, shaking his head. "No, she's alive. And well, I'm sure. Just busy."

"Doing what?"

A smile flickered across his face, one that somehow seemed like the opposite of a smile.

"Other things."

"Where?"

"Somewhere else."

"Can we go see her some time?"

He took so long to answer that I thought maybe he hadn't heard me. Finally, he whispered, "I don't think so."

There were a hundred more questions I wanted to ask, they were practically jumping off my tongue, but I knew from experience that Gordon had already said all he was going to say. I decided not to push my luck and just be satisfied with the answer I'd been given. After all, I had learned something important: my mother truly existed, she was *out there* somewhere. I turned my attention back to my new treasure. I rolled onto my side and examined the items in the box. I took them out one at a time, turning them over slowly as I ogled them, already inventing imaginary histories for each of them.

Gordon moved away from the bookshelf and went over to a small armchair in the far corner. While I marveled at my new possessions, he sat there quietly, rubbing at his beard with a heavy hand, his mind in some far-off place. He was still sitting there when I eventually fell asleep.

The funny thing is, before that night, I pretty much never thought about my mother. I know that sounds weird. What kid doesn't think about his mother, especially a kid who doesn't have one? But the fact is since I'd never had one, I didn't know the first thing about her. All I'd ever known is my life with Gordon. Which must have been enough for me, because I never asked him anything about her. What her name was, what she looked like, why she wasn't around. Nothing. Nor had Gordon ever volunteered anything on the matter before that night.

Later, I understood that he'd been carrying that cigar box around my whole life, stowed somewhere out of sight, waiting for the right moment to give it to me. I have no idea what it was about that particular night that made him decide to hand it over. Maybe it marked some important anniversary. Maybe the date had been predetermined. Maybe nothing. The reason didn't really matter. What matters is that he did it. And in doing it, he planted a seed in my mind, a simple idea that grew into something bigger and took on a life of its own.

From that night forward, I thought about my mother, in some way or other, every day. The cigar box and its contents, I decided, were special items from her childhood, talismans she wanted me to have, links that connected us, bound us together. Before long, I had reconstructed her entire childhood from them. I went on, in turn, to construct her teenage and college years, her time with Gordon, the vitally important work that forced her to be apart from us. For a while, I pestered Gordon about her, sometimes by way of what I thought were clever hints, sometimes point blank. He never answered, of course, just grumbled something incomprehensible under his breath before quickly changing the subject. Mostly, though, my questions were met with total silence. Not that it mattered, really. I heard in his silences the answers I wanted to hear, read in his avoidance confirmation of my every hunch.

I'm sure it's not what Gordon intended when he gave me the cigar box. In fact, it's just as likely that night was just a rare moment of weakness on his part, one he probably regrets. For that reason, I'm careful to keep my time with the box private. And believe me, I spend *a lot* of time with it. That box is more than a gift, more than a simple inheritance. It's tangible proof, incontrovertible evidence, that my mother exists, that, somewhere out there, she is thinking about me.

Early morning sun streamed through the rear windows of the van, shining directly on my face and forcing me awake when I would have been happy to keep on sleeping. Blinking against the relentless light, I looked around me. Gordon was already up and nowhere to be seen. Somehow I knew not to be worried by his absence, knew that, for the moment at least, he was fine. It was day three of The Plan. One way or the other, I told myself, it would be the last. Either Gordon would have another bad day (and as bad as things have gotten, he's yet to suffer three bad days in a row) and I would have the chance to finish the drive to Riverside, or he would be fine, figure out what I was doing, and put an end to it. To be honest, I wasn't sure which one I wanted more. Or less.

 I rubbed the sleep from my eyes and stretched, trying in vain to stifle a series of short yawns. I stretched again, then yawned again, the spasm forcing my jaw so far open that it cracked. Taking advantage of Gordon's absence, I clambered from the back of the van up to the passenger seat. Once seated, I reached out and lowered the sun visor, carefully examining my reflection in the little mirror on its underside.

Like any fourteen-year-old, I would imagine, I spend some time checking out my reflection. A lot of time, actually. In fact, I've probably spent more time looking up at the sun visor or standing in front of some rest-room mirror, staring intently at my reflection, than even the most self-absorbed adolescent.

Not that I'm some kind of narcissist or something. I don't spend this time in front of mirrors out of vanity. The thing is, whenever I stand in front of the mirror examining my face, I'm not actually examining *my* face. I'm examining a *version* of my face, one upon which Gordon's is superimposed. I lay a mental image of his face over my own, then strip away all the similarities between them. After removing all the physical traits we share, whatever is left, I figure, must be from my mother. And those features, those little pieces of her, form the canvas on which my idea of her, my image of what she actually looks like, is painted. Performing this exercise every day keeps that image from fading, keeps the idea of her alive. I understand it's not the same thing as *knowing* what she looks like, but it's better than nothing.

I do my best to overlook the fact that in the end I don't really have a lot to go on. It's pretty clear most of my features come from Gordon. Same small mouth with lips that are neither thin nor full, same naturally straight teeth with the same pointy canines. Same large, "proud" ears that glow bright red when we get excited or eat mustard. Same tall forehead (though Gordon's is lightly creased while mine is smooth), same natural right-side part to our equally unruly hair. Same thick-but-not-bushy eyebrows, pulled together by the same furrow at the bridge of the nose that makes us look slightly angry even when we're not.

So, what else is there? What do I get from my mother? Symmetry, mostly. While Gordon's face is handsome enough (in my opinion, anyway), it's not exactly symmetrical. The bend at the tip of his nose, for example. His left ear is a little more proud than the right, just as his left eye is set just a little higher than the right one and seems somehow larger. My nose, in contrast, is straight, my eyes are level and the same size. Another difference between us is our skin tone. Gordon's skin is somewhat pale, with a light dusting of freckles on his face and forearms that darkens a little in the summer, while mine is quite a bit darker, and will start to tan within five minutes of exposure to the sun.

The biggest physical difference between us, however, is the color of our eyes. While the shape of our eyes is similar, Gordon's are a sort of greenish-brown, with little gold flecks in them. Nothing at all like my eyes, which are gray. Pale gray.

When I stand in front of the mirror staring at my reflection, I mostly focus on my eyes. It's weird ("uncanny" as Gordon would say), staring into your own eyes. If you do it long enough, you start to get the feeling that you are looking into the eyes of someone else, the eyes of another person, strange and mysterious, gazing back into yours. Sizing you up, questioning you, somehow forcing you to account for yourself. The eyes that stare back at me from the other side of the mirror are my mother's. I'm certain of it.

Symmetry, skin tone, eye color. Not much of a basis for building up a concrete image of someone you've never seen, someone imaginary. You need imagination too, and luckily, I've got plenty of that. In the same way that I invented an ethnic background for Gordon, simply deciding he was Welsh (a pure guess on my part. I have no idea what his true heritage is, since he's never uttered a word on the matter), I invented one for my mother. I flip-flopped between Italian and Spanish, found I couldn't decide one way or the other. In the end I settled on the general idea: *Mediterranean*.

But even with a cultural underpinning, the image still wasn't stable. It needed some weight, some kind of physical model to hang on. For a while I took to studying the figures of women I encountered on the street. Surely one of them, I reasoned, possessed my mother's size and shape. I was certain I'd recognize it when I saw it, but I never did. One day, while leafing through a musty old book on the Louvre, I came across a photograph of a marble statue of Artemis—*Huntress With Stag*. I knew instantly that I'd found what I was looking for, a physical shape, a kind of classical mannequin on which I could drape my idea of her.

Whenever I think of my mother, then, I see a gray-eyed, olive-skinned Mediterranean goddess with perfect symmetry. Not entirely realistic, I know. I'm sure I'm compensating for something. Whatever. It's what I have, and until I'm proven wrong, I'll stick with it. And believe me, I would be happy to be proven wrong. Really, I'd love that. It would be great.

I was still gazing into the sun-visor mirror, locked in a staring contest with myself, when Gordon returned. He held a cup of coffee in each hand, and a small white paper bag, filled with warm croissants and strawberry jam packets, was clenched between his front teeth. He looked rested and refreshed. Normal. One look at him was enough for me to know it would be a good day. For today at least he would be himself. Good old Gordon. Intelligent, rational, in control. No episodes, no embarrassments, the potential for calamity basically zero.

We sat on the back of the van, eating our breakfast in silence, as was our custom. We stared off at the distant hills, covered in windmills, just as we had the afternoon before. Eventually, Gordon's chewing slowed, then stopped altogether. He cocked his head ever so slightly. He had just come to the realization, I knew, that we were not in Visalia. He put a hand to his face and rubbed it hard, as if trying to wipe away his dismay, shaking his head with that frustrated sadness that came whenever he was presented with the evidence, the residue, of an episode. Finding himself in a different place than he remembered, for example.

Life has recently has taught me that it's possible for things to be simultaneously a blessing and a curse. Take Gordon's episodes, for example. They're simply awful. A curse in every sense of the word. Bewildering, unsettling, terrifying. *Uncanny*. Not that he remembers them after they happen. Not the details anyway, which is good. It would kill him to know. He prizes his rationality above all, the balance and self-control and dignity of bearing that comes with it. Knowing that he's losing that, being aware of his behavior, of what he's like when he goes under, would be the worst thing that could happen to him. So, it's a blessing that he doesn't remember.

I stay pretty quiet about it, for my part, thinking it best to keep the gory details to myself. I don't volunteer information unless he asks for it, and even then I try to be as succinct as possible, which is easy enough. I've learned the art of secret keeping from the master himself, after all.

Still, he *knows*. The gaps in his memory are enough to tell him something has happened, that he was not in control of himself, and I think it terrifies him. The worst part for him is the implication that I am the one shepherding him through it. He has always taken care of me, placed my well being before everything. So the idea that he is no longer a father to me but a burden is undoubtedly hard to bear.

Gordon rubbed his eyes and took a deep breath and lifted his head, turning his gaze back to the hills.

"Where are we?" he asked

"Tehachapi."

He nodded, saying nothing. Gordon could not have known the state of California better if he'd laid down every one of its roads himself. He knew perfectly well where Tehachapi was and how far it was from Visalia. And he knew that I was the one who'd driven that distance.

For a second, I thought he also knew *why* we were in

Tehachapi, that he'd figured out The Plan. I chased the thought away. He didn't know anything about it. He was simply frustrated, sad, humiliated. I could only imagine the whirlwind inside his head. I knew, based on how these situations have unfolded in recent months, he would either apologize, briefly but sincerely, or he would say nothing.

"Jesus Christ, Sam," he said, shaking his head in a mix of shame and disbelief. He exhaled unsteadily.

I waited for him to go on, but he didn't. *Jesus Christ*. That was it. I understood. What more could he say, really?

We went back to eating in silence, nibbling halfheartedly at our croissants. I finished mine and stood up, brushing the flaky crumbs from my shirt. I crumpled up the empty paper bag and walked across the parking lot to the nearest trashcan. I stopped a few feet short, tossing the bag toward the can like a last-second basketball shot. Not even close. I shook my head and walked over to the can, picking up the paper bag ball and dropping it in.

When I got back to the van, Gordon was standing by the driver's side door, swirling the contents of his coffee cup, squinting slightly as he scanned our surroundings. He was, I knew, trying to determine how our day was going to be spent.

"How's the library?" he asked.

"Not the best," I replied. "Closed, mostly. And on the three days it's open, it's in a strip mall."

"Right," he said, nodding. The kind of nod that meant we would be leaving Tehachapi momentarily.

Taking a slow, deliberate sip from his cup, he turned to me and said, "Where to, then?"

Maybe it was a kind of thank you, a reward offered in recognition of my efforts of the past couple days. Or maybe he simply wasn't in the mood to make a decision. Whatever the case, he wasn't in the habit of asking me where I wanted to go.

His question caught me completely by surprise, and not just because it was such a novel situation. It also hit me that we were at a kind of crossroads. I could either attempt to steer us in the direction of Riverside, stick to The Plan at the risk of Gordon figuring it out, or I could say that I didn't really care, wherever he wanted to go was fine. Which would mean giving up, basically, chucking The Plan and going back to not dealing with what was happening, pretending it was only temporary and hoping that things would magically fix themselves. I knew The Plan was stupid. But not the idea that we needed help. There was no denying it. And where else were we going to get it?

I thought for a second about just coming out with it, telling Gordon about my idea, why I thought it was the right thing to do, try and convince him to go along with it, but decided not to risk it. I just couldn't tell what kind of mood he was truly in. Instead of choosing, then, I decided on a kind of compromise, telling him where I wanted to go but not why.

"Well?" he prodded.

"Riverside?" I suggested, as if acting on a whim. I cringed at the strangely high-pitched sound of my voice.

The little shake of his head was almost imperceptible. But it was there. If he wasn't on to me before, he was now, I was sure of it.

I found myself backtracking. "I don't know," I shrugged. "Just a thought. You know, just south. Somewhere south. We haven't been down there for a while. Riverside just popped into my head." I shrugged again, hoping I hadn't inadvertently given myself away in my effort to sound innocent.

He stood there and looked at me, his expression unreadable. He drew a deep breath, then smiled.

"Okay," he agreed. "Riverside it is."

Maybe he was just humoring me, playing along with my ruse to see how far I would take it. Or maybe he really didn't know what I was up to. Either way, I wasn't going to question my luck. We were heading to Riverside and he was driving, an unwitting accomplice.

He opened the door and climbed into the driver's seat. I went round to the back, hopping in through the open rear doors and closing them behind me. I clambered through the van up to the passenger seat. I felt relieved, happy almost, for the first time in days.

Gordon seemed happy too, an impression confirmed by the fact that he let me pick the first tape of the day. I decided to reward his generosity with some of my own. I popped side two of *Generic Flipper* into the deck and cranked the volume. We made our way through the spacious, sunny streets of Tehachapi accompanied by the dirty bass and grating guitars and screaming poetry of "Sex Bomb," our heads bobbing in unison, each of us more or less happy in our own way.

It would be natural, based on appearances, to peg Gordon for a classical music buff, or maybe a jazz aficionado. With his tangle of Beethovenesque hair and his Bohemian-slash-noble bearing, he certainly looks the part. You would be surprised to discover, then, that he listens almost exclusively to punk rock.

For someone in the neighborhood of fifty, Gordon has accrued very little. It's not that he's against ownership, or thinks it's wrong to possess things. I don't think it's a question of not being able to afford things, either. We're not rich, to be sure, but we're not poor. Not dirt poor, anyway. Gordon never mentions anything about money, how much or how little he has or where it comes from. All I know is, his bank account has never run dry, and just because he takes it out in dribs and drabs doesn't mean there's not plenty in there. And it's not like he doesn't have an appreciation for things, either. He never fails to stop and admire something well-engineered: a fountain pen, a fire hydrant, a vintage automobile, a minimalist door handle, a Walther PPK. He just doesn't seem to have any need or desire to own things, almost like it doesn't occur to him that possessing things is a possibility. He has a son, a Volkswagen Vanagon, various items necessary for our day-to-day living, some camping equipment, a few changes of clothing, whatever he keeps in his backpack. Practically nothing, in other words. And apart from yours truly, the only things he has genuine affection for are the Vanagon and his tape collection.

Housed in an ancient, battered orange crate, Gordon's collection of cassette tapes maintains a permanent residence on the Vanagon floor, wedged between the front seats just behind the parking brake. There are fifty-three cassettes in all, twenty-six of which contain the "music" of punk bands from what Gordon calls "The Golden Age," which is to say late seventies and early eighties. Most of them are California hardcore bands, The Dead Kennedys and Flipper and The Dickies and Black Flag and the like, though there are a few East Coasters, like Bad Brains and Minor Threat. About a third of the punk tapes are live recordings of shows Gordon attended in the flesh, bootlegs made by his "friend and co-conspirator," Billy Sepulveda.

I like the music too, up to a point. I've been raised on it for one thing, listened to it all my life. It's what I know. And there's no denying it makes for great road music, which is important considering our traveling lifestyle. Mostly, though, I like it because it's pretty much the only open window I have on Gordon's past, the only thing he's chatty about. More than chatty, actually: unabashedly verbose.

Tight-lipped on the best of days, when it comes to talking about his punk days he can hardly contain himself. He gets downright nostalgic, going on and on about the bands, their assorted exploits and outrageous antics, the overdoses and suicides of numerous key figures. Before long, he starts talking about *himself*, recounting in great detail the clothes he wore and how he wore them, the "constant architectural and chromatic transmogrification" of his hair, the hijinks of his "crew" at shows and parties, his various "puerile, anarchistic" political gestures. Compared to the meager diet of biographical crumbs on which I am usually forced to subsist, these reminiscences are like a holiday feast.

When listening to Sepulveda's bootleg *Flipper/Avengers/ Lewd/Mabuhay Gardens/SF/3.13.81* for example, not only do I know that Gordon was there, I also know that he was sixteen years old, that his hair was "phosphorus-orange" and "generally hexagonal," that he and his "cohorty nemesis" Dennis Bricker crashed the stage during Flipper's performance of "Brainwash," whereupon Bricker attempted to urinate on the amp of guitarist Ted Falconi while Gordon delivered an "impromptu harmonica solo." (It's probably true. You can actually hear the solo on the tape. For a few seconds, anyway, after which it is replaced by a *whump*—which Gordon claims is the sound of him taking a nearly full beer can to the right eye socket—and a few sarcastic cheers.)

Although he's told this story more times than I can count, I never tire of hearing it. Similarly implausible anecdotes go along with most of the other tapes. They are, when it comes right down to it, our home movies. The act of listening to one is as much a visual experience as an audio one, as I picture a young, cocksure Gordon, his whole life ahead of him, game for anything, a live wire throwing himself with reckless abandon about this mosh pit or that. When he refers to the "Golden Age," I think he's not so much talking about the music as about that part of his life.

Punk rock accounts for twenty-six of the tapes, then. What about the other twenty-seven? They can be divided into two groups, the Kraftwerk tapes and the non-Kraftwerk tapes.

For the longest time, these other tapes were something of a mystery. The twenty-one non-Kraftwerk tapes are a completely random assortment: Peter Frampton, Roy Clark, Poco,

Herb Alpert & The Tijuana Brass, Foghat, Genesis, Spyro Gyra. These tapes are never listened to, with the sole exception of *The Slider* by T. Rex, and then it's only for the sake of one song, "Telegram Sam," which used to be something of a nickname of mine. Whenever he was in the best of moods, Gordon would drape an affectionate arm over my shoulder and sing, "Telegram Sam, you're my main man!"

The mystery behind the presence of all these not-to-be-listened-to tapes in the bottom of the crate was solved the day Black Flag's *Damaged* started to sound a little squirrelly. Gordon immediately ejected the tape and tucked it into his shirt pocket. Later that evening, as we lounged in the back of the van, he pulled a portable tape deck from deep beneath the driver's seat, then grabbed the cassette crate. He thumbed through it quickly and took out a tape from the bottom row, *Life Support* by Air Supply. After fiddling with the bottom of the cassette with a small screwdriver, he slipped it into one of the portable deck's two slots. He took the Black Flag tape from his pocket and put it in the other one. He pressed a couple of buttons, then played the Black Flag tape through with the volume turned all the way down.

Fascinated, I asked him what he was doing.

"The cassette tape," he replied, "is a particularly sensitive storage medium. The magnetically imprinted source information is easily degraded, and the tape itself is susceptible to wear, becoming stretched and thin over time. The result is a gradual, and inevitable, loss of the recorded information. In other words, the music on a cassette eventually begins to sound like crap, which can't be tolerated, even when that music is punk rock and was intended to sound like crap in the first place."

"Right. So what are you doing?"

"Over-dubbing."

"Neat. What does that mean?"

"It *means*, I'm erasing the crap that was intentionally placed on this tape," he waved the Air Supply case in the air, "and using its pristine substrate to store the infinitely less crappy information that is *Damaged*."

I asked him why he didn't make use of a better storage medium. He just smiled thinly at me and said nothing.

When he'd finished dubbing, he took the original Black Flag cassette out of the deck and put it in the Air Supply case, which he then threw away. The *Life Support* cassette was placed in the original *Damaged* case, the spirit of which it now contained. In a kind of nice two-for-one, not only was the mystery of the non-Kraftwerk tapes solved, Gordon's over-dubbing session also explained why you got The Dead Kennedys' *In God We Trust, Inc.* when you put in Kansas' *Point of Know Return*, or Pürple Hëlmet instead of Fleetwood Mac.

The Kraftwerk tapes are another matter. Why? Well, for one thing, we actually *play* them. There's also the fact that there are six of them, which leads me to believe their presence in the crate isn't completely random. They're a *collection*. And a collection cannot be random, because it takes a person to have a collection. The question then is whose collection?

Not Gordon, certainly. It's pretty clear he doesn't much care for the music. And if he wasn't the person who collected them, the only other possibility is my mother. The tapes, I've decided, were hers, and for whatever reason—*Nostalgia? An intention to return them some day?*—Gordon kept them. Once the thought took hold that they were hers, I demanded that I be allowed to play them. Eventually—reluctantly—Gordon obliged.

No sooner had I popped *Computer World* into the deck then I knew it was the music for me. Futuristic, artificial, precise, equal parts happy and melancholy. More importantly, it just sounded right to my ears. I felt calm, restful, at one with my surroundings. The music made my brain feel clean, like it had been coated with a super thin layer of liquid metal.

I mentioned how the music made me feel. Gordon, who did not appear to share my response, smiled glumly. Instead of acknowledging what I'd said, he proceeded to lecture me on why it is that different people experience the same music differently. Each person's brain, he told me, resonates with different types of sound, different frequencies, so different people find pleasure in different types of music. "It's a question of Delta-wave modulation," he explained. "Of innate neurological wiring."

According to him, different brain states—awareness, relaxation, sleep, anxiety—correspond to different ranges in the frequencies of brainwaves, electrical currents running through our brains. I don't remember the exact frequencies of these wave ranges, but I do know that each of them is named after a letter from the Greek alphabet. For example, the normal state of alertness and anxiety is called Beta, deep relaxation (like when you're meditating) is called Theta, deep sleep is called Delta. The kind of light relaxation you might feel when driving long distances is called Alpha.

Alpha, beta, gamma. Whatever. I don't remember the exact frequencies, but that wasn't the important part. What was important was that since my response to Kraftwerk was a matter of brain-wave synchronization, it was physical. Physical things are mostly inherited things. And since Gordon's brainwaves were definitely not in sync with the music, my physical, material affinity for it had not been inherited from him. Which could only mean that I had inherited it from my mother. It was scientific proof, basically, of my suspicion that the tapes were hers.

With a flash of insight, I understood that the tapes were like the cigar box: something she had passed onto me so I wouldn't forget her, so I would know she was out there. Thanks to the fact that our brains flowed with the same waves, she knew her music would become my music. Thanks to Kraftwerk, our brains were connected—*we* were connected—across time and space.

It would have been asking too much of the cosmos to think we could just drive straight on to Riverside. The first hour or so out of Tehachapi went well enough, Gordon taking 58 southeast for a while before turning due south along Highway 14. He drove along happily, playing finger drums on the steering wheel while he sang—or growled, or barked—in tuneless harmony with Will Shatter. For my part, I decided to count my blessings and be happy with the fact that I didn't have to drive.

I'd already worked out the quickest way to get to Riverside: 14 to I-5 south, then east on either the 10 or Highway 60. Gordon had other ideas, and merged onto I-5 only long enough to leave it again a mile-and-a-half later, heading east on the 210. That wasn't a problem, in itself, since east still took us in the direction of Riverside. What worried me was the fact that he had chosen to skirt the Angeles National Forest. I began to suspect that Gordon had formed a plan of his own, a suspicion that was all but confirmed when we stopped in the well-to-do suburb of La Cañada Flintridge in order to stock up on what was unmistakably *campground* food. Sure enough, as soon as we reached the outskirts of town we veered due north, straight into the endless wilds of the San Gabriel Mountains.

I wanted to ask Gordon straight out where we were going, to make sure he wasn't taking us somewhere completely beyond the reach of civilization, but I couldn't. He was still in high spirits, and I didn't want to put a damper on that. I knew how important it was for him to feel in control, not only of himself, but also of our life. So instead of speaking up, I let my concerns go, surrendering myself to whatever he wanted, telling myself that it would just be a temporary detour.

We made our way further and further into the mountains, Gordon driving with a calm, almost annoying deliberateness up the winding two-lane road. We climbed steadily through the various woody zones Gordon had taught me to identify, passing from the Riparian zone of Sycamore and Black Oak and Big Leaf Maple, into the properly Alpine zone of White Fir and Sequoia and Jeffrey Pine. *Thank you, Ranger Gordon.*

The air was clear and fresh, and the scenery truly amazing, but I found myself unable to enjoy it. For one thing, I'd had just about enough of Gordon's music. Three hours and counting of hammering guitars and angry, semi-coherent shouting was more than I'd signed on for. I leaned forward in my seat and punched the STOP button with the knuckle of my index finger, bringing the Dead Kennedys' grating "Holiday In Cambodia" to a blessed end. The soft ringing that entered the ensuing silence was a noticeable improvement.

Gordon shot me a questioning glance, seemingly amused by my sudden testiness. I smirked at him and went back to looking out the window, trying to work out exactly where he was taking us. We've been to the Angeles National Forest a few times, but it's a big place and most of it looks pretty much the same. So even though the area looked vaguely familiar, we could just as easily have been heading somewhere new as somewhere we'd been before. Either way, I tried to pay attention to road signs and possible landmarks, just in case I was the one who drove us back out.

We were forty-five minutes into the mountains when Gordon eventually turned off the main road, pulling the van into the empty parking lot of the Mt. Waterman ski area. He hopped lightly from his seat and went to the back of the van, where he immediately set about organizing his pack. By the time I joined him, he'd already fixed his sleeping bag and pad to his pack and was busy filling it with some spare clothing and the recently purchased dry goods. I was still rooting through my things when he slung his pack onto his shoulders and turned on his heel, giving me a quick punch on the arm to signal the lightness of his mood. Carrying the tent, apparently, was my responsibility.

I made up my pack as quickly as I could, slung the tent over my shoulder, and followed after Gordon, who'd already disappeared into the trees by the trailhead on the other side of the lot. Not that I felt a need to catch up with him. I was quite happy to lag behind and leave him to himself. I just wanted to keep him in sight.

The names chiseled into the trailhead sign all designated other trails except one: Buckhorn Campground. The name had a familiar ring to it, but I couldn't remember if we'd been there before. According to the sign, the hike from the ski area to the campground was a mile-and-a-half, climbing steadily up to sixty-five-hundred feet. I spent most of it about twenty yards behind Gordon, thinking my own thoughts and cursing the stupid tent, which swung back and forth from the shoulder strap as I marched along, banging repeatedly into my hip.

When we got to the campground I was surprised to find it nearly empty, considering the season. Of the thirty-six campsites, less than ten showed any sign of being occupied. Even so, we had to crisscross the entire place before Gordon found one to his liking, the most remote of the three vehicle-free, tent-only sites on the campground's southernmost edge, as far away from the other occupied sites (and the restrooms) as you could get. Gordon stood in the middle of the site for a while, looking out at the endless view of mountains and valleys, then unshouldered his pack and set it on the ground next to the fire pit.

"What do you think?"

I shrugged, tossing the tent next to his pack.

"It's fine." I said flatly, not wanting to give away the fact that I actually really liked it. It was a little more out in the open then the others, so it was lacking that cozy sense of shelter you get from being nestled in among trees and shrubs, but the view was definitely amazing. I also liked how separate it was from the rest of the campsites. If Gordon had a bad night, we would be far enough away from the other campers for them not to hear *our* noise.

My answer, to say nothing of the irritation I tried to convey through it, didn't seem to register with Gordon, who set about making camp. He transferred the food from his pack to the bear proof box, and laid out the tent. He moved fluidly and with purpose, as if following a carefully choreographed sequence. If anything, his spirits were still on the rise. He whistled jolly versions of songs from the day's drive as if they were easy-listening ditties. Still determined to hold out against his infectious mood, I left him to his work and made a quick reconnaissance of the "facilities."

I don't mind roughing it in the least. Usually, the more remote a place is, the more I like it. When toilets and sinks *are* available, however, I like to verify that they're in passable condition, so I know what I'm getting into in the middle of the night. I took my time wandering about the campground, taking a census of our fellow campers. By my count, there were only eight occupied campsites. In two there were tents only, while the other six had both tents and vehicles. The only people I saw were an older couple, sitting in folding lawn chairs beside their pop-up trailer and drinking wine from plastic cups. I waved lamely in response to their friendly calls of "good afternoon."

The restroom was the standard wooden shack with an open-air entrance and a shingled roof. Apart from a faintly pungent odor, as if something had died there recently, it was in pretty good shape (i.e. the toilet seats weren't smeared with other people's feces, and the water from the faucets was cold and clean). Most importantly, it seemed to be well lit. Satisfied that I had nothing to be afraid of should I be forced to pay a visit to the commode in the middle of the night, I returned to our camp.

Gordon was climbing out of the already-pitched tent as I approached. The camp, naturally, was spotless, the tent perfectly situated. Our packs, I knew, would be inside it, our bags and pads neatly laid out. Gordon zipped the tent closed behind him and stood up, arching his back and stretching his arms skyward before standing there with his hands on his hips. When he saw me coming, he raised a forefinger, and mouthed a silent "Ah!" as if remembering something. He unzipped the tent and climbed back inside.

It was now almost six, and though the sun was far from setting, the mountains to the east glowed with a soft orange light. The air was fresh and clear, the visibility extending to forever. I stood there taking it all in, finally allowing the petty annoyances of the day to fall away. I watched a pair of buzzards riding thermals out of a distant canyon. Like them, I felt light and buoyant and suddenly at peace. It had been, I had to admit, a pretty good day. The best in a while. And it only got better when Gordon re-emerged from the tent with our gloves and a ball.

Among our few permanent possessions we count a pair of well-worn baseball gloves. Gordon's is a catcher's mitt, chocolate-brown with age but still stout and well padded. Mine is a floppy but reliable Rawlings infield glove. On the darkened leather of the palm you can still make out the simulated autograph of some guy named Mark Bolanger (according to Gordon, he was a sure-handed but light-hitting shortstop, back in the day). Gordon re-laced the whole thing with new rawhide about a year ago, and it fits like the proverbial glove.

We have played endless hours of catch over the years. Apart from hiking, swimming, and the occasional jog, it's pretty much the only sporting activity we engage in. Over time, Gordon has taught me the mechanics of pitching. I'm not sure where or when he acquired the art, though I assume it was when he was a kid, probably from his own father.

However he came by his knowledge of pitching, I'm glad he decided to pass it on to me. Like language, I like to think I have a knack for it, and if I were on a team, I would expect to pitch. Of course, having grown up in libraries on a steady diet of fruits and nuts and cheese sandwiches, I'm not exactly your corn-fed Iowa farm boy. So my fastball—and by extension, my change-up—is a little weak. But I have a good snap in my wrist and all manner of pretty mean junk, including a curve with a six-inch break and a forkball that the bottom falls right out of.

A while back, Gordon got into the habit of taking us to the Little League field of whatever town we happened to be in. If it was deserted, I got the chance to pitch from an actual mound, digging in and pushing off against an actual rubber. If there was a game in progress, we'd watch a few innings from the aluminum bleachers or from the grass along one of the outfield foul lines. The games themselves were usually sloppy, error-filled affairs, invariably dominated by the Hüsker Dü (Gordon's euphemism for a larger-than-the-others-soon-to-be-fat kid) who always seemed to be on the mound. The Hüsker Dü is by definition a bully, and it was always pretty clear his success on the mound had as much to do with the batters' fear of getting beaned than with the quality of his stuff.

I was only mildly interested in the other kids, concerning myself mostly with trying to decipher the underlying meaning of their various semi-aware gestures: the exaggerated and almost continual spitting, the packing of cheeks with wads of bubble gum, the incessant crotch tugging, the hair flipping, the swatting of imaginary home runs while standing out in right field during the middle of a game. It was hard to escape the feeling that childhood is just one big, bored game of make-believe.

The parents were far more interesting to me, the basic mystery of their lives endlessly fascinating. What kind of houses did they live in? What kind of jobs did they go off to every day? How did they treat their kids? Did they teach them anything truly useful? Did they love each other?

I always felt a little embarrassed for the fathers, at least in comparison to Gordon, who sat in their midst like a lion among house cats, stroking his beard and smoking his pipe and missing nothing, while they ate soggy nachos from cardboard platters and drank liters of soda and yelled at the umpire or their kids or poked away at their pocket phones.

As for the mothers, well, I couldn't get enough of them. Unlike the fathers, I had nothing to compare them to. I was less concerned about their inner lives than about what you might call their comportment: their shapes, their manners, how they styled their hair, how they wore their clothes, how they smiled and frowned, how they looked upon their children. Occasionally, a certain feature would stand out—a hairstyle I liked, or a neat way of dressing, or a pleasing laugh—and I would immediately assign that trait to the composite image of my mother, flesh and blood to go with inert marble.

Gordon, when he wasn't observing the game, observed me. After a while, I realized he was on the lookout for any sign that I somehow yearned to be out on the field with these silly little fellows, my so-called peers, for evidence that I might actually want to trade in the life I had for the one unfolding before me. No chance. I would shoot him a look that said "enough already" and off we'd go, in search of a small diner, a cheap but clean motel, or, if it was still early enough, the town library. Eventually, he seemed to accept the fact that I wasn't really interested in the *other life* and we stopped going.

We tossed the ball back and forth, each of us standing in one of the empty campsites on either side of our own. Long, easy throws. The only way to properly warm up a pitching arm.

The conditions were absolutely perfect. Low seventies, the air dry and clean, the late afternoon sun getting softer and more orangey by the minute. Gordon puffed away at his pipe, the mild breeze occasionally carrying a pleasant whiff of burnt cherry to the spot where I stood.

We threw the ball fifty times without saying a word. Then Gordon cleared his throat.

"I love this place," he said through clenched teeth, his pipe wedged in the corner of his mouth.

"Me too," I replied, sounding a little less positive than I wanted to.

"You remember the last time we were here?"

"I do." In truth, I did not. Not entirely, anyway. For some reason, I remembered the trail but not the campground. In my defense, I've stayed at a lot of campgrounds. They start to blend together after a while. Then again, so do hiking trails.

I was taking a mental inventory of campgrounds and trails, thinking of making a list of my favorites, when Gordon's voice broke in again.

"I've been coming here for a long time," he said.

He paused for a moment with the ball in his hand, then turned to look at the mountains and valleys in the distance. After ten seconds or so he turned and faced me again.

"A long time," he repeated, tossing the ball in a long, looping arc.

There are certain words and phrases I have come to understand as veiled references to my mother. The word, *Her*, for example. Or *Once*. Rare utterances that always cause my ears to prick up, hungry as I am for even the most meager scraps. *A long time* is another such phrase. It means not only *Before you were born*, but also *When your mother and I were together*. Sometimes Gordon will expand ever so slightly on these hints, and I will listen with every fiber of my being, straining after even the tiniest innuendo. Most of the time, though, he simply falls silent, and I have to content myself with knowing he's thinking about her, about those earlier days.

This was one of those times.

The ball sailed back and forth through the early evening air, Gordon catching and throwing with that fluid, easy motion of his. I followed the lazy flight of the ball into my glove, which I hardly needed to move. We were so in sync by that point I could have caught his tosses with my eyes closed. Every one of them landed right in the middle of the pocket, as if our gloves were connected by an invisible wire.

Without warning, Gordon removed his glove and wedged it beneath his arm, bringing the game to an abrupt halt. He took his pipe from his mouth and tapped it against his palm, knocking the burnt tobacco loose, then set it down on top of a small boulder next to him. He turned and looked again at the view from the mountain, then shook his head and muttered something.

"What?" I asked, even though I was pretty sure I knew what he'd said.

He sighed and repeated, "I'm *sorry*, Sam."

He put his glove back on and threw the ball to me on a frozen rope. It lodged itself in the palm of my glove with a loud snap, stinging my hand.

"Oh," I said, wincing. "About what?"

We'd had this conversation a few times already during the past year, so I already knew where it would go. It wasn't one I enjoyed having. Basically, it amounted to Gordon beating himself up over what was happening, blaming himself for everything, telling me how unfair it was to me, and how sorry he was about it. My assurances that it was okay, that it was no big deal, only made things worse. Instead of feeling better, he would grow moody and withdrawn. It wasn't a place I wanted to go. What I wanted, right now, was just to play catch, to enjoy the one thing that hadn't changed.

I threw the ball back and waited.

We stood facing each other from our respective campsites, Gordon with his head slightly cocked, looking at me intently while carefully choosing his words, me just standing there, trying not to seem irritated.

"About what?" I repeated.

"About all of it."

"All of *what*?"

Normally, Gordon would have narrowed his eyes and chastised me for playing—or being—dumb. Instead he kept gazing at me with his head cocked, his expression serious but full of affection. I couldn't help but look away.

"All of the things I've subjected you to," he said.

Yep, I thought. *Here we go.*

"All of the things you've been denied, thanks to me. Thanks to my choices."

Choices. Another coded word. Suddenly, I realized his apology might be about more than just our recent troubles.

"When you start out," he went on, his voice catching on the words, "when you start out, of course you don't see things from far enough out, how can you? You don't have the perspective, the experience, to see where they'll end up, let alone the ability to control them."

I looked into my glove, pretending to be interested in the honey-colored leather, the laces, the fake autograph.

"I ... you ... you just don't know how things are going to turn out, you really don't. You do your best, of course, I like to think I've done my best, but if you're honest about it, you have to admit—"

It felt a little strange, having this conversation while standing so far apart. I couldn't help thinking that it was actually the distance between us that allowed Gordon to open up, as if he required a buffer of isolation in order to bare his soul.

He stepped over to the boulder where he'd placed his pipe and sat down, resting his forearms on his knees. He rubbed at his eye. "It's selfish, Sam," he said. "That's all it is. When it comes right down to it, it's just selfishness, pure and simple."

I shrugged. How long had I waited to hear this, an admission, a confession, an explanation? I don't have the slightest idea why, but now that it was happening, now that I was finally hearing it, I realized I didn't *want* to hear it. I just wanted him to stop, to get up off the rock, put his glove on, and throw the ball back to me. I felt powerless and small, like a human plaything in some Greek myth, tossed about according to the whim of a bored god. My helplessness only made me more irritated.

"I don't know what you're talking about," I shouted across the distance.

Gordon smiled ruefully, ignoring the testiness in my voice. "I'm talking about the way I've raised you," he said. "The life I've given you." He shook his head. "The life I *haven't* given you would be more accurate. I wish I could tell you that it's all been mapped out, that everything is going according to plan—"

Me too.

"—but it's not. Probably never was. All these years it's just been me running, keeping us on the move just to stay ahead of ... I don't know what, somehow getting by, turning a series of defeats and compromises into a set of habits, a routine, and then passing that routine off as a way of life, it's ... it's not what I intended."

And then I knew what was irritating me, why I didn't want to hear what he had to say. He was talking about us, about our life, about the thing that matters more to me than anything else. And he was being critical of it. The life, the set of *choices* he was disparaging, was all I had, and I wasn't going to hear it belittled, not even by him.

"Oh," I said cynically, removing my own glove as if readying for a fight. "What *did* you intend?"

He slipped his pipe into the pocket of his shirt and stood up. "I always told myself our situation was just temporary," he said. "That eventually I'd get everything figured out, get us settled, normal, apply myself to your long-term well being, to your happiness."

Who cares about normal?

"I'm happy as a clam, Gordon!" I snapped. He recoiled a bit at that, the ensuing silence making me aware of just how loudly I'd shouted it. I took a deep breath, held it in, let it out slowly.

"I'm happy," I repeated quietly.

Gordon looked at me and shook his head. "That's because you don't know any better, Sam. Because you don't know anything else. Jesus Christ! It was always my intention to make everything right, *tell* you everything, explain it all to you. I owe you that. And now … with what's happening now … it's all … everything's—"

"Everything's fine Gordon!" I insisted, shouting again despite myself.

We stared at each other across the divide while I tried to figure out how to bring this "conversation" to an end.

I shrugged apologetically.

"You don't need to *explain* anything," I said. "I'm happy. I've always *been* happy. Happy to be me, happy to be with you, happy to do what we do. You're a good father—a great father—and I wouldn't change a thing. Not a thing." *Got it?*

His expression tightened and he looked away, blinking rapidly.

"You know what would make me happy right now?" I called.

A deep sigh and a shake of the head. "No."

"Some fastballs, that's what. And some sliders. And maybe a few breaking balls. Could we do that? Please?"

Gordon nodded in defeat, a pained smile on his face. "Sure," he said. "You bet."

"And then maybe we could eat something. I'm starving."

The sun was like a stubborn child that simply refused to go to bed. Even after it had dipped behind the snaggletoothed line of low mountains to the west, the sky continued to glow with its radiance, the thin layer of high clouds that had assembled out of nowhere lit up with a beautiful pinkish-orange light. Gordon set up the stove and began preparing our dinner while I rooted around the campground collecting firewood. Gathering up as much as I could carry, I returned to the campsite, dumping my haul of twigs and small logs next to the fire pit. I made four trips in all, and by the time I was done, I had built a two-foot tall pyramid of kindling.

As I set about arranging the fire, I soon lost myself in a naturalist's game of identifying the different types of wood I'd gathered—Ponderosa, laurel, coastal sage, manzanita—each according to its shape and color and bark and, especially, its smell. According to Gordon, scent, like music, is a mnemonic device, and it was the combination of woody aromas, the unique scent of them all blended together, that triggered my memory of the time we'd been here before.

It was two years ago. We stayed in this very same campground, maybe even this same campsite. It was a little confusing, forgetting something so recent. I like to think my memory is better than that, but the more I thought about it, the more it made sense. There was very little about that particular trip to make it stand out from dozens of other identical trips. The only notable thing, in fact, the only memorable part about it, is that it was the first time Gordon revealed his *concerns* about plastic.

We'd gone for a long hike, setting out from a trailhead adjacent to the campground. I remembered now how quickly we found ourselves in the middle of true wilderness. Apart from the dusty trail itself, there were no obvious signs of human civilization. No power lines, no roads, no cars, no houses or rooftops. Not even other people. Nothing apart from the litter.

It was everywhere. Cans, juice boxes, cigarette butts, bits of paper. But mostly it was plastic. Plastic bottles, plastic wrappers, plastic six-pack holders, plastic bags. We began picking things up as we walked along, stuffing them into our pockets. These were soon filled to overflowing, so we used a couple of plastic grocery bags we found stuck to a bush. By the time we returned to the campground, we'd each filled two bags with plastic crap.

The presence of litter on a public-use trail is not exactly remarkable. But this time, something about it—maybe just the sheer amount of it—really got to Gordon. He ranted and raved the whole time, something he never did. He might talk at length about the most obscure subjects, but he almost never ranted, and he certainly never raved. His rant that day began as a fairly standard piece of Gordon-style edification.

After retrieving the remnants of a Styrofoam coffee cup from the clutches of a chaparral broom, he turned to me and asked, "What would you say is the most durable material on earth, the material that will last the longest?"

"I don't know," I answered earnestly, thus walking right into his trap. "Lemme think about it for a second." I crouched down to pick up a Ziploc bag at my feet. "Diamond, maybe? Limpet teeth?"

Gordon frowned, completely missing the attempted humor in my response.

"Right," he said, clearly meaning *wrong*. "Let me rephrase the question. Which *man-made* material will be around the longest?"

That was easy. "Glass," I said, feeling rather clever. It's true; while glass may be broken or shattered easily enough, it actually takes a million years for an individual piece of glass to biodegrade. Contrary to my expectations, however, Gordon's frown only deepened, pulling creases in his forehead and next to his eyes. It was then that I had my first inkling that our quarry was something other than the truth.

Gordon rooted through his bag, then held out his hand. Three objects were displayed in his palm: a piece of cork, a metal bottle cap, and a red cap from a plastic soda bottle. Categorical symmetry, typical Gordon.

"Let me re-rephrase the question. Of these *man-made means of keeping liquid in a container*, which will be around the longest?"

"You mean as a method?"

Gordon closed his eyes and pinched the bridge of his nose, something he only did when he was frustrated with me. Ignoring the fact that my question was entirely reasonable, it usually took about five rounds of obtuseness on my part to warrant a nose pinch.

"No, Sam," he sighed, as if already beyond the limits of patience. "As an object. Which of these three *objects* will outlast the others?"

I usually enjoyed playing Socrates with Gordon. But it was clear that was not what we were doing. This conversation was not heading toward a teachable moment. Whatever the game was, I didn't feel like playing. I just wanted to hike and pick up litter. Instead of giving him the right answer, which was obvious enough, given the context, I just tossed one up to the winds.

"The metal one?"

"Wrong!" he exclaimed, an odd note of triumph in his voice.

I'm not exactly sure why my being wrong made him so happy, but it did. Which was fine. I was clearly not essential to the dialogue, so there was no reason to take it personally. *Whatever floats your boat*, I thought.

Gordon tossed the metal cap and the cork back into the bag, then held the red cap up between his thumb and forefinger, inspecting it like it was a jewel or a rare coin. "It is *not* the metal one. It's this one, right here. The plastic one."

"Neat," I said indifferently, scrambling off the path in pursuit of a bendable slushie straw wedged between two boulders.

"And which one will outlast man?"

"All of them," I grunted, struggling to remove the straw. My hand, so long as it held the straw, was too big to exit from the crack. Sighing in frustration, I let the straw go and slipped my hand free, turning my thoughts to devising some new strategy for extracting it.

Gordon frowned at me for a second, as if puzzled by the fact that I wasn't giving him my full attention. Proving my intellectual superiority over rock, I steered the straw from its prison with a twig, tossing it ceremoniously into my bag. Filled with the sense of satisfaction only a bona fide tool maker can feel, I returned to the path, where Gordon was still holding up the plastic cap for inspection.

"Come on, Sam," he said. "Think about it."

Okay fine. "The plastic one."

"Yes! The plastic one. Good. And how long do you think it will be around?"

I shrugged helplessly. I didn't care. I really and truly didn't. I found myself wondering how many students Socrates typically lost after the first week of incessant dialoguing.

"Forever," Gordon answered for me. "It will be here, on this planet—lying in the dirt, or floating out at sea, swirling around in the great Pacific Gyre—along with a billion other pieces of *fucking plastic*—forever."

The edge in his voice, along with his choice of words, had my attention. I stared at him intently, though he no longer seemed to notice me.

"Forever," he repeated. "Or until the sun goes supernova, anyway. As recently as a hundred years ago, the world had never known plastic, and was hardly lesser for it. Four and a half billion years and no plastic. Now, thanks to the *ingenuity* of the mutant, hairless ape that is man, the earth will never again be without it. And do you know why? Convenience. That's why. That's what we place our ingenuity in the service of! And what is convenience? Laziness. Indifference to life, to the challenge of being alive. It's always been that way, too. That's what the history of technology is, the history of humanity: the constant, inexorable creep of convenience. It's what humans value above all. More than life, more than nature, more than the future. Plastic is the pinnacle, the apotheosis of convenience. Which is why we shouldn't be surprised by the fact of its fucking ubiquity. Ubiquitous. *U-bi-qui-tous.* Do you know what that means?"

I did, which was beside the point. It was clear I wasn't supposed to answer.

"It means *everywhere*. On everything, *in* everything. Omnipresent. That's the word for plastic. Four-point-five-billion years and no plastic. Clearly, it's not an essential material, as far as the rest of the cosmos is concerned. But it is for us. We can't live without it, can't *imagine* living without it. And no wonder. It's everywhere, *in* everything, clogging our living space, choking fish, strangling turtles. Sure, you can make it smaller, you can keep cutting it in half until the end of time, but you'll never be rid of it. It's Zeno's dichotomy, with the indissolubility of plastic in the role of the Unity of Being. And man oh man, are we ever proud of it! And we should be. It's our baby, after all, our true legacy. It will be here, all of it, a testimonial, an indictment, of us and the culture we stood for, long after our own atoms have been returned to the cosmic dust."

He went on and on, growing more agitated and more vehement as we walked, not stopping until we'd returned to the campground and deposited our bags of litter in the bear-proof trashcan. He was quiet for some time after we got back to camp, and when he did start talking again a little later, it was about other things. It was almost as if the rant had never happened. When he did address it later, over dinner, it was only to make light of the whole thing. "So. Today. On the hike. Sorry if I got a little carried away." He winked at me and said, "Nothing to worry about, Sam. Just a bit of a personal bugaboo, I suppose."

Bugaboo: Gordon's word for the irrational hang-ups that impede clear thinking. He was ever on the lookout for them and quite adept at pointing them out. The thing about bugaboos, they were something that only afflicted other people. Not him.

At the time, I was more annoyed than anything. It was mostly just the simple fact of his acting so irrationally. I wasn't used to it, and my response was to be irritated. If plastic was indeed a bugaboo of his, he had never shown it before. Afterwards though, I couldn't help but see it. He would shake his head and mutter under his breath whenever he saw a piece of plastic lying on the ground, or notice someone drinking water out of a plastic bottle. He refused to drink coffee from Styrofoam cups, and started using his index finger to mix the milk and sugar in his coffee. Every extraneous piece of plastic—anything, basically, that wasn't attached to it—was banished from the van.

The headaches wouldn't become apparent for another year, but as I sat there building my little lattice of twigs for the fire, I couldn't help thinking that maybe that was the day when it all started, the day the first little crack appeared.

I forced myself not to dwell on it, focusing instead on the here and now, on what was right in front of me. Overall, it hadn't been such a bad day. Sure, my plan had been derailed, but that was only temporary, and only because Gordon was in good spirits. I wasn't going to do anything to jinx that. The night was warm, the first stars were out, and the food was on.

We ate our dinner with relish, and sat by the fire in contented silence, staring into the flames and following the rapid ascent of the occasional spark. We tended the fire for a while then let it be, gazing up at the starry sky until the flames had lowered to nothing and the softly glowing embers barely warmed the soles of our shoes. We made our evening *toilette* at a nearby spigot, then crawled in the tent and into our sleeping bags, dropping off quickly to what I hoped would be an uneventful night's sleep.

It was dry and clear and warm as we set out from camp late the next morning. Day four of The Plan, which was now very far off script. We hiked from Buckhorn Campground to the junction of the Burkhart Trail, a dusty single-track winding through shallow canyons covered in chaparral and coastal sage. The idea, according to Gordon, was to make the daylong hike to Cooper Falls and back. It wasn't long before I realized that the Burkhart Trail was in fact the same one we'd taken two years ago. Which made me a little uneasy. What if the trail was still filled with litter? What if it was worse?

It turned out to be completely free from litter of any kind, which was something of a surprise. Who knows? Maybe a Boy Scout troop in pursuit of their ecology badges came through or something, scooping up every piece of litter along the way. Whatever the case, it was a relief to be hiking on a clean, uncluttered trail. Not only did it make for a more beautiful day, it also reduced the likelihood of Gordon coming unglued.

Although it was only about three miles from camp to the Falls, it seemed like we hiked through five different ecosystems.

One minute we were walking through a shady forest of Jeffrey Pine, the ground along the path blanketed with ferns and wildflowers and tall green grass, the next we were out in the open sunshine, the foliage suddenly sparse and rugged, with scattered spruce and rocky outcrops and views that went on for miles. Other scenes were straight out of Sir Walter Scott, with sylvan streams trickling along lush canyon floors, while off in the distance red cedars clung to the sides of steep and rugged mountainsides, sometimes growing straight out of giant granite boulders.

Gordon seemed to be on another solid day. He strode effortlessly along the path, whistling jaunty versions of his favorite punk tunes as he went, the spring in his step enhanced by the fact that the path to the Falls sloped gently downward.

We reached the Falls just before noon. As it was almost the end of summer, it would be more accurate to describe the waterfall as an intermittent trickle, one that had its hands full just keeping the moss covered rock face damp. The pool at its bottom was still and shallow and a little scummy around the edges. None of which made the spot any less refreshing. The day had been getting steadily warmer, but the canyon was completely shaded and still held the cool, fresh air of morning. We scrambled from the top of the falls down to the canyon floor, then climbed onto a large, flat rock next to the "frog pond" and ate our lunch. As we sat, munching on cheese sandwiches and gorp, drinking water from our reusable *metal* bottles, my thoughts wandered aimlessly, eventually settling on an activity—a kind of game, actually—that Gordon and I used to play.

The game is played in a busy place, a big city bus station or, better yet, an airport. You wade into the middle of a busy terminal and find yourself an inconspicuous spot on a bench or comfy chair. Then you sit and watch the people as they stream past, this way and that, lost in their thoughts or in conversation with one another, all on their way to or from some other place. Gordon and I would take turns picking people out of the crowd. The object of the game was to uncover something good about your person before they disappeared from view. Something that proved you had looked deeper than the surface, past their physical appearance or the style of their clothing. Something that indicated they cared about someone, or that someone cared about them. Something special or redeeming. Something to love.

We each had our own method for discovering the lovable. Mine was basically sympathetic. I tended to focus on physical traits, especially things that somehow showed a person's perseverance: a limp, a slight disfigurement, like a facial scar or a gnarled hand, any indication that a person was not the picture of perfect health. For some reason, I found it easier to love people who had something "wrong" with them. Gordon typically zeroed in on relationships. A dad with his little girl perched on his shoulders, steering him this way and that by tugging on his ears. A hard-edged teenage couple with heavy packs and grubby clothes, runaways maybe, but laughing and holding hands as they made their way to the bus that would take them somewhere new. Sometimes he would pick out someone who seemed completely and utterly alone, and describe their missing half, the parent or child or spouse or partner out there somewhere, who they loved and who loved them back.

I'm not sure why sitting by a mossy pool in the middle of the Angeles National Forest, with no one around but Gordon, made me think of time spent in busy bus terminals and airports. Maybe it had to do with how happy I always felt when we played that game, how it made me feel peaceful and reassured about life, convinced that people were good and things were going to be okay. I guess that's how I felt sitting in the little oasis with Gordon, like somehow everything was going to work out. I couldn't help feeling that things were looking up. The last two days had been good. Not great, but better than expected. Maybe it wasn't asking too much to hope that Gordon was actually getting better, that he was finally slipping free of whatever darkness had been afflicting him.

We finished our lunch and stood up, stretching out the little aches and kinks that had crept into our muscles. We secured our packs and climbed back to the top of the Falls, heading for camp. The sun was now straight overhead, strong and hot. We'd be back at the camp before long, with plenty of time to spare for a nice, leisurely game of catch.

The hike back to camp was actually harder then the hike out. For one thing, the slightly downhill slope of the trail to the Falls was now a slight uphill. For another, the temperature rose steadily the whole way back. The strong afternoon sun, combined with the total absence of any wind, made for a pretty hot afternoon. We were barely halfway home when we ran out of water, and we had to stop in the shade a couple of times to try and cool off. When we did finally make it back to camp we were tired, grimy, and probably a little bit dehydrated. Gordon was quiet and seemed to have shrunk. Relieved to be back, I felt somehow wary, though I was too tired to bother trying to figure out why.

I'm not afraid of too many things, for a kid. Insects, spiders, rodents, clowns, spaces open or closed; none of that stuff gets to me. The so-called scary movies I've seen didn't really scare me or give me nightmares or keep me up at night. I'm not particularly squeamish at the sight of blood, including my own. And while I'm generally wary of strangers (which is to say, everybody), it's a pretty rare occasion that I'm actually frightened by one. If there's one thing I am a little afraid of, it would be the dark.

Well, not a little afraid. I'm pretty much terrified of the dark. Not your basic, hard-to-make-things-out-in dark, but pitch-black dark. Absolute, can't-see-your-hand-in-front-of-your-face darkness. I think it has something to do with the fact that the absence of light, of even the faintly visible outline of objects, places me entirely at the mercy of my imagination. And my imagination, it turns out, prefers to go to scary places.

Luckily, I don't have to confront this fear very often. Night usually finds us in the back of the van or maybe a motel room. Motel rooms get plenty of light, so long as you keep the blackout curtains drawn, which Gordon is kind enough to do. The Vanagon, too, lets in all sorts of light: moonlight, floodlight, light from passing traffic, parking lot lights, streetlight. While I love the comforting powdery orange of the streetlights, Gordon absolutely hates it. Before the thing with plastic came along, orange streetlight was his only bugaboo: "Just who, exactly, called for every inch of the known world to be slathered in this soul-sucking orange shit, anyway?"

When I do find myself in genuine darkness, it's usually because I've been caught off guard, like the time in a gas station restroom when the ceiling light suddenly burned out. One minute I was peeing contentedly, the next, everything was black. Not a speck of light found its way in from outside, not even through the crack at the bottom of the door. It was not a big space, maybe six feet by six feet, so it wouldn't have been a problem, for the average person, to zip up and calmly find their way to the door. Not me. I couldn't move, I couldn't breathe. Completely paralyzed, I was unable to think beyond the single thought that the entire world had simply flashed out of existence, that everything I had ever known was just an illusion, a flimsy construction that could be wiped away with a simple flip of the switch, leaving nothing but an endless black. Well, someone *had* flipped the switch and thrown me into nothingness. One problem with being afraid of the dark is you can't hide from it. You can only try to get out of it and into the light. But you can't get to the light if you don't know where it is, if you can't move. I stood there, inert, for I don't know how long. Gradually, I managed to regain a jot of composure. I zipped up my pants and, putting my hands out in front of me like the blind man that I was, inched my way through the dark until I bumped into the wall. I felt my way along it, stooping beneath the immense weight of pure nothingness pressing down on me. I made my way to the door. Gripping the handle like a lifeline, I jerked it open and stepped out into the blinding, beautiful daylight.

I was covered in sweat and shaking uncontrollably. By the time I had climbed back in the van I was crying. Alarmed, Gordon leaned over and placed his hands on my shoulders, lowering his face to mine and trying to look into my eyes, which I averted, for some sign of what had happened. I'm sure he thought someone had attacked me or something. For my part, I was embarrassed. It had taken everything I had to get myself under control. When I had calmed down enough to look him in the eye, he asked, in the most serious voice I had ever heard him use, "What happened, Sam?"

"Nothing," I answered with a sniff.

He wasn't buying it. He sat back in his chair and waited.

I closed my eyes and shuddered. "The light in the bathroom went out," I said. "I panicked."

Gordon knew all about my phobia, so took me by the shoulders again and nodded. "Hey," he said softly. "Are you okay?"

"I'm fine," I said. "Let's just go."

He threw the van into gear and pulled out of the station. My mind was swirling so rapidly it almost hurt, like when the feeling returns to a limb that's fallen asleep. After we'd driven along for a while, I turned to him and asked, "Is it possible to be afraid of nothing?"

He mulled the question over. "Well," he began. "Not sure. That's sort of a semantically ambiguous question, don't you think?"

"What?"

"It depends on what you mean by 'afraid of nothing.' Whether you're referring to fearlessness or nihilophobia."

"Sorry?"

"Nihilophobia," he repeated. "The fear of nothingness, of non-being."

"Um, yeah," I agreed tentatively. "That one."

"Well, that's a tough one, Sam. I mean, it's pretty much *the* primordial question, isn't it?"

"The *what?*"

"The primordial question. The first, the most basic, of all questions, the starting point of all philosophy: *Why is there something and not nothing?*"

"Right. And what's the answer?"

Gordon laughed. "Aye, there's the rub. There is no answer. At least there's no final, definitive answer. To be sure, plenty of history's finest minds have pondered the question—your pal Leibniz, for example—and taken a stab at formulating an answer."

As was often the case, Gordon became absorbed in his own reflections, seemingly forgetting that we were in the middle of a conversation.

"*And?*" I prodded.

"Hmm?"

"The answers? To the primordial question?"

"Oh, yes. Well, the best of them are basically circular nonsense, and the rest are pretty much cheap knockoffs of the ontological argument."

I could only throw my hands up in the air in response to that.

"The ontological argument," Gordon said, shooting me a sideways glance that somehow felt like a mild reproach. "A type of proof of the existence of a Supreme Being, of God, by way of arguments based solely on so-called reason."

"What does God have to do with it?"

"Exactly."

The Vanagon continued chewing up the miles while we sat in silence.

"What do you think?" I asked finally.

Gordon thought it over for a bit, his eyes fixed on the road.

When he replied, his voice was full of conviction. "What I think is that having unanswerable questions is a good thing. Not knowing everything, being *unable* to know everything, is what makes knowing possible, is what makes anything that is possible, *possible*."

Speaking of possible, it's possible that Gordon's plan was to help me to forget about my bathroom ordeal through misdirection and confusion. If so, it had worked. Experience told me if I didn't change the course of things soon, he'd just take me further down the rabbit hole.

"Why do people have phobias, anyway?" I asked.

His answer came so quickly it was like he'd rehearsed it in anticipation of my question. "Phobias, like all human behavior, originate in the brain, in discrete structures that deal with potentially threatening stimuli, such as a lion or a menacing facial expression, as well as those that process emotions, like fear and anxiety. These are not little people inside our head making certain rational decisions for us; they're anatomical structures, biological mechanisms. Electrochemical machines that operate entirely within the bounds of established physical laws. They do what they're told, nothing more, nothing less. With me so far?"

"Sure."

"Okay. Now throw in the fact that some of these little fear machines also have a hand in the formation of memory, and it becomes possible for the physical experience of an instance of actual fear—let's call it a *trauma*—to become attached, often quite strongly, to the memory of that experience. Taking that logic a step further, it's possible for the experience of fear to become attached to a component of memory, like a smell, or a color, or a sound, something incidental to the memory that is not fearsome in and of itself."

I could only sit there with my mouth open, equally impressed and dumbfounded at how far from my original question he'd taken us in so short a time.

"To take an example," he went on, "it's possible for a child, after being stung by a bee while running through a field of wildflowers, to harbor from then on not only a justifiable fear of bees or other flying insects, but also an irrational fear of flowers, for the simple reason that they were present at the scene of the trauma."

It made sense, I guess. I wondered what trivial, harmless trigger lay behind my fear of the dark.

"Are people ever born with phobias?" I asked.

"I should think not. I mean, the mechanisms are there in everybody, part of our biology, so the capacity is certainly inherited, but while the formation of fear as a means of self-preservation is most likely instinctual, individual fears are not. Take fetishes, for example. You can't reasonably describe a shoe fetish as innate when the brain function responsible for such things probably predates the existence of shoes by about a hundred-and-sixty-thousand years."

"I'm sorry?" I said, shaking my head in confusion.

Gordon rewarded my obtuseness with a disdainful sigh and an arched eyebrow. "We're born with the container, but not the content."

"Got it. So basically, anything can become a phobia?"

"Probably. You just take the Greek or Latin root for that thing and tack a *-phobia* onto the back of it. Claustrophobia, for example, is derived by adding the Latin word for a closed-in-space, *claustrum*, to the Greek word for fear, *phobos*."

"Cool," I said, nodding appreciatively. "All right then: Flowers?"

"Anthophobia," he answered without missing a beat.

"Bees?"

"Melissophobia."

"Nice. Heights?"
"Acrophobia."
"Balloons?"
"Globophobia."

Okay, I thought, *time for a curve ball or two.*

"Phobias?"

"Easy," he laughed. "Phobophobia."

"Mmm-hmm. Big words?"

"Sesquipedalophobia."

"You're making that up!"

"I'm not," he laughed again, holding up the middle and index fingers of his right hand. "Scout's honor."

I shook my head. This was the fruit of a life spent in books: knowledge. I wondered if I would ever find Gordon's lacking.

"Truly anything then?"

"Anything, Sam. Anything at all." A serious look crossed his face then, like a dark cloud sweeping across a sunny field, and he added, "Even children."

A somber silence came over him, leaving me alone with my own thoughts and concerns. I still hadn't learned anything, I realized, about my own phobia.

"All right," I began again. "How about my fear, fear of the dark?"

"Acluophobia," he answered indifferently, as if no longer interested in the tedious game of naming phobias.

"No. I mean, why do I have it; what does it mean?"

"Oh, I don't know Sam," he answered, his voice sounding tired. "Being afraid of the dark is a pretty common thing, especially when you're young."

"Okay. The thing is, it's not actually the dark I'm afraid of. It's the nothingness inside of it. Do you know what I mean?"

"Maybe," he said with a shrug. "Sometimes things get crossed up, one thing is substituted for another, and a seemingly obvious fear turns out to be a mask for something deeper."

"Like what?"

"Like fear of the dark standing in for the more primordial fear of non-being, itself just a substitute for the one fear behind all the others, the fear of death."

I smirked. I was not afraid of death.

Gordon smiled and shook his head. "I know. You're not afraid of death. Which isn't quite the case. The truth is, it's not so much a question of your being unafraid of death as the fact that you never *think* about death, which is quite different."

I was about to object to this assumption, but then thought about it for a second and realized he was right. I nodded faintly to show my acceptance.

"Don't worry," he went on. "I only know about this stuff because it applies to me, too."

Whatever else, my moment of terror in the men's room was by then a distant memory. It's possible our little dialogue helped me to better understand my fear. Then again, it's possible that it did nothing at all. I thought about asking Gordon what he was afraid of, but decided against it. I told myself he probably wouldn't answer me anyway, but that wasn't the reason I held my tongue. What kept me from asking was the slight possibility that he *would* answer. And I knew, in my heart, that if there *was* something he was afraid of, I didn't want to hear it.

When I woke, naturally, it was to the purest, deepest black imaginable. To the most absolute darkness I have ever experienced. I could just as well have been in the bowels of the earth, or at the bottom of the Mariana Trench, as inside our tent.

I searched the darkness for my small flashlight, even as I felt the first slight stirring of darkness-panic. I started to shiver as I patted the ground beside me, not out of fear, but because I was cold. And I was cold because I was wet. The right side of my sleeping bag—my hand confirmed it—was quite damp. I reached inside the bag and felt the right leg of my pants. Also damp, but less so than the outside of my bag. Bringing my hand to my face, I caught a faint but unmistakable whiff of urine. Somehow, at some deep-down, animal level, I knew it wasn't mine. Still punchy but growing rapidly more alarmed, I reached out to my right, where Gordon was sleeping. His bag, like mine, was wet. But unlike mine, it wasn't just damp, it was completely soaked. And empty.

In an instant my childish fear of the dark, the irrational preoccupation with what *might happen*, vanished, replaced by the authentic fright of discovering that something bad was *actually happening*. I had slept too soundly, and so I missed it: sometime during the night, Gordon had crossed over into that other place, losing control of himself and wetting his bag. He woke up and then went wandering out into the night.

Wriggling out of my bag, I crawled around on my hands and knees, searching as calmly as I could for the flashlight. I eventually found it right where I had purposefully left it, in the small pocket sewn into the side of the tent. Cursing my panicky self I turned the light on, breathing in the relief that came with even that little bit of illumination. I managed to get myself under something like control, then took a last deep breath and scrambled out of the tent.

Zipping the tent closed behind me, I stood up and flashed the light into the chill night air. The beam appeared solid as it moved through the dark, casting narrow cones of light about the campsite. It would have been too much to ask, of course, to simply find Gordon sitting there, perched on a rock. Instead, I found the campground empty and still. The bear-proof box was still closed, as it had been since our arrival the day before. The fire pit was completely dead, not a single trace remaining of the fire that had blazed there just a few hours earlier: no heat, no embers, not even a wisp of smoke. I walked over to the Vanagon, rubbing dew from the windows and peering inside, even though I knew he wouldn't be there either. That would also have been too easy. I made my way nervously to the edge of our campsite, perched atop a pretty steep hillside, if not an outright precipice. A vivid image of Gordon, lying broken and bloody at the bottom, flashed through my mind as I looked over, but my sweeping flashlight revealed only an empty gully.

I felt a brief moment of relief, then the enormity of the situation hit me: I would have to begin searching the surrounding area.

Alone and in the dark.

I turned the flashlight off so my eyes could begin adjusting to the darkness, but also to get some sense of what it would be like for Gordon out there, walking around the woods without a light. There was no moon to fill the cloudless sky with its glow, no softly luminous heavenly orb to reassure me, to guide me through radiant woods. The light from the millions of people in the cities and towns in the sprawling valley below wasn't much help either, visible from this height as little more than a weakly twinkling field, an upside-down sky of stars. Seeing the faint light from so many homes all filled with people sleeping safely in their beds only made me more aware of how alone and isolated I was. I stood for some time in the darkness, doing my best to keep my fear of it from seeping back in, trying to build up the necessary resolve for the search ahead, waiting as patiently as possible for my eyes to adjust.

I drew up a mental map of the campground, trying to picture its numerous hazards, the literal pitfalls it would present to someone walking around in the dark, someone who had neither a flashlight nor his wits. Trees, roots, boulders, gullies, fire pits, logs, bear-proof boxes; there were dozens of things for Gordon to hurt himself on. I had to acknowledge that there wasn't the slightest chance Gordon could see where he was going out there. I couldn't help imagining him stumbling about blindly. I was convinced that he'd fallen. The only question was where.

In a way, the physical dangers were actually the least of my concerns. I was far more worried about him stumbling into one of the other campsites. How would someone react to a deranged, urine-soaked man barging into their tent in the middle of the night? While the fact that there were only a few other campers around made the possibility of an unfortunate encounter less likely, I was still concerned enough to start my search there. My initial sweep turned up nothing, even though it wasn't completely thorough, since I was careful not to make any noise or shine my light on any of the other tents.

My relief at not finding Gordon tangled up with other campers was short-lived. I had to acknowledge that my search had just begun. My chances of finding him in the middle of the night, armed with nothing but a small flashlight, were pretty much zero. The only positive thing was that the night was not as chilly as it had first felt—it was almost mild, in fact—and even though my pants were still a little damp, I was warmer now than when I first woke up. At least Gordon, wet or not, was not at risk of hypothermia.

Where to look? I tried to consider the situation calmly and rationally, the way Gordon would have. A person had gone walking off into the night. That person was not in the campground, meaning he was somewhere in the neighboring forest. Even if that person had a logical destination in mind—which he didn't, because this person also happened to be suffering from some form of lunacy—he was not likely to find it, since it was pitch dark out and he had no flashlight. Clearly, the only rational thing to do was to wait until morning, when it was light out, and enlist the aid of others.

Which just so happened to be the last thing I wanted to do. I wanted to *act*. There was no way I could handle just sitting there, waiting, doing nothing. I needed to keep myself busy, and the only way to do that was by searching. More importantly, the questions that would arise from enlisting the aid of strangers, involving them in our situation, was not something I was ready to risk. Finding him was up to me and me alone. So I started searching, beginning with the area around the Burkhart trailhead, hoping against hope that I'd just get lucky and stumble across him, walking aimlessly but harmlessly along the trail.

After nearly an hour of randomly roaming around, sometimes on the trail, sometimes in the brush beside it, lurching over rocky, uneven terrain, I had to admit that it was pointless. I'd lost Gordon, and I wasn't going to find him. Not in the middle of the night. Not by myself.

My flashlight was spitting out a dull yellow light, so weak it barely managed to make it as far as the ground. Feeling the darkness closing in on me, I began jogging for the safety of our campsite. I was lucky I even made it back to the campground. Exhausted, my limbs buzzing with the last few molecules of adrenaline left in my body, I collapsed onto a log bench in front of the empty Ranger's shack. I sat beneath the flickering light of a dying fluorescent bulb and buried my face in my hands.

The full weight of it hit me, like a million gallons of water dumped right on my head by one of those forest-fire airplanes: it was over. Done. All of it. Everything. Our life together, our way of being in the world. Gordon's way. My life, the only life I'd ever known, was over. Gordon could already have been dead or dying for all I knew. Even if he wasn't, there was no way I was going to find him by myself. The only chance I had of finding him was to get help from other people. People who would find out about our life, about what had been going on for the past year, about what I was doing, and it would be over. My mind alternated between images of Gordon lying in some ditch, his eyes open and unmoving, and me, sitting in a remedial math class in some state run institution for orphans and delinquents.

My face still in my hands, it wasn't until my head started to hurt that I realized I was crying, openly crying. Even as I sat there blubbering, I couldn't help pointing an accusing finger at myself. Why? Why had I allowed him to drive us out here, to the middle of nowhere, when I knew it couldn't possibly end well? A river of stupid, hot tears merged with the salty snot leaking from my nose, coating my palms and my face. Sitting up, I rubbed my hands on my thighs, and wiped the ignoble slime from my face with a swipe of my sleeve.

Fuck.

That's all I could think, even though I'm not prone to cursing: fuck. *Fuck, fuck, fuck.*

What did I think I was doing, really? Why was it so impossible for us to acknowledge—for *Gordon* to acknowledge—that we needed help, that without it something like this was bound to happen? What, exactly, was the point of trying to keep our life ticking along like normal, like everything was peachy, when it was clearly impossible, when the black clouds had already massed overhead?

Typically, even in this moment of crisis, my thoughts wandered. I recalled one of our birthday dinners, Gordon's, I think. He drank two small carafes of red wine during dinner, and only poked at his steak. I had already come to recognize the connection between his rare indulgences in drink with the even rarer bouts of disclosure. Wiping a dribble of wine from his beard with his white napkin, Gordon leaned back against the maroon leather of the low-backed booth. He looked at me carefully, as if weighing the pros and cons of telling me what he was about to tell me. He tugged at his shaggy beard, his eyes sparkling in the low light of the steak house. His eyes narrowed and his chin dipped toward his sternum. I waited with baited breath, eager for whatever nuggets of information he was about to reveal.

He blinked once, slowly, then nodded to himself. "Things come apart for people," he said, his voice quiet.

I smiled awkwardly and waited, wondering how he was going to tie that sentiment to the pending revelation.

"Not *fall* apart, though that happens too," he continued. "Things *come* apart."

He reached for the nearly empty carafe and tilted it toward

his equally empty glass, taking no notice of the fact that only a few ruby drops trickled into it.

"Things come apart and there's nothing people can do about it, because it's in the nature of the universe."

I tried not to let my disappointment show. This wasn't going to be one of those rare let-me-tell-you-a-little-something-about-your-mother conversations. It was going to be one of those far less rare nature-of-the-universe-and-its-relation-to-the-human-condition conversations.

He raised his glass to his lips, tilting it until it was nearly upside-down, letting those last few drops fall onto his tongue.

"The universe is expanding," he intoned, "at something on the order of seventy kilometers per second per megaparsec. And not just expanding, it's accelerating. The most distant stars—you've never seen them—are very likely moving away from us faster than the speed of light."

He paused long enough to squint at me and take a drink of air from his empty glass.

"All of which implies, quite clearly, that the ultimate purpose of the universe is to pull itself apart."

He waved his hand in the air, as if batting away a question I hadn't asked.

"Smaller bodies, of course, planets and solar systems, asteroid belts, are bound by the weak force of gravity, so the effect of this expansion on them is negligible. This gives them the *appearance* of stability, of something like permanence. People, *human beings*, fall into this category of smaller bodies, adding the weak force of their will to that of gravity. Human will. Pure futility. It's just an illusion, you see, the greater force is, in fact, constantly subjecting those seemingly stable *small bodies* to its superior will, undoing them, joylessly unraveling the pointless efforts of those bodies to hold themselves together. What, after all, is human will compared to the desire of the universe?"

He looked away from me and into the bottom of his wine glass, a slightly puzzled expression on his face, as if only just then aware of its emptiness. I just stared at him, unsure of what to say. What was the point of this?

"Things come apart," he repeated. "For people and for everything else. It's built into the nature of things, into the *fucking fabric* of it, there's nothing anyone can do about it."

He regained his composure a little bit then, a small degree of here-and-nowness, making up for his harangue by letting me order a hot fudge sundae for dessert.

I didn't make much of it at the time. Cosmic digressions were a bit of a thing with him, and while they were often entertaining, they just as often flew right over my head. As far as 'things coming apart for people' was concerned, I assumed he was talking about other people, not us.

Sitting there beneath the dying fluorescent light, I understood what he meant quite clearly. Because it was happening to us—to me—at that very moment. The world as I had known it, the little solar system comprised of me and Gordon, seemingly stable and orderly as clockwork, was being pulled apart from the inside out, just like the rest of the universe. There was no stopping it, no reason for it. It was simply in the nature of the universe to pull things apart. It happened to everything and everyone. Why fight it?

Why not?

That was the answer that popped into my head, delivered by two voices simultaneously. My voice, and Gordon's too.

Yes. *Why not?* Why give in, *why not* resist the inevitable? That's how *we* did things. Why do what's expected, why *be* what's expected, just because it's expected? Just because it happens to be in the nature of the universe? I thought of Gordon's definition of free will: "The ability to affect the interim, not the outcome." And I still had something to say about the interim.

Sometimes, the harder way is the only way. Time to stop crying.

Pressing a fingertip to the side of my nose, I blew out a tenacious stream of snot, clearing first one nostril, then the other. I wiped my eyes with the back of my hand. Streaks of grime showed clearly in the flickering light, and I realized that it had been days since my last proper shower. I was filthy, equal parts sweat and dirt and tears and Gordon's urine. I don't like being filthy.

I needed to gather myself, to be mentally and physically prepared for the morning, for the coming day. I would resume my search in the light of day, and this time I would get help. From the Ranger and other campers and anyone else who offered it. I needed other people. There was no other way. Maybe we would find Gordon, maybe we wouldn't. Maybe life as I had known it would change, maybe it wouldn't. I would deal with whatever happened when it happened.

Whatever my fate might be, I preferred to meet it all clean and shiny, and not coated in grime and smelling like an animal. I took as much air into my lungs as I could, then exhaled slowly. I got up from the log bench and headed for the washroom.

Instead of heading straight to the washroom, I made a quick detour to the campsite, grabbing a towel and some soap from the van. If I was going to wash up, I might as well do a proper job of it. I popped into the tent, swapping my tired flashlight for Gordon's fresh one. Draping the towel around my neck, I jogged off to the washroom.

I paused by the washroom entrance, momentarily distracted by the dense cloud of insects swarming around the big yellow light. They circled it in crazed orbits, making soft tinking sounds as they crashed headlong into the bulb, their carapaces and compound eyes no match for the glass. I found the sound strangely beautiful, though I understood it came at the expense of living beings braining themselves.

The men's washroom consisted of two open-air sit-down toilets, two small sinks, set into the cinder block wall beneath a pair of scratched metal mirrors, and two small shower stalls hung with tattered, opaque-plastic shower curtains, all gloomily lit by a naked fluorescent light in the center of the ceiling. I was relieved to discover that the dead animal smell from the day before seemed to have disappeared, though the dank air still held a whiff of unclean toilet.

I walked over to one of the sinks and turned on the faucet. I tried to avoid looking at myself in the mirror, but I couldn't help catching a quick glimpse of the complete mess I had become. I looked like a real Struwwelpeter. I took off my shirt and draped it over the top of a toilet stall. An ancient rubber stopper was attached to the end of a rusty chain anchored to the base of the chrome faucet. I wedged the stopper in the drain and filled the small porcelain sink. Leaning over the bowl, I closed my eyes and splashed my face with clear, cold water. I rubbed my face vigorously, almost angrily, then splashed it some more. Cupping my hand to the mouth of the faucet, I took a long, cool drink. I stood up and patted my face dry with the towel. Opening my eyes, I found I could at least tolerate the person reflected in the mirror. The water in the bowl was now dark gray, almost black.

I pulled the plug and watched the water drain slowly from the sink. It made a slight sucking sound as it emptied. This sound grew louder as the sink drained, so it took me a second to realize that it had been joined by another. A low, guttural sound. An animal sound. A sound from what Gordon called *the lower order of being.*

I turned my head slowly, trying to zero in on the source of this other sound. It stopped for a few seconds, and started up again. It was definitely coming from inside the washroom. From one of the shower stalls, in fact. It went on for five seconds, ten, low and ominous, then stopped again.

I felt a surge of panic, my pulse pounding rapidly in my ears. Apparently, I needed to add moaning wild animals to my list of fears. I resisted the urge to turn and run, thinking any sudden noise might alarm whatever was lurking behind the shower curtain. Marshaling every ounce of self-control, I backed away slowly, inching as quietly as possible toward the door. I was nearly there when the noise returned. I was practically free and clear, I only had to turn and run, but for some reason I hesitated. The noise, it seemed to me, wasn't angry or threatening. It was more pathetic than anything. Like the sound of something wounded. Or dying.

Something needed my help, which changed things. My natural impulse to help, reinforced by a lifetime of Gordon's example, pushed my fear of the unknown into the background. I walked over to the shower stall. I stood in front of it for a moment, holding my breath, then reached out and slowly pulled the curtain aside. I looked down at the floor, at the animal making the strange moaning noise.

It was Gordon.

My father was lying on the moist, concrete floor of the stall. He was curled up into a ball, his knees pulled up close against his chest with his arms wrapped around them. He was completely naked, save for his dirty under shorts. His entire body, from the soles of his bare feet to his thick, matted hair, was covered in dirt. His eyes were shut tight, his face contorted into a grimace, his lips trembling. His awful moaning stopped again, replaced by uncontrollable shivering.

Seeing Gordon—a kind, intelligent being, a lion of a man, a loving father—reduced to such a state, imagining the harrowing path that had led him to it, was like taking a series of sledgehammer blows right to the heart. I pounded my fist against my forehead in frustration. I leaned my head back and stared at the ceiling. A deep, dull ache closed around my chest. I felt lost, helpless. For the first time in my life I felt truly homeless. The days or weeks or whatever it was since we'd last enjoyed the familiar comforts of a library felt like a thousand years. I found myself desperately wishing this nightmare would end and I would wake up in a small, cozy library in some out-of-the-way town, wrapped up in my fleece blanket, Gordon working away beneath the soft, green glow of a nearby desk lamp.

Only the fact that there was so much to be done, right here, right now, saved me from completely caving in on myself. An immediate course of action presented itself in the form of a list: make sure Gordon was not seriously injured; get through to him somehow, try to calm and reassure him; get him cleaned up; get him dry and warm and into fresh clothing; get him resting comfortably in the van; break down the campsite and pack up our stuff. By the time all that was done, I figured, it would be light enough to drive back down the winding road to the valley, then straight on to Riverside.

I got down on my knees and examined Gordon more closely. At first glance, he seemed unharmed. When I helped him lift his head from the ground, however, I saw that the entire right side of his face, the side he'd been lying on, was covered in blood. The hair above his ear was also matted with blood, and there were reddish-brown streaks of it on his shoulder and collarbone. Feeling panic surging forward once again, I closed my eyes and took a series of deep breaths, pushing it back. *I was not afraid of a little blood.* Leaning in closer, I checked his face and head for wounds. There was nothing major that I could see, no cuts or punctures or gashes. I wiped his face gently with my towel. Most of the blood came off easily enough, except for whatever was stuck in his hair and beard. It was thickest on his mustache, and I realized, with a strange sense of relief, that it had simply been a nosebleed.

At first, Gordon responded to my ministrations with a weak whimpering. Then he growled threateningly, lashing out at me with his left arm. I tried to ignore him as he barked at me, catching only snippets—*No! Who? That's not!*—as I was more concerned with getting him into an upright position so I could move him out from beneath the shower head. I couldn't turn it on with him where he was, as there was no telling how he'd respond to the shock of getting hit with cold water. Because of our size difference, I found him almost impossible to move. In response to my prodding and pulling, he curled back up into a stiffened ball, which was actually a stroke of luck, since it allowed me to just kind of roll him over to the corner of the stall. Once there, it wasn't so difficult to heave him into an upright position.

Seated with his back against the wall, Gordon swatted at the air in front of him. His eyes still closed, he growled menacingly, "Is this it? Is this what you want? Is it? IS IT?!" He threw a jerky punch at an imaginary assailant, mumbled a few words I couldn't make out, then fell back into his low, injured-sounding moaning.

Breathing heavily from the effort, I stood up and turned the shower on. The pipes pinged and clanked, the water spitting and spluttering before finally pouring out in a steady stream. Twenty seconds later and the it was quite warm. I bent down and whispered reassuring words to Gordon, telling him that his son was here and that everything was going to be okay. I told him he was going to have a shower and that it would feel nice and warm. He opened his glassy eyes, looking at me but not seeing me.

"We're going to stand up now," I told him. "It's okay. Everything is going to be okay. Are you ready?"

He didn't answer. In fact, he gave no sign that he understood or even heard me. I could almost taste my desperation. I did not have the strength to fight him every step of the way. But when I put my hands under his arms he stood right up, mostly under his own power, and allowed himself to be ushered into the water. He stood stock still beneath the steamy spray, his arms held stiffly at his sides, his hands balled up into claw-like fists.

A parent bathing a child is, I imagine, a wonderful thing, natural and right in every way. There's nothing right about a child bathing a parent. It's awkward and humiliating and physically exhausting and there is an unmistakable feeling of something being very wrong. Not morally wrong. Cosmically wrong. Contrary, as Gordon would say, to the nature of things. As difficult as moving Gordon had been, it turned out to be nothing compared to the labor of cleaning him. It took just about everything I had.

When it was finally over, when I had scrubbed every last bit of dirt and filth from his body, when I had rinsed the last rosy traces of blood from his hair and beard, things felt just a tiny bit better. He was no longer shivering, for one thing. He was balling and unballing his hands, and his lips moved as he silently mumbled, but he seemed to have one foot, or part of one anyway, back in the real world. He looked into my eyes in a way that acknowledged that he knew I was actually there. Whether he knew it was *me*, I couldn't tell.

I began drying him off, doing the best I could with a towel that was already pink with his blood and damp from my own wash-up. He stood there impassively while I wiped away at him, drying his torso and arms first, passing quickly over his privates, then toweling off his hair.

I had just crouched down onto my knees to do his calves and ankles and the tops of his feet when I heard the sound of sandaled feet outside the washroom. The sound grew louder as the footsteps approached, slapping loudly onto the washroom's concrete floor and coming to a stop a few feet behind me.

Fuck. The word of the day.

I did not move an inch, thinking—*hoping*—whoever was there would just turn around and walk out, leaving us in peace. I held my crouch and waited. Apart from the dripping of water from the showerhead and the heavy breathing of the person standing behind me, the room was quiet.

"Uh, *o-kaaay*," a voice rang out, uncertain but slightly

amused. "Interesting. What exactly're you guys up to there?"

Fuck.

"Nothing," I said, trying my best to sound as if it were true. I rose to my feet, placing the towel in Gordon's unquestioning hands, hoping he would cover himself with it, maybe even wrap it around his waist. No such luck. He just stood there, holding it in his outstretched hands. I pushed it gently towards him so it at least blocked the guy's view of his nakedness, then turned around.

I couldn't decide whether I was relieved or disappointed to find that it wasn't a Park Ranger. The guy was in his mid-thirties, maybe, a little shorter than me and very stocky. His hair was close-cropped, his face wide and simple and, as far as I could tell, understanding. Apart from the rubber flip-flops that announced his arrival, he was wearing a pair of baggy canvas shorts that hung below his knees and a loose fitting T-shirt with a Mexican beer label on it. A blue towel was draped over his shoulder and he held a plastic shaving kit in his right hand. For the life of me, I couldn't figure out what he was doing coming to shower in the middle of the night.

I scanned his face over and over, looking for some sign that he might get ugly somehow, but it was clear he was just trying to be helpful. Which was kind of amazing, I guess, when you looked at the scene from his perspective: a campground restroom in the wee hours of the morning, with a half-naked teenage boy and a spaced-out, middle-aged man, completely naked except for the wet, bloody towel held loosely in front of him. I decided I could trust this guy, to a point.

"He's my dad," I explained.

He looked from Gordon back to me a couple times, as if trying to gauge some degree of resemblance, and nodded. "Yeah, okay. Are you all right? Is he—" he tilted his head at Gordon, "—is he all right?"

A number of different answers came to mind. Only one of them was the truth, and I decided not to use it. "He just had a little too much to drink," I said. "He tripped and bloodied his nose. I was just helping him get cleaned up." I tried to make it sound like a shameful truth, one I would have preferred not to admit, one I'd had to confess before.

The guy's expression changed a little bit then, becoming less sympathetic somehow. He looked at Gordon again, staring hard with his brow furrowed. He frowned and I thought he was going to give Gordon a piece of his mind, offer me a word of advice or something, but he didn't. He just shook his head and sighed.

"Man," he said, shaking his head again. "Sorry, kid. That sucks. You need any help?"

I could tell by the sound of his voice that he really was sorry for me, maybe even for Gordon. Something the size and consistency of a small stone appeared suddenly in my throat. I had to open my mouth in order to breathe properly, to stem the flow of tears this offer of help from a complete stranger had started.

"No, thanks," I said, swallowing hard and smiling weakly at him. "I've done this before."

He frowned again at that.

"Okay," he said, the disappointment in his voice unmistakable. "If you say so. I can come back later."

He sniffed and turned to leave, then stopped. He sniffed again, before exhaling loudly.

"Look," he said. "You seem to know what you're doing, so I'm just going leave you two alone. But if you need anything, anything at all ... I'm in campsite thirteen." As if to prove that his offer was serious, he allowed his expression to return to its earlier openness.

"My name is Teddy," he said, then left.

I stared at the empty doorframe for a while, my heart thumping in my chest. I repeated the man's name again and again, until it had become a meaningless chant: *teddyteddyteddyteddyteddy*. The stone in my throat dissolved with a loud gurgle, returning me to my senses and my situation. I turned my attention to Gordon, still standing there motionless, the towel held lamely in front of him. His giant head drooped and his eyes were almost shut. I took the towel from him and finished drying him off. By the time I'd shepherded him back to our campsite day, had broken.

I dressed him in one of his last sets of clean clothes, wrapped him up in a blanket and helped him into the passenger seat, which I reclined back as far as it would go. I cleared our things from the tent, stuffing the damp sleeping bags and our soiled clothing into the canvas laundry bag. I broke down the tent and stowed it in the van along with all of our food and supplies. By the time I finished, Gordon was sleeping heavily.

I should have been exhausted but I wasn't. My whole body hummed with an odd, low-level energy. Or maybe that was just what exhaustion felt like. Who knows? Whatever it was, I felt alert and strangely alive as I climbed into the driver's seat. A little bit lucky, too. As terrible as the night's ordeal had been, it was nothing compared to the prospect of losing Gordon forever. The horizontal beams of daybreak streamed through the trees as I drove slowly through the still-sleeping campground. I had no trouble finding the winding road that led to the valley below, my head, for once, blessedly empty of thought.

Uncle Don

"Uruk, Troy, Machu Picchu."

I ticked the names off on my fingertips, one by one.

"Minoan Crete, Carthage, the Library at Alexandria. The workshop of Leonardo DaVinci. Uh ..." I glanced quickly at the list in my lap, reminding myself of what I had written next. *Ah, yes:* "Victorian London." I shrugged, still not entirely sure about that one. I saved the best for last: "Mougins," I said with a smile. "On the Mediterranean. With Picasso."

Gordon corrected my French pronunciation, but did not tilt his head in the way that meant I might want to rethink my choices. He did, however, narrow his eyes slightly, indicating that he *had* taken issue with something, most likely my "basic assumption." That being, in this instance, time travel.

It was a little over a year ago. I had been scribbling lists in my journal for almost a year. In all that time, Gordon never showed any obvious interest in my activity, though I think he more or less knew what I was up to. So when he glanced over from the driver's seat and asked, as casually as you like, what I was writing, it caught me a little off guard. Instead of thinking it through, picking a list I knew would meet his approval, I blurted out the one I'd only just finished: *People and Places to Visit with a Time Machine*.

There are few areas of knowledge (zero, in fact) where I can hold my own with Gordon. Physics, for example. I can rattle off a smattering of factoids concerning some of its major figures—the fact that Tycho Brahe wore a false brass nose, say, or that Sir Isaac Newton spent as much time searching for the Philosopher's Stone as he did studying mathematics, or that Albert Einstein was married to his cousin. Einstein also came up with the General Theory of Relativity, I know, but that doesn't mean I *understand* the first thing about it. Gordon, on the other hand, seems to have some understanding of what's *actually going on*. I don't mind this state of affairs. It puts Gordon in a position to teach me things, and I'm as happy to learn about things straight from him as I am from books.

If there's one subject I've learned to avoid, however, it's science fiction. I like science fiction well enough as entertainment, as a form of fantasy offering temporary escape from reality. When it comes to movies, for example, the choice between science fiction and hard-hitting family drama is not really a choice. For Gordon, though, science fiction is something other than mere entertainment. He takes it very seriously, especially when it's wrong. There is nothing he enjoys more than debunking a sci-fi story, exposing the "fatal flaws" in its premises, plot or conclusions.

My tenth birthday, for example, which we celebrated with a double feature of *The Matrix/The Matrix Reloaded* at the Sunset Drive-In in San Luis Obispo. The next morning Gordon monologued over a diner breakfast of eggs and hash browns, taking the films to task for everything from their "facile appropriation of orthodox Gnostic cosmology" to the "preposterous notion" of humans as batteries: "A poor choice indeed, one no AI overlord worth its assembly code would be likely to make, not least because the energy costs of keeping humans alive would far outweigh the paltry amount of energy generated by their bio-processes."

When it came time to talking about my list, then, I should have known better than to admit that its title included the phrase "time machine." Especially since the point of it wasn't really the possibility, or impossibility, of time travel; it was just an innocent list of times and places I would love to see for myself. Whenever I read about something from history—whether it's an ancient city, a great battle, a famous person or a discovery—or look at illustrations of ancient temples and dwellings and artifacts, my thoughts turn to what it would be like—what it *would have been* like—to be there, alive and contemporary and in the flesh. What did it really look like? How did it smell? How were things made? What were the people like? Were they just like us, or completely different? What was it like to look into their eyes? I can't help it; I'm fascinated by the past, by ancient peoples and places, by temples and palaces and castles, by weapons and armies and battles, by emperors and nobles and serfs and peasants. I'm sure knowing basically zip about my own past has something to do with it. Honestly, the irony of the fact that I know more about Sumerian history than I do about my own is not completely lost on me. So I sat there holding my breath, hoping Gordon would be magnanimous enough to let my careless remark pass without commentary. Not a chance.

"Interesting notion, Sam," he began innocently enough. "Visiting the past. How, exactly, do you propose going about it?"

"I don't, Gordon. The list has nothing to do with building an actual time machine. It's not about that. It's just a prop, a means of thinking about history. A *Gedankenexperiment*," I said, throwing one of his own ten-dollar words at him.

He waved off my perfectly reasonable response. I rolled my

eyes, cursing my own stupidity. I had wandered straight into science-fictionland. It was no longer a question of what was reasonable. I took a deep breath, bracing myself for the coming tidal wave.

"Humor me," Gordon urged humorlessly. "If you *were* somehow able to travel in time, how do you think it would work?"

I haven't given serious thought to the notion of time travel any more than the next person. So of course I botched my response, fumbling my way through a poorly thought-out patchwork account of time travel, filled with lame science fiction clichés and other stuff I made up on the spot. I ended the whole sorry story with the statement that I would of course avoid doing anything that might compromise the time-line and thus alter the future/present.

The word *time-line* had barely passed my lips when Gordon launched his assault. Beginning with an entirely predictable "Not even wrong!" he dismissed my "theory" as "standard and naïve" before proceeding to honor me with a time-travel primer, complete with detailed analyses of such things as Gödel spacetime, quantum entanglement, Leibnizian compossibility, and the Novikov self-consistency principle.

He took a brief hiatus after the initial onslaught, presumably to allow sufficient time for his knowledge dump to sink in, before continuing. "Now. Given all that, you will doubtless be surprised to know that a type of time travel machine does, in fact, exist."

"Doubtless," I echoed.

"Care to guess what it is?"

I could only stare at him. *Not really.*

"No?"

I shook my head.

"It's the human being, Sam. The human being is a time-travel machine. Oh yes, it's true. The thing is, this particular machine travels in only one direction: forward. And in the process of traveling forward in time, the human being encounters a certain periodicity, according to which the forward movement is broken up into discrete units. Only one of these units may be physically occupied at a time. Such a unit of time is called *the present*. It is physically impossible for the human being to occupy any unit of time that is not a present unit of time. A properly functioning time-travel unit is content to move in this fashion. With me so far?"

I gave him a *whatever* look. At this point it didn't really matter whether I was "with him" or not; he was a runaway train. My role in the dialogue could have been handled perfectly well by a dog, or an ashtray.

"Now, it *is* possible for this time-travel machine to *imagine* itself occupying other, non-present, units of time, which is of course not the same thing as physically occupying a discrete unit of time, i.e. the present. Which is unfortunate, when you consider the likely outcome of the machine getting ahead of itself and thus becoming lost in the future, that is to say, in *imaginary* moments that *don't really exist*. Similarly, it can become obsessed with *former* moments of present time, which are no longer accessible to it, save through the *illusion* of memory. Such attempts to live outside the present result in *disorientation*, which is harmful to the machine, since it leads, inevitably, to *sadness*. In either case, the result is that the machine becomes unmoored from the now, from the sole reality. The sad fact is the vast majority of time travel machines are damaged in such a manner."

It was suddenly clear to me what the "conversation" was really about: the here and now.

It was the biggest difference between Gordon and me: I love the past, and I love it precisely *because* it is such a mystery to me, whereas he hates the past because it isn't. Hates it so much, in fact, that he puts everything he has into the present. Maybe he's right; maybe people escape into the past, or the future, to avoid dealing with the present. But how was his fixation on the present any better? What was he really doing, if not taking refuge in the present the way other people take refuge in the past or the future?

I had long since come to accept Gordon's refusal to engage with the past, to keep it to himself, but for some reason, it made me angry this time around. I wanted to shout at him, let him know that if I *did* have a time machine I wouldn't care one iota about the space/time continuum or any of that hokum, that the first thing I would do is go back in time to when he and my mother were together, then hide the machine or blow it up and stay there forever.

But I didn't. Instead, I said, "I don't care about time travel, Gordon. I just like history."

His face took on a slightly puzzled, almost apologetic expression, as if he realized that he'd been haranguing, that he'd pushed too hard.

He whistled softly through his teeth. Then, in a tone that was clearly meant to indicate a change of subject, he said, "Do you remember what Taylor said in the Forbidden Zone?"

I should have seen that one coming. *Planet of the Apes*. Gordon's favorite film and one of the few blind spots in his critical sense. For whatever reason, talking apes riding around on horses, shooting rifles and smoking cigars, did not activate his debunking faculty the way almost every other sci-fi film did. He quoted from it constantly, probably as an excuse to show off his Charlton Heston impression.

"Taylor said a lot of things, Gordon," I replied wearily. Hoping he would see the obvious parallel to our present situation, I added sarcastically, "He did *most* of the talking, in fact."

"Right you are, Sam."

An apologetic dip of the head indicated the point had been taken.

"I was thinking," he went on, "of the part near the beginning of the film, before the encounter with the apes. Specifically, the scene when Taylor is riding Landon. He's ostensibly doing it for Landon's benefit, to get him oriented to core facts of their situation, but more likely he just enjoys it. Anyway, after two-plus days of trekking through the Forbidden Zone, Landon is still preoccupied with getting a fix on their actual location in space and time. Taylor turns to him and says, 'There's only one reality left. We are here and it is now. You get hold of that and hang on tight, or you might as well be dead.'"

I couldn't help laughing. Gordon's Heston truly was flawless. We petered off into silence, Gordon staring intently at the road ahead while I waited for the relevant point to be made.

"Well?" I asked, tired of waiting.

"Well what?"

I laughed again. "*Well*, what's your point?"

Gordon shrugged. "Ah! Nothing really. The quote speaks for itself, I think."

That, apparently, was that. He said nothing more on the matter, losing himself in his thoughts, or the act of driving, his eyes narrowed and his shoulders slightly tensed.

Why did this conversation from a year ago keep playing itself over in my mind as I nudged the Vanagon eastward along the 210, toward Riverside? Probably because it had taken place the last time we were in Southern California, driving along a freeway just like the one we were on now. Association by place, basically. But then I realized that it was also one of the last "normal" conversations we had, that it was the last time Gordon was truly Gordon, twenty-four hours a day. The bad headaches started the next day, which he spent in a darkened corner of the Mesa Verde branch of the Orange County Public Library, hunched over in a chair with his hands pressed to his eyes. It was the first time in my life I'd seen him doing anything in a library besides reading and writing and devouring knowledge, and though it was weird, seeing him like that, I had no idea that things would never be the same.

We made it to the outskirts of Riverside a little after ten. Day five of The Plan. Riverside is not technically a major city, the kind with an international airport and a Chinatown and a financial district filled with skyscrapers, like San Francisco or Oakland. Even so, it was the biggest, busiest place we'd been in for quite a while, and my limited experience driving into new places did not prepare me for the hustle and bustle of it. I was amazed, overwhelmed almost, by the sheer number of people already going about their business. The streets were full of cars and delivery trucks, all honking and speeding and swerving in their hurry to get wherever it was they were going, the sidewalks crowded with people walking this way and that, the offices and restaurants already filled.

So many people, living lives filled with other people, with friends and family and coworkers. I could not help thinking how small, how isolated, our little life was in comparison, what little we really had. Where was *our* family, where were our friends? Who, apart from the two of us, even knew we existed?

The protocol for arriving in a new town typically involved

driving around a bit to get the general lay of the land, taking note of potential places to eat and sleep, and, of course, finding the library. I completely abandoned this approach upon coming into Riverside. I was too impatient to find Donald Coleman to think of doing anything else. Never mind that the only genuine fact I possessed concerning the man was that he taught at UC Riverside. I didn't know which department he taught in, or when he taught, let alone the location of the campus itself.

I was a little over my head in the busy morning traffic. A slow and careful driver even on my best days, the concentration required to simultaneously navigate the busy streets *and* look for signs of the campus had me driving at a snail's pace. Other drivers honked impatiently, cursing at me or giving me the finger as they raced angrily by. In the end, it was all I could do to drive the same circle over and over again. My fingers ached from gripping the steering wheel too tightly and my palms were sweating. Eventually I just gave up, pulling the van over to the side of the road and parking it.

I was well and truly exhausted. The invigorating full-body buzz I'd felt just a few hours earlier had been replaced by a deep weariness, a dull ache that throbbed in time with my heavy pulse. My unhappy stomach gurgled and growled. It hurt in a way that made me suspect it was eating itself. Maybe it was: I'd put nothing in it since our late afternoon dinner the day before.

Gordon hadn't eaten in all that time either, which was not a good thing. He was still sleeping—deeply but fitfully—in the seat next to me. He was clean enough, thanks to the previous night's shower, but apart from that he looked worse than I'd ever seen him. His great mane of hair was a mess, having been pressed by the headrest into a lumpy trapezoid. His eyes were hollow and ringed by large dark circles. The skin of his face was pale, almost bloodless; it seemed older somehow, *looser.* His lower jaw was slack, his mouth hanging open and oddly aslant. The left corner of it quivered periodically, causing the saliva pooled there to spill out onto his beard. Every so often his limbs twitched violently, and he must have called out to Kai a dozen times. I couldn't help thinking that the previous night's ordeal had lowered him somehow, that he had lost some important piece of himself, a piece he would never get back. I couldn't look at him.

I sat at the wheel, staring at the now lifeless dials on the control panel, listening absently to the ticking and pinging of the engine as it cooled down. In contrast to my blank expression, my head was a beehive of random, unwanted thoughts. Completely at a loss, I didn't have the slightest idea of what to do next.

Luckily, my stomach *did*. Its continual growling grew louder and louder, until I finally decided the first order of business, for both of us, was getting something to eat. Taking a full minute to work up the nerve to do it, I reached over and took hold of Gordon's elbow, jostling it gently. I held my breath as I waited to see what it was that would be waking up.

He mumbled and moaned, stirring slightly. He sat up slowly in his seat, his eyes still tightly shut. He grimaced as if in pain, then opened his eyes, squinting against the sunlight. He spent the next thirty seconds alternately scrunching his eyes closed and then opening them wide again. He sniffed and cleared his throat, then turned and looked at me.

He smiled.

A crooked smile, sneaky and mistrustful. I could tell that he didn't recognize me. He was still on the other side, in that other place.

My heart sank.

"Good morning, Gordon," I said quietly.

He snorted disdainfully in response to my friendly greeting.

He stared at me suspiciously, his head tottering, drool trickling onto his beard. He narrowed his eyes, and nodded sagely, as if to show that whatever game I was up to, it wasn't fooling him in the least. He laughed melodramatically and said, "You should probably know that you are quite recognizable despite your ridiculous disguise."

What could I say? How could I possibly respond to that? There was nothing I could do, really, other than simply remain quiet and wait.

"Nothing to say for yourself, eh? I thought as much." He laughed scornfully, dismissing my imcompetence with a wave of his hand. "So be it. It's your move, old boy. The ball, as they say, is in your court."

He turned in his seat and faced forward, straightening his back until his posture was perfectly erect and placing his hands primly in his lap, like a chaste schoolgirl.

More than once during the past few months, Gordon had gotten it into his head that we were being followed by agents of some shadowy organization. Never mind that there's no reason for anyone to be following us. We're not exactly important people. But reality, I've learned, has nothing to do with it. And the most important thing about dealing with someone stuck in an alternate reality is not trying to force them into the real one. It's better just to humor them, to play along until the fantasy runs out of steam and they come around. Instead of trying to convince Gordon that he's being paranoid, that we are alone as always, I just go along with him, joining his attempts to give our "tail" the slip: abrupt backtracking, walking serpentine, observing the street behind us in store window reflections.

This was different. This was the first time that he'd turned his delusion on me, treating me like some sort of enemy, like one of *them*. But I could see no reason to change my usual approach: I would play the role Gordon gave me. I pretended to ignore him and kept quiet, as if under orders not to divulge any information. It seemed to please him. He turned to look at me again and said, his voice full of sarcasm, "So, would you care to enlighten me on your master plan? Or would that be asking too much?"

Master plan. If he only knew.

"The *plan*," I said, injecting a slightly adversarial tone into my voice, "is none of your concern."

I started up the van and put it into gear. Pulling away from the curb and merging back into the heavy Riverside traffic, I tried my best to look like someone in control, like someone who knew what he was doing.

It wasn't easy, finding a place to eat. There were plenty of places to choose from; that wasn't the problem. It was just that they were all busy, all filled with the same people who filled the sidewalks and streets. I just didn't have the energy to waltz into a crowded restaurant with Gordon in his muddled state of mind. Finally, I spotted a falafel shop across from a concrete and glass office building. It was tiny and inconspicuous and, most importantly, empty.

    I pulled the van into a parking spot a little way up the street. I got out and walked around to the passenger side, opening the door and reaching up to help Gordon out. He swatted my hand away testily, warning me not to lay "a single dirty finger" on him, then climbed unsteadily onto the sidewalk. Once there, he more or less allowed himself to be shepherded toward the falafel shop.

    I pushed the rickety wooden screen door in to the accompaniment of a small, ringing bell. I held it open for Gordon, and followed him into what proved to be a truly tiny place. Half of it was taken up by a large stove and a deep fryer. A narrow,

L-shaped prep counter, with napkins and plastic utensils and a cash register on the short leg of the L, separated the cooking area from the customer section, which could not have held more than five or six people. An open door at the far end of the counter led to a storage room. At the sound of the bell, a small, hairy man with a big smile emerged from the storage room, wiping his hands on a white towel, bowing and nodding his head repeatedly to us and mumbling a friendly greeting in a language I had never heard before.

I said hello then asked Gordon what he wanted. He refused to answer, shrugging his shoulders and holding his hands up a few inches apart, as if they were shackled by invisible handcuffs. *Fine.* I took a quick look at the chalkboard menu and ordered two falafel sandwiches and two pomegranate lemonades.

Luckily, Gordon did not seem inclined to make a scene, probably because he was just as famished as I was. We stood in front of the counter, each of us cloaked in the heavy silence of the deeply hungry, completely mesmerized by the sure-handed manner with which the man made our sandwiches, a dollop of creamy humus spread smoothly across the pita, followed by the freshly fried falafel, crushed with a spoon, a sprinkling of purple coleslaw, a generous squirt of tahini and a few shakes of what looked like hot sauce, all deftly rolled up and wrapped in paper and foil. With great care, he packed the sandwiches, lemonades, and a handful of paper napkins in a white paper bag, folding the top of the bag over twice so that it took the shape of a sturdy rectangle. I took the bag and handed it to Gordon, thinking it would be good to keep him involved, while the man punched the order into the cash register. Still nodding and smiling, he said something to me in his friendly-but-cryptic mumble. He repeated himself in response to the uncomprehending look on my face, then simply pointed at the digital display on the register: $14.53.

Only then did I realize that I had no money on me. Embarrassed, my heart pounding like a jackhammer, I could only offer up my own form of incomprehensible gibberish, pretending to rummage through my pockets as I did so. The sound of the door bell, followed by that of the door itself slamming shut, told me what I already knew from the falafel maker's nervous smile: Gordon had exited the shop, taking our unpaid-for lunch with him. Apologizing profusely, I held up an index finger in what I hoped was the universal sign for "one moment please." Praying the man wouldn't start shouting or hop over the counter with a baseball bat, I turned and hurried outside.

Thankfully, Gordon had not left the shop with any real purpose. He was just standing there, in the middle of the sidewalk, peeking into the lunch bag. He turned and looked at me, a vacant expression on his face.

"Come back inside please, Gordon," I said, not even pretending to be anyone other than myself.

"*Gordon?*" he echoed with a frown. "So *that's* your name, is it?"

Please, I thought. *Not now. Just give me two minutes, two normal minutes. Then we'll play any game you want.*

"Sure," I said. "Whatever you say. Look, we have a little problem."

"*We?*"

"Yes, *we*," I said impatiently. I nodded at the bag in his hands. "Unless you don't feel like having that lunch."

That got his attention.

"Okay," he said. "What's *our* little problem?"

I pulled my pants pockets inside-out, making rabbit ears out of them. "No money," I said apologetically.

Gordon laughed. It was actually kind of perfect, something he could easily fold into his delusional narrative: an inept kidnapper who couldn't manage to buy lunch. Sure enough, he gave me a withering look and sneered, "Quite a show you boys are running there. Can't even afford lunch."

He handed me the bag and wobbled back into the shop. I followed him, smiling reassuringly at the falafel guy, who was genuinely relieved that we had returned.

"What's the damage?" Gordon asked, pulling his wallet ostentatiously from his front pocket.

The man pointed again at the register again. With a scornful but satisfied shake of his head, Gordon took a twenty dollar bill from his wallet. He waved the bill mockingly in front of my face and said, "You can put it on my tab." He gave the man a wink, then handed the bill over with a flourish before turning on his heel pompously and walking toward the door, calling out over his shoulder, "Keep the change."

Gordon has always been a generous tipper, twenty percent at a minimum, even for mediocre service. I hope to emulate that generosity some day, I really do, but given our present uncertain circumstances, there was no way I could let him just give away five dollars and forty-seven cents. Amazingly, the man seemed to understand the situation. He opened the register drawer, tucked the twenty into the cash tray, then pulled five one-dollar bills and a handful of coins from it and gave it all to me. I put the change and four of the bills in my pocket. I tried to hand one of the dollars back to the man, but he held his hands out in front of him, steadfastly refusing to take it. He nodded once more, and disappeared back into the storeroom. Bowing in profound gratitude, I took the bag and left the shop.

I found Gordon back in his spot in the middle of the sidewalk. He wasn't waiting for me; to be honest I think he had already forgotten about me. He was simply lost. His arms hung loosely from his slightly stooped shoulders, his great head bowed slightly. His face was completely blank, his mouth open just a little, his eyes empty. He swayed a little on his feet, like a slim tree in a heavy breeze. In the space of seconds, he'd slipped another level.

I placed my free hand gently on his elbow.

"Come on, Gordon," I said quietly. "Let's go eat."

He allowed himself to be led across the street and to the sunken concrete plaza in front of the glass office building. It was fairly busy, with people coming and going and sitting around eating their lunches, but I managed to find us a place to sit on a rectangular concrete slab, off to one side and under the shade of a small maple tree. I led Gordon over to the slab and helped him sit down. I could feels his limbs stiffen as he sat and he was breathing in short shallow puffs.

I took our lunch from the bag, which I tore open and flattened, spreading it on the concrete between us like a tablecloth for the sandwiches and drinks. I poked straws in the plastic lids of the lemonades and offered one to Gordon. He didn't seem to notice, and only accepted it after I had practically placed it in his hand. He put the straw in his mouth absently and then took a series of short drinks, in time with his breathing. He drained half of it in one go. It seemed to do him some good. He cleared his throat and sat a little more upright on the bench.

I unwrapped one of the falafels halfway and handed it to him. He regarded me with a puzzled expression as he took it, as if wondering why a complete stranger was giving him food. He seemed, at least, to have let go of the notion that I was his nemesis. He took an exploratory bite, testing the morsel with mouse-like nibbles. Satisfied that it was edible, he proceeded to eat voraciously, the biting and chewing and swallowing all seeming to take place at once. He stalled when he came to the end of the unwrapped portion, unsure of what to do next. I took the sandwich from him and peeled the foil and paper back like a banana, leaving an inch or so at the bottom so the contents wouldn't spill on him, then handed it back. He promptly recommenced with the devouring of it. I turned my attention away from the spectacle and focused on my own falafel. I ate as calmly and deliberately as I could, which wasn't easy considering that my hunger was genuinely painful. I drank sparingly from my lemonade, thinking to save some of it for later.

We sat quietly on the bench after eating, soaking up the midday sun and biding our time. I waited for the effects of the food to kick in, for it to turn into the energy I needed to carry on, at the same time hoping it would help lift Gordon from his low state, or at least lull him to sleep.

I didn't have to wait long. I could feel energy returning to my tired limbs, the almost painful buzzing of my fatigue growing fainter by the minute. A welcome feeling of calm spread throughout my body. My head began to clear as well, and I soon found myself composing a mental list of next steps: *relax, find a library, get some rest, get back on The Plan, locate Donald Coleman, talk to him ...*

I was enjoying this upward trend in my mood when Gordon said, in a slow voice full of meaning, "That can be no Christian bear."

I cocked my head and looked at him. "What?" I asked, confused. Apparently, the food had worked on him too, restoring him, at least, to his earlier level of paranoia. Something, or someone, had caught his wary eye.

Gordon indicated the opposite side of the plaza with a subtle nod of his head. I followed his gaze, searching among the many people, some passing through on their way to somewhere else, others standing around conversing in small groups. Nothing obvious caught my eye.

I looked at Gordon again, trying to read his line of sight and determine exactly where he was looking. As far as I could tell, the object of his interest was directly across the plaza from us. The only person in the vicinity of his gaze was a thin man, who sat eating his lunch on a concrete square like ours, one long leg crossed over the other. He looked to be about Gordon's age, with grayish blonde hair cut short and parted at the side. He was dressed in the white coat of a doctor. He held a half-eaten apple in one hand and a pocket phone in the other. There was nothing about this man, as far as I could tell, that could have struck Gordon as suspicious ... apart from the fact that he was staring straight at us.

I looked away from the man quickly, then looked again, secretly, a couple seconds later. I did this a number of times. Each time, he was staring at us intently.

Considering how bothersome Gordon's paranoia can be, it was almost a relief to find a genuine source for it. Just because the man was staring at us, it didn't mean he was following us, that he was spying on us. But at least he was actually *there*.

I glanced at Gordon to see if he was still on his guard. He was not. He had slipped out of awareness again, and was all but asleep. His eyes were closed, his head dipping, the bearded chin below his open mouth slowly sinking to his chest.

I looked back toward the man in time to see him stand and prepare to leave. He glanced briefly at his pocket phone then slipped it into the breast pocket of his lab coat. He took another bite of his apple, then tossed it into a trashcan and walked off, away from us. So much for that.

I turned my attention back to Gordon, who was now most definitely asleep. I decided it would be best to rouse him now, before he sank too deep. If I could get him back to the van and have him sleep there, it would make my search for the university a lot easier. I was about to take him by the shoulders in order to shake him gently awake when I heard footsteps approaching. I waited for them to go by, but instead of passing us they came to a stop right in front of us. I looked up from my seat to see the man in the lab coat standing in front of me.

He was tall, taller than Gordon even. Six-four, maybe six-five. Looking up into his face from the bench, my head tilted all the way back, was like looking up at a giraffe; it didn't seem possible for a head to be perched that far off the ground. Everything about the man was tall: his arms and legs, his face, even his ears and fingers seemed not so much long as *tall*. He might also have been the cleanest person I've ever seen. His narrow face was clean-shaven and shiny, his close-cut and immaculately combed blonde hair sprinkled here and there with gray. His spotless white lab coat was unbuttoned and pushed casually back behind his wrists, his hands floating in the pockets of his perfectly creased charcoal gray slacks. The breast pocket of his coat was neatly embroidered in dark blue: *Stephen R. Moser, MD, PhD Neurology*.

I didn't have the slightest idea what this stranger wanted with us. I sat and waited for him to explain himself.

He looked intently at Gordon, a thin but sympathetic smile on his tall face. "Hmm ... no. Not vascular," he said, scratching his chin. "Definitely not vascular. MCI? Maybe, *may-be*—"

I cleared my throat, forcing him to acknowledge the fact that I was there too, a couple of feet away from him.

"Ah!" he exclaimed, as if genuinely surprised to find me sitting there, watching him watching Gordon. "Yes, well. Sorry. I don't mean to intrude." An obvious white lie; he could not keep his eyes off Gordon. "Your father?"

I confirmed his assumption with the slightest of nods.

"Right, of course," he *hmmed* again. "He is a patient with us?" He had a faint European accent, maybe German, maybe Scandinavian.

"I'm sorry?"

"Your father. He is a patient here, at the medical center?"

I could only stare at the man in confusion.

He took a hand from his pocket and pointed behind me. I turned and looked over my shoulder, at the office building to which the plaza was attached. Only then did I notice the large aluminum letters spanning the front of the glass and concrete building: UC RIVERSIDE MEDICAL CENTER.

"Oh," I said. "No, he's not. He's not a patient anywhere."

The man frowned. "Not a patient? Anywhere? Really?"

If the man's goal in approaching us had been to cause confusion, he'd succeeded.

His frown deepening, he tried again: "But you *are* here to visit the hospital, no?"

"No. We're here to eat lunch."

He smiled thinly, tipping his head. "Right. My apologies. My name is Dr. Moser." He pointed at the embroidered patch on his coat, as if I required additional proof of his claim. "I am head of the Neurology Department here."

"Congratulations," I said. "I'm Sam."

Dr. Moser chuckled. "Nice to meet you, Sam. Forgive me for interrupting your lunch. To be totally honest, I can't help myself sometimes. It's just," he glanced at Gordon again, "people like your father, it's what I do."

People like my father. What was that supposed mean?

I nodded curtly and looked away, having decided I was ready for him to leave.

"And also," he went on, "I wanted to commend you. I have been watching the two of you for some time now, since you left Falafel Palace. I want to say that you seem to be doing a fine job, considering."

"Considering what?"

Dr. Moser smiled his thin smile and pursed his lips.

"Considering his condition, of course."

"What condition?"

He seemed genuinely taken aback by my question. The muscles in his jaw tensed slightly, his eyes narrowing as he resumed his earlier scrutiny of Gordon. He mumbled to himself again as he did so, though this time I couldn't make out what he said. Eventually, he nodded to himself, pursing his lips again and looking back at me.

"*Louie?*" he asked, though it sounded more like a statement than a question.

"No," I answered instantly, out of reflex. "No, his name is Gordon."

The doctor tutted softly, shaking his head. "I was not asking your father's name," he said. "I was inquiring about his condition. It is Louie body?"

I could not have been more lost. "I don't know what you're talking about," I said.

"Louie body, spelled *l-e-w-y*. It's a form of—" he stopped abruptly, frowning again. "So what you are saying is true?" he asked. "You don't know? You have no idea, exactly, what is the matter with your father?"

"I'm fourteen," I replied.

"Okay, right." He rubbed his chin, thinking. "And you

are not here for an appointment, you are just here for lunch? Coincidentally?"

"*Yes*," I said warily. "And to rest a bit. He's tired."

"Of course he is. That's good, letting him rest. Smart. Best thing you can do."

This conversation was making me uneasy. It wasn't just the unsolicited intrusion of this nosy doctor, or his keen interest in Gordon. It was the fact that I couldn't remember the last time I'd spoken to anyone other than Gordon. I didn't dislike this Dr. Moser, there was something intriguing about him, something kind. I just wanted the conversation to be over.

"Well, thanks," I said. "It was nice to meet you, Doctor, but we have to go, we were just getting ready to go."

The doctor's eyes narrowed again, though they were now focused on me. He stared at me so intently I had to look away. Which was a good thing, since Gordon, who was still dozing, was beginning to teeter forward. I managed to jump up and catch him by the shoulders just as he was about to fall from the bench. The force of the catch jolted him momentarily awake.

It was not Gordon who woke but some other thing. Through heavy-lidded eyes, this creature looked at me without seeing me. Its face was gray and its mouth hung open, exposing a pasty tongue and teeth filled with great globs of doughy food. Its head pulled back from mine, as if trying to gain the distance needed to properly focus. It blinked once, slowly, then its head fell forward onto my shoulder. Gordon was asleep again.

I stood there in a kind of half-crouch, wedging myself against the dead weight of my slumbering father/creature. There's no telling how long we would have remained in that position, Gordon half on and half off the bench, if Dr. Moser hadn't stepped forward and helped me reposition him.

Turning his face to me, Dr. Moser offered me a kindly half-smile and asked, "How long has he been like this?"

"Since he woke up this morning,"

"No. What I mean is, when did this all start, when did he stop behaving, say, completely normally?"

"Oh." I felt a flush spread across my face, embarrassed at misunderstanding him. "Um, about a year ago, pretty much."

He nodded, as if it was precisely the answer he'd expected to hear. "And how did it start?"

"Um, well I don't—"

"Headaches?" he volunteered.

"Yeah."

"Bad dreams? Fluctuating cognition?"

"Pardon?"

"Sorry. He sometimes phases in and out of awareness, seems completely normal one minute and then distant, not fully there the next?"

"Yes."

"And certain times of the day are worse then others?"

I nodded, looking at him with a mixture of suspicion and something like awe. *Who was this man? How did he know all this stuff? How was it that a complete stranger could know more about Gordon's troubles than me?*

I suddenly realized how much I wanted to know, too. I was tired of not knowing, it was stupid that I didn't know. All of the doubt and fear, the accumulated worry of a whole year of not knowing, welled up in my chest, came rushing forward before I could stop it.

"Do you know what's wrong with him?" I blurted. I expected the question to come out as a shout, the emotion behind it was so strong, but a knot had formed in my throat, and it came out instead as a strangled, barely audible whisper. I sounded, even to my own ears, like a frightened child.

Dr. Moser smiled. "I don't, Sam. Not exactly. But I'm pretty sure I could find out."

"Really? How?"

"Speaking with your father's doctor, for starters."

I frowned, unsure about how much I really wanted to tell this fellow. I liked him. More importantly, I *trusted* him. But we'd only just met. How did I know what he really wanted? How could I be sure I wasn't walking into some kind of trap? I couldn't. I couldn't be sure of anything, really. All I could do was go with what I felt was right. And at that moment, trusting him felt right.

"We don't have a doctor," I said.

"I see."

He uttered it like any other statement of fact. For some reason, I was not surprised to see that *he* was not surprised by my admission.

"Okay. Well, is there someone else who—"

I shook my head, cutting him short.

"No one? It's just the two of you?"

"Yes."

It was his turn to frown, though it seemed more a frown of concentration than consternation. He was the kind of person, I could tell, who thought deeply but quickly, cutting right to the heart of things. A man who formed *real* plans, and then put them into action. A clear thinker, like Gordon.

Plunging his hands into the pockets of his crisp white coat, Dr. Moser nodded to himself and said, in a voice that indicated the matter was already settled, "Here's what I would like to do: I need to keep your father here, overnight. He will have his own room, with a comfortable bed. He can rest, get a little more nourishment in him. I will run a few tests, do some imaging—standard stuff, nothing painful or invasive—then let him rest some more. We will keep a close eye on him, take good care of him, make sure he gets a good night's sleep. By late tomorrow morning, I will have a pretty good idea of what's causing all the trouble. If he is feeling better by then, we can talk about what to do. How does that sound?"

It sounded great. No, it sounded like a dream. It was obviously far superior to my own plan, to anything I could have come up with. More than that, it was an offer of help. *An offer of help.* My throat tightened even further. I was unable to make a sound.

"So. What do you say?"

I wanted to say *Yes!* I opened my mouth to say it, but found I couldn't. I knew that no matter how much I wanted to, I wouldn't be able to say yes. The offer sounded perfect, and I have no doubt Dr. Moser meant what he said, but that didn't change the fact that it *was* a trap. If I said yes, there was no telling what the final outcome would be. I would be giving up what little control I had of our life, of *my* life. I shook my head: *No.*

Dr. Moser made no attempt to convince me further. He reached out and put his hand on my shoulder, squeezing it gently, turning the plum stuck in my larynx to a grapefruit. How many times had I been touched by someone other than Gordon? With a shock I realized I didn't know. I stood there gaping like a goldfish that had flopped out of its bowl.

I was about to lose it completely. Luckily, Dr. Moser's phone buzzed in his pocket. He took it out and began poking it, momentarily too busy to notice my distress. He nibbled at the bottom of his lip while he poked. Returning the phone to his pocket, he gave me a hard stare. "Do you live here?"

"No," I said, massaging my throat back into shape. "We're visiting. From out of town."

"Visiting?"

"My uncle. On my mom's side. He's a professor. He lives here. We're staying with him."

I knew that Dr. Moser knew I was lying but he decided not to press me on it. "Great," he said. "That's great."

He unclipped a pen from his breast pocket, then reached into his one of his side pockets and pulled out a small piece of white paper. "This is my card," he said. He circled the phone number on the card with his pen and handed it to me.

"If you change your mind, if you decide you would like for me to take a look, just give me a call. Any time."

I slipped it into my pocket without looking at it. "I don't have a phone."

For the first time, Dr. Moser looked confused. "No phone?"

"Nope."

He glanced at Gordon. "Your father?"

"No," I said. "We don't have a phone."

"Really?"

"Yes, really."

He scowled, as if our not having a phone was the most absurd thing he'd ever heard. "Right. Well, I'm sure that's fine." He stroked his chin for a bit, then said, "Okay. Well, maybe your uncle has a phone."

"Maybe."

"Okay then, Sam," he said, still slightly perplexed. "It was nice to meet you." He offered a thin, tall-fingered hand.

I did my best to shake hands with the doctor solemnly, but mine was no match for his and disappeared inside it. His palm was dry as dust, his grip almost entirely slack.

"Remember what I said. If there's anything I can do, please let me know."

"Thanks," I said.

A tight-lipped smile creased the doctor's tall face. He cast a final look of appraisal at Gordon, and nodded at me with a kind of reluctant finality.

"Actually," I said as he turned to go. "There is one thing."

"Yes?"

"Can you tell me how to get to the University?"

The university was close enough to walk to. But the day was growing steadily warmer and I had no reason, given Gordon's state, to believe that walking even a short distance would be easy. I roused him as gently as I could and helped him shuffle over to the van. He was practically asleep on his feet and leaned heavily on me. I opened the rear doors and guided him inside. He crawled, moaning, onto the pile of blankets and collapsed. I stood there for a while, watching him as he fell into sleep, the corner of his mouth quivering in time to his quiet whimpering, his left hand twitching every few seconds.

I followed Dr. Moser's directions to the campus and parked the van in a shaded spot on the street next to one of the many nearly empty parking lots. Accepting the obvious risk, and hoping my mission to locate Donald Coleman would be successful *and* quick, I left Gordon asleep in the van and hurried onto the campus. It was far from crowded—compared to the city it seemed almost deserted. I was already regretting not taking Dr. Moser up on his offer, if only because it would have meant being free of the burden, of the overwhelming, ever-present obligation, of looking after Gordon. I began to imagine, I couldn't help it, what it would be like to be free. Free from this worry and fear, free from having to do a job that was beyond me. Free to be a boy, a plain old fourteen-year-old boy.

I pushed this daydream, with all of its stupid little temptations, out of my mind. There was nothing else for it.

In the closed off atmosphere of the van, I became aware of just how tired I was. My ears were ringing and I was numb. A total, all-encompassing numbness, a strange kind of heavy weightlessness spreading out from deep inside, filling me from head to toe, making it impossible to tell where my body began and where it ended. I felt transparent, like a spirit trapped in a physical world. The sensation of not being there was heightened by the fact that no one in this busy city (apart from Dr. Moser) seemed to notice me.

I found it easy, under the circumstances, to believe in a soul, in a part of myself that was real but somehow not made of matter, because like the rest of me, my soul was numb too. It was different than the kind of numbness where you can no longer feel something you know is there. It was the kind that comes from a thing *not being there*. I only knew my soul through the outline of what was missing: the things that had always made up my life, the things that were real to me. The Gordon I had always known—the *man* who was my father—was disappearing, and I was losing more of him every day, a process that seemed like it would go on until he had disappeared completely. What I used to think of as reality was no longer real, the days and weeks all blended together in a grayish pea soup, the individual sights and sounds and perceptions I'd always found it easy to fix in my memory now slipping through it like water through a sieve. I no longer even felt homeless, as I had in front of the ranger station only the night before. No, not even homeless. Lost. Utterly lost. Was this really what life was going to be like? Was *this* what I could expect from here on out?

I wandered about as if in a dream. Actually, it was more like the opposite of a dream. It wasn't my surroundings that felt unreal. The buildings, three- and four-story concrete jobs for the most part, bordered by green lawns and rows of leafy trees, could not have been more real, more imposingly solid. The same was true of the handful of students I saw, sitting beneath the bright sun on wide green lawns or walking along alone or in small groups. And the birds, chattering loudly to one another from trees and bushes, darting gracefully between the walnut trees and hemlocks and miniature eucalyptus. Even the background details, like the far-off mountains and the small plane humming high overhead, seemed hyper-real, somehow more *there* than anything I'd ever seen. The only thing that was unreal, the thing that made it all seem like a dream, was me.

A soft, warm breeze whispered through the trees, sweeping across the lawn, ruffling the blades of grass. It blew on my face, causing the sweat on my face to tingle, the goose bumps on my arms convincing me that I *was* really there.

Enough! The voice of Charlton Heston interrupted my self-pitying daydream: *You are here and it is now. You better get a hold of that fact.*

Hard to argue with that. And I had a job to do in the here-and-now.

I took a deep breath. I was here, at UC Riverside. Donald Coleman was here too. Somewhere. I just had to find him, talk to him, explain things to him, and then they would start getting better. Compared to everything else, it was simple.

I crossed the lawn to a walkway that led toward a cluster of buildings. The walk entered a kind of open-air tunnel, a series of concrete arches painted white and topped by a low roof. The air inside was cool. I drank it in like water from a fountain, the coolness in my lungs adding further proof that I was indeed real. I continued along the sheltered walk until I came to the first, and largest, building. A brass plaque next to the entrance read: TOMÁS RIVERA LIBRARY. Perfect. At the very least, I thought, the lobby would have one of those YOU-ARE-HERE maps. I followed the entrance path to the revolving front doors and pushed my way in.

The lobby was surprisingly spacious and, like so much of the campus, all but deserted. The lights were turned off, the only illumination coming from the light filtering through the tall, narrow windows set on either side. The lobby was gray and shadowy, as if it were a rainy day. Not that there's anything wrong with a library on a rainy day.

A library! I felt an overwhelming urge to slip through one of the metal turnstiles and wander the stacks, lose myself in the endless rows of books, whole floors of them, to sit down in some quiet corner and disappear into the pages of one giant tome after another. No. I scanned the gloomy interior, looking for the reference desk. It was on the far side of the lobby, near the empty checkout counter, a rectangular workstation with eight computer terminals and piles of reference materials.

I sifted through the course catalogues and department brochures until I found a phonebook-sized faculty directory. I opened it eagerly and rifled through the flimsy pages to the *C-Os*. I felt stupid, like what I was doing was hopeless, pointless. And then, just like that, there it was, right in the middle of the page: Coleman, Donald. 1993. Professor of Earth Sciences. Geophysics/Geohydrology. Geol 205.

I let out a triumphant yip of joy. On the back cover of the directory was a campus map. I ran my index finger over the surface of the page until I located the Geology building. I made a mental map of the route and sprinted across the lobby to the exit.

•

Like the library, the lobby of the Geology Building was empty, and illuminated by indirect sunlight. Something about that fact was odd. Then I made the connection that it was August. August is summer. You don't have school in summer. Trying not to think about what that implied for the likelihood of Donald Coleman being around, I set off along the main hallway of the first floor.

The hallway was lined with glass display cases, filled with geological artifacts, cross-sections of petrified wood, fossils and bones of extinct animals, posters on the ecology of forest fires, scale models of the San Andreas fault. I paused for a while in this unexpected museum, losing myself in the miniature worlds inside each cabinet.

Reluctantly, I made my way to the staircase at the end of the hall and trudged up to the second floor, preoccupied with thoughts of obsidian and trilobites and tectonic plates. Reaching the top of the stairs, I turned absently into the second floor hallway and found myself staring right into the face of a giant, stuffed mastodon, encased in glass.

The suddenness and utter strangeness of this confrontation wiped all other thoughts from my head. At first I could do nothing but stare in awe at this prehistoric relic: the long, bristly hair only partially covering its massive body, like the sparse coat of a mangy coyote; the gleaming yellowish tusks, covered with small pits and deep gouges; the massive, flat-bottomed feet which made me think, like the feet of elephants always did, of upside-down bongo drums; the rectangular sections cut into the hide of the front leg, revealing a massive femur and the bones of the lower leg.

It had to be a bad omen. I mean, how else was I to understand it? When I looked into the giant brownish-black eyes,

I felt it had been waiting for me, a tireless sentinel, a guard whose only task was to prevent me from entering the second-floor hallway. The weirdest thing was, even though I knew the eyes were not real but simply glass substitutes, I couldn't shake the feeling I was looking into living eyes. It was more like *it* was looking into my eyes, accusing *me*: *Why are you here? What do you want? What do you hope to achieve? Who do you think you are?*

Feeling once again like some kind of ghost, I drifted forward, leaning onto the case and pressing my forehead against it. I looked intently into the mastodon's giant, glassy orb, feeling myself more and more deeply under interrogation. I sighed and pulled back from the case. My focus shifted as I did so, and suddenly I was looking into my own face, reflected in the glass. Me. Samuel P. Furlong. Here. Now. The mastodon was not a sentinel, not a gatekeeper. It was not blocking the way to anything. It was a stuffed animal, an object. The only thing standing in my way was me, and the imaginary obstacles I kept inventing.

I wiped the glass with the side of my hand, cleaning the little smudge my forehead had left on it. I nodded respectfully to the mastodon, then turned and made my way down the hallway. I read the number on every classroom and office door out loud until I came to the one I was looking for: Room 205. The office of Prof. Donald Coleman. *Uncle Don.*

My hand floated up and I knocked on the door. It made no sound. Of course. Ghosts can't interact with matter. I shook my head and took a deep breath, holding it in for as long as I could. I knocked again, more forcefully this time. I waited, my heart a gorilla fist pounding in my chest. Five seconds, ten. No answer. I tried once more and waited. Still no answer. It was as inevitable as it was predictable: Professor Coleman was not in his office.

I did not get angry. I did not curse fate. I didn't even sigh. I simply blinked—once, twice—accepting the situation for what it was. And not just this latest little setback, either. The *whole situation*. The headaches, the sleepless nights, the nightmares, Kai, the wandering, the disappearing, the delusions, the craziness, the *need*. It was time to give up, that was clear. There was no reason not to. No reason not to forget all about the stupid plan, no reason to do anything other than just sit and wait for it all to be over, the disintegration of my father's life and my own.

No reason, except for the fact that it's just not how it's done. Not for us, anyway. It's not what Gordon would do, and in my heart of hearts, I knew it wasn't what I was going to do either. The better thing, the *harder* thing, was not to give up, to stick to The Plan, and that's what I would do.

It occurred to me that I *could* leave a note. I didn't know when Donald Coleman would be coming in. Maybe tomorrow, maybe next week, maybe not for another month. Then again, maybe he'd be here in an hour. Whatever the case, I wasn't going to leave Riverside until I'd found him. I could at least let him know Gordon and I were in town, that we were hoping to see him, that I would keep checking his office in case he was in.

My notebook, along with my pen, was in my backpack, which was in the van, on the other side of campus. *Ugh!* Whatever else could be said, the evidence was piling up that yes, life really was like this, each of us merely the butt of his own personal inside joke. There were probably twenty pens sitting in Donald Coleman's desk, just on the other side of the office door, along with reams of paper. On impulse, I reached out and pulled down on the door handle. I didn't expect anything to happen; I knew the door would be locked. It was a small miracle, then, when I heard the latch click and felt the door slip open. I gave it a little push and it swung inward. Warm air escaped from the office breezed past my face. I stepped cautiously into the office, my hand going out instinctively, searching the wall to the right of the door for a light switch. It was a moment before I realized the room was already lit. Two small table lamps, one on a bookshelf on the far wall, another on a metal desk, cluttered with papers and folders, bathed the windowless office in soft yellow light.

The opposite wall was lined with books, as was the wall to my right. A large rug, covered with abstract patterns, hung on the wall to the left. A man sat in the center of the room, reclining in an old office chair with his feet propped up on the desk, a large pair of headphones on his head. He was staring straight at me. It was Donald Coleman.

I stood in the doorway, my hand poised in mid-air, a statue entitled *Boy With Light Switch*. For a second I thought I was seeing things. A phantom projection of my over-active imagination. An illusion. Maybe, after all the ups and downs, all the frustrations and disappointments of my journey to find this man, my brain simply felt sorry for me and decided to allow me the momentary happiness of thinking I had reached my goal. But he wasn't an illusion. He was there. Well and truly. In the flesh.

His stillness matched my own. He stared across the room at me, waiting, clearly hoping that whoever I was, I would acknowledge my mistake, turn around and go and leave him be. After I'd stood there too long for my presence to be a mistake, however, a pained grimace spread across his face. Sighing heavily, he swung his feet from the desk and pulled himself upright in his chair. He rolled forward, taking his headphones off and placing them on the desk next to the shiny little device they were connected to. He pressed the front of the device with his finger, bringing the sound of faint, tinny music—maybe violins, maybe trumpets—to a halt. He clasped his hands together, placing them on the desk in front of him. He looked at me and waited.

I stood there, with no idea what to say. Somehow, during all the ups and downs of The Plan, I hadn't given a moment's thought to what I would say to Donald Coleman when I actually found him. My muteness was compounded by the fact that he didn't look at all the way I remembered him. The Donald Coleman of my memory was a lean man, not quite as wiry as Gordon, but tall and athletic, with a full, well-shaped Afro, a friendly open face, and a smile that was broad and ready. The man in front of me, in contrast, was far from trim. He was actually a little portly, and though seated, I could tell he wasn't much taller than me. What was left of his hair—he was mostly bald on top—was speckled with gray and cut short. His round face was far from friendly. Nor was there any evidence of the famous smile I remembered so well.

Okay, I told myself. *People change.* It had been half a lifetime since I last saw him. Then again, that's half of *my* life, which is only seven years, and there's no way the person I thought I remembered could have changed so much in seven years. If it wasn't for the fact that this Donald Coleman, like mine, was African American, I would have thought I had the wrong person.

He raised his eyebrows as if to say, *Yes?*

I continued to stand and stare, unable to utter a word.

My silence only added to the irritation he clearly felt at my presence. Clearing his throat loudly, he said, "Can I help you?"

Do something. Say something.

"Um, you're Donald Coleman?" *Great question, Sam! Well done!*

"That's correct."

"It is? Oh, okay."

I laughed awkwardly. What was wrong with me? Was language, my sole strength and ally, really going to desert me in my hour of need? Donald Coleman went back to waiting while I tried to get it together.

"Well, yeah," I went on, stalling. "So. We ... *I* ... I've been looking for you."

"Okay." He unclasped his hands, holding them out to either side to indicate the obvious. "And now you've found me."

"Yep."

"*Yep*. And you would be?"

I put his failure to recognize me down to the fact that I too had probably changed a lot since the last time he'd seen me, but his tone did nothing to inspire confidence. A big, gleaming smile, like the kind I remembered from my childhood—the kind I *thought* I remembered—would have gone a long way.

"It's me," I said, smiling for the both of us. "Sam. Sam Furlong."

If the name meant anything to him, he didn't let it show. If anything, the expression on his face told me that we had already arrived at the limits of his patience.

"Gordon Furlong is my father."

Nothing. Not a flicker, not a spark.

"You remember my dad? You guys used to work together? Right?" I couldn't believe I was asking these questions. I felt unsteady, like I was standing in a wobbly canoe.

His eyes narrowed in concentration. Somehow I knew it wasn't because he was combing his memory; he was trying to decide whether or not to answer me.

I found it hard to hold his stare, and after a few seconds I looked away. My eyes wandered about the room, completing a full circuit before I had the courage to re-engage those of Donald Coleman.

His expression had softened. "Yes, I remember you," he admitted at last.

"Oh?"

He sighed. It was pretty clear talking to me was the last thing he wanted to be doing. "Yes. Your father brought you to my house once."

Once?

"You were little then, six, maybe seven. You were a little bit under the weather, too, stomachache or something like that. You slept on the couch for the afternoon."

No, I wanted to blurt out. *You have it all wrong, We spent the night, we spent many nights. Like the time Gordon gave me a special box, full of things from my mother.* But I didn't.

"An unexpected visit, really. I hadn't seen your father for years, since before you were born, then he shows up out of the blue. I knew about you but I hadn't met you. It was funny, actually ..."

He went on talking, but I had no idea what he was saying. I couldn't hear him. I saw his mouth moving, heard garbled sounds coming from it that were like words, but my brain simply could not decode them. My ears were filled with a steady, ringing hum, and there was a strange pressure in my head, like I was standing at the bottom of the ocean, beneath a thousand feet of water. The pressure, I think, came from a sudden and intense need to not be there, a need to not to be anywhere, to not *be*. What was the point of anything if you couldn't even trust your own memory? I turned away from the droning mush that was Donald Coleman's voice, my hand reaching out for the door handle.

"... and not just your mother."

At the sound of those words, I snapped back into being. I spun around from the doorway, completely focused on the babbling figure sitting in front of me.

"My mother?"

"Hmm?"

"You said something about my mother. Just now."

He cleared his throat.

I waited, but he said nothing.

"You knew my mother?"

It was his turn to look away, uncomfortable.

"You knew her?"

He sighed. A heavy sigh, the meaning which was beyond me. "I did," he said. "I do."

I do. My being was expanding so rapidly I found it hard to breathe. It was like a form of the bends. Which makes sense. I'd just shot from the ocean floor to the clouds in the space of thirty seconds.

Despite my shortness of breath I pressed on. "*How?*"

"This is not something I need to be talking about," he said, shaking his head. "Not something I'm supposed to be talking about. I made a—"

"Please," I interrupted. "Can you please just tell me?"

He fixed me in a cold, hard stare, deliberating. Finally he said, "We were students together, friends. In graduate school." He shrugged. "A long time ago."

There was a hint of finality in his voice. It was clearly the last word he intended to say on the matter. Despite all of the questions crowding my brain, stumbling over one another in a desperate scramble to be asked, I didn't push him. A lifetime of living with Gordon had conditioned me to accept that life itself was close-mouthed.

Quietly, almost as if he were talking to himself, Donald Coleman asked, "You really don't know anything? ... He never said anything about? ... " He cut himself short, shaking his head again and scratching at his chin with obvious agitation.

"About what?"

"Look, Sam. What are you doing here? Why did you come here today?"

I wanted to keep quiet, show him I could keep things to myself too, but found I couldn't. I was there for a reason, after all.

"Gordon is not well," I said.

"Not well?"

"Yeah. Not well."

"How do you mean?"

"I mean *not well*. As in *not good*. You know, bad, terrible. *Sick*. I think he's losing his mind. So I just thought ... we don't ... there's not a whole lot of people we ... you came to mind. I thought you were friends, thought maybe you could help. It's my mistake, I remembered things differently." My jaw was tightly clenched. I relaxed it as much as I could and said, "I ... its stupid, I know."

He looked at me, an unreadable expression on his face.

Uncle Don. How could I have been so wrong?

"I'm sorry I bothered you," I said, turning to leave.

"Sam."

"What?"

"Your father. Where is he now?"

"He's at the medical center," I lied.

"I see. How bad is it?"

"I already told you."

"Right, sorry. What is it, exactly, that's wrong with him?"

"I don't know," I shrugged. "We don't know."

He nodded, thinking. "How long are you here?"

"Not long," I lied again. "We're heading out later today."

He frowned. "Really? Where to?"

"I don't know. Somewhere else."

He rubbed his forehead. "I wish I could help you, Sam, I do. But I'd need to sort a few things out. I mean, maybe I can give you some—" he stopped, frowning again. "Look. Can you come back later, before you leave? With your father?"

"No," I said flatly. "I can't."

Once again, we found ourselves staring at each other in silence.

"What about your mother?" he said finally. "Does she know what's happening?"

"My mother?" I asked bitterly. "I really don't know who you're talking about. I've never met her. I don't even know her name."

Donald Coleman's expression was sympathetic enough—in any other situation I would have been moved by it—but I found I didn't really care. I was done here. I couldn't take any more. I was angry and confused. And I was tired of being confused.

"I'm sorry to have bothered you," I said formally. "Thank you for your time."

I turned and opened the door, slipping through it quickly and closing it behind me with a soft click.

Life, I've decided, is almost certainly one big practical joke. Not a cruel joke, necessarily. Not entirely anyway. You can even laugh along with it once in a while. But it's most definitely a baffling one, the kind you never completely get, where the punch line goes on forever. Case in point: as if things weren't bad enough, as if I wasn't in over my head in every way, I think I might have fallen in love.

After closing the door to Donald Coleman's office, I sprinted down the second-floor hallway, moved by an overwhelming urge to be out of there, to get away from myself. I clattered down the stairs to the lobby and kept running, leaving the Geology Building and the UC Riverside campus behind.

It turns out you can't run away from yourself. The thing that is you, with its world full of problems, the thing that attracts frustrations big and small, like some kind of existential flypaper, stays firmly attached to you, follows you wherever you go. My attempted flight took me as far as the van, the container of everything that had gone wrong with my life.

I sat beneath the shade of a giant linden tree across the

street from the van and glared at it. It was as close as I wanted to get right then. I couldn't help wishing it had been towed away while I was gone, and Gordon along with it, hauled off to some unknown location where I would never find it. I didn't care if he was still asleep or awake. I didn't care if he was delirious or coherent, happy or sad. I didn't even care if he was still inside.

I needed a break, half an hour of calm somewhere quiet where I could put my head on straight. I suppose I could have gone back to the university library, but for some reason that didn't occur to me. It was now late afternoon, the first hints of orange seeping into the clear blue sky. The air was soft and warm. I breathed in the pleasantness of my environment, letting it arrange itself around me like a cocoon. I decided to go for a walk. I got up and set off down the sidewalk, pretending I was simply a man of independent means, strolling along at his leisure. I grew calmer with every step.

A few blocks from the van, I entered a small business district, with restaurants and bars and clothing stores and specialty shops. The metal sign of a coffee chop, jutting out from the white-painted wall of a low, cinder block building, caught my attention. The metal had been cut away in parts to form the stencil of a turreted castle, floating on a foundation of clouds. Letters were cut into the bottom of the sign, the empty spaces spelling out the word, *Luftschlösser*. There were three tables on the sidewalk in front of the café, but they were all taken, occupied by people busy poking their pocket phones, ignoring their coffees and muffins and the world around them. The double doors of the entrance were propped open, allowing the slightly cooler air of the interior to pour out onto the sidewalk, along with the sound of some kind of jazz. I peered into the long, narrow room, filled with people seated around small tables and plopped on couches, engaged with their computers and pocket phones, some of them even reading. The bare brick walls were lined with small framed drawings, all the same size and evenly spaced. The service counter was all the way to the back, beneath a large chalkboard menu. It was perfect.

I made my way to the counter, taking note of an empty corner seat on one of the couches as I went. I hovered back a few feet from the counter, reading the menu and trying to figure out what I could afford. According to the chalkboard, a double cappuccino was $5.45, which would leave me with two cents.

The girl behind the counter was already smiling at me as I approached it. "Hell-o," she said, her voice pleasant and songlike. "What can I get you?"

"Uh … I um … I'll have a cappuccino please. Double."

"For here or to go?"

"Here, please."

"You got it. Name?"

"Hmm?"

"Your name?"

"Oh, right. Sam."

She leaned back on her stool, calling out to a bearded, heavily tattooed guy manning the espresso machine, "Double-cap-house-Sam." She turned to me and smiled again. Her teeth were incredibly white and perfectly straight. She was pretty, very pretty actually, tan and athletic looking, with straight blond hair pulled back into a long ponytail. If I had to guess, I would say she was about eighteen.

"Is that all?"

"Pardon?"

She smiled, apparently her face's natural state. "Would you like anything else?"

"Oh. No, thanks. Just the coffee."

She poked at the register. "Five eighty," she sang.

"What?"

"Five dollars and eighty cents."

I felt a jolt of panic.

"Um, the sign says five forty-five?"

"Yep," she smiled. "That's before tax."

"Oh." Panic turned quickly to embarrassment. My face flushed. I felt silly, childish, a little boy who didn't even know about tax. "Right. Crap. I'm sorry," I said. "But I've only got five forty-seven."

She frowned for a fraction of a second, then smiled. "Don't worry about it!" She gave a quick wave of her hand, wiping the missing money from existence.

"Really?"

"Really, no problem. I think we can spot you thirty-three cents."

"Wow, thanks," I said, reaching into my pocket and handing over a fistful of money. She untangled the jumble of bills and coins nimbly, placing everything in its proper slot in the cash register. She took three dimes and three pennies from a little dish of coins next to the register and tossed them in too.

"Thank you!" she sing-songed.

"Thank *you*," I said gratefully. Relieved but still embarrassed, I drifted away from the counter and waited for my coffee. A bald, middle-aged man with a pointy white beard and a tight fitting T-shirt emerged from the bathroom and walked past me grumpily, limping slightly and massaging his right butt cheek. I watched him mince across the room over to the couch, where he plopped down into the very spot I'd already mentally reserved. Like I said: *life*.

"Double cappuccino for Sam!"

C'est moi.

I walked to the counter and picked up my coffee, thanking the bearded guy, who nodded curtly. I dropped two brown sugar cubes into the foamy cup and stirred it with a stick. Holding the saucer with both hands, I shuffled slowly into the big room, trying figure out where to sit.

The couches were full, and while there were a few unused chairs, they all belonged to occupied tables. Only one of those tables had two empty chairs. I found myself walking over to it by default.

The table was occupied by a girl about my age (a fact which *should* have factored into my decision but somehow did not). An open book, a pad of paper and a clear glass coffee mug, half-filled with watery coffee, sat on the table in front of her. She was writing away on her pad of paper with a number two pencil. I approached cautiously, then stopped at a respectful distance and waited. And waited. After giving her more than enough time to notice that I was standing in front of her, I mumbled tentatively: "Um, excuse me?"

She scribbled out a couple more characters before finally glancing up, just long enough to confirm my presence. Without a word, she turned her attention back to her work.

"Um," I said again. Why did I keep saying that? Apparently, as the f-word had been the night before, 'um' was today's word of the day. "Excuse me? Are these seats taken?"

She flipped her pencil neatly so that the eraser end faced the page. She rubbed a few characters out of existence, then flipped the pencil back to the lead-forward position.

"Nope," she said, wiping the little nubs of eraser debris from the page with a casual swipe of her hand. "Help yourself."

"Thanks," I said. I placed my saucer on the table carefully, but still managed to spill some coffee down the sides of the cup. I sat in the chair directly across from her and looked around, making a show of taking in the artwork on the café walls. It was actually pretty good, intricate pencil and ink drawings of intertwined tentacles and krakens and other imaginary sea creatures. I sniffed, then blew softly onto the foam in my cup.

I sniffed again, wishing I'd thought to grab my own notebook and pen from the van, if only so that I too had something to do. Thinking of my notebook naturally set me to list-making. Imagining my notebook laid out in front of me, I wrote the title for a new list in my head: *Plan Two: Preliminary Considerations*.

That was as far as I got. Unable to concentrate, I didn't come up with a single element of this new plan. It wasn't fatigue or lack of inspiration that hindered me. It was the fact that I couldn't take my eyes off of the girl sitting two feet from me.

I thanked whatever gods were responsible for the fact that she was completely ignoring me, since it meant that I could look at her without her knowing. There was almost nothing that wasn't perfect about her. The longer I looked, the more perfect she seemed. Her light brown hair, pulled back in to a short, jagged ponytail. Her head, her neck, her nose, her ears, her fingers, the little knobs formed by the bones of her wrists; the work of a Pygmalion, I thought. Her gestures, too, were basically perfect. The way she tucked the strands of hair that slipped from her ponytail behind her ear, or nibbled on the inside of her lip as she wrote, the way her eyebrows knit in concentration as she read from her book, the way she made a fist to hold her pencil. Any one of these details would have been enough to capture my attention. All of them taken together were like a conspiracy to make me forget to breathe.

I've always scoffed at the examples of love at first sight I've read in books. Aeneas and Dido, Romeo and Juliet, Lancelot and Guinevere. Great stories, all ruined by love. Apart from the fact that thunderbolt love always ended poorly, I just couldn't bring myself to believe in it. It was fairy tale stuff. Fantasy. Now, sitting in a strange coffee house in a strange city, I found I'd been converted. A bolt from Cupid's quiver was sticking straight out of my forehead. The initial impact of that arrow was as painful as a real one. I could feel its effects spreading out across my being. A new hum enveloped me, a happy kind of numbness this time. It seemed to me in that instant that everything missing from my life—including a few things I hadn't known were missing—combined to form a hole, a hole that was exactly the size and shape of the girl across the table from me. I felt like I was going to be sick.

I was staring at the little hollows on either side of her collarbone when she suddenly looked up from her work and stared back at me, allowing me to see her face in full. Another arrow thudded into my sternum, almost knocking me out of my seat. Her eyebrows were darker than her hair, full and arched, like the wings of a falcon, the eyes beneath them big and brown and almond-shaped. Her left eye looked directly into mine, locking onto it and preventing me from looking away. Her right eye, however, was slightly adrift, floating up and to the right. Of all the things that were perfect about her, that beautiful hovering eye was the most perfect. I had to remind myself to breathe. It was awful. It was wonderful.

Her eyes narrowed suspiciously, and I knew if I went on staring like a village idiot all would be lost. I needed a diversionary tactic, something to draw attention away from the fact that I was basically powerless. Like using words. I needed to say something, anything. Somehow I managed to tear my gaze away from hers and nod at her cup. "What are you drinking?" I asked, my voice practically breathless.

She looked at me neutrally for a moment or two longer, then turned her head slowly to look at her cup before looking back at me. "That would be tea," she replied. "English Breakfast with honey."

Of course, I thought, kicking myself. *Watery coffee! What a moron!*

"Oh," I said lamely. "Right. You don't like coffee?"

"Not really."

"Not even lattes?"

"Not my cup of tea," she said with a wink, pointing her finger at me and cocking her thumb like the hammer of a pistol.

I'm a strong enough swimmer. I'm not afraid of currents or deep water. But in that moment I understood what it must feel like to be unable to swim and find yourself in the middle of the ocean. My heart was beating fast as a rabbit's, and snow had begun to fall near the periphery of my vision. I would have been happy to sit there and say nothing, to just watch her scribble and erase and chew her lip and tuck her hair behind her ear. I could have done it for hours, but I knew that would get me nowhere. I *had* to continue talking to her.

"What are you reading?" I asked, my voice still sounding partially strangled despite my attempt at nonchalance.

"It's algebra," she said, with a note of disdain. I could only hope it was for the subject and not me. "You don't read it. You do it."

"Oh." I was starting to reconsider the decision to open my mouth. "Right. So what are you *doing*?"

"Algebra," she repeated.

Ugh! All right idiot. Step back, regroup, try again. "No. I mean, what are you doing here, in this place?"

She threw me a skeptical look, clearly debating whether my question deserved an answer.

"Well," she began. "Apart from *drinking tea* and *doing algebra*, I'm waiting for my sister to get off. She works here." She nodded toward the back counter. I turned and looked at the pretty, smiling girl who'd let me off the hook. Pretty, sure, but not beautiful. I turned back to find *beautiful* looking at me. It was a little frightening.

"How about you, Sam," she said. "What are *you* doing, *in this place?*"

I stared at her with a look of utter bewilderment. How did she know my name?

"How do you know that?" I asked in amazement. "My name?"

She laughed. "Timba told me."

"*Timba?*"

"Yeah. Timba. The guy who made your fancy coffee. I heard him call your name when it was ready." She made a serious face. Dropping her voice down low in imitation of Timba's, she said, "Double cappuccino for Sam!"

Her laugh. It was like two hands reaching out and twisting the arrows in my forehead and chest. My ruin was complete.

I wanted desperately to hold up my end of the conversation, but could only manage basic sounds. "Oh."

"So. Are you new here? I've never seen you before, and I'm here almost every day."

"Um, yeah," I said, nodding my head thoughtfully. "This is my first time."

She smiled. Maybe she had a soft spot for dopes? I could only hope.

"What brings you here?"

"Just visiting," I said, feeling a slight panic at the truth of it. What I wanted was to be able to say, *Yeah. I just moved in, right next door to you.* "With my dad." I pushed the pang of conscience that accompanied that sentence away. Was it too much to ask to enjoy the present moment for once?

"He's in a meeting," I lied. "Until tomorrow."

"Wow. That's a long meeting."

"No. I mean, we're here until tomorrow."

"Oh," she said. "Then you're going back home?"

Maybe, just maybe, she sounded a little disappointed. My heart jumped at the thought.

"Yeah," I said. Another lie.

"And where is home?"

I didn't know how to answer that one. I didn't want to talk about me, really, or Gordon, or our life. Hoping to change the subject I blurted out, "What's *your* name, anyway?"

She tilted her head, then laughed. "Magda," she said. "My name's Magda. It's short for Magdalena."

"Yeah I know," I said, a little too quickly.

"You do?"

"Well, no. I don't actually. But that's what I would have guessed."

She tapped her bottom teeth lightly with her pencil. "It's German," she said. "But you probably would have guessed that too."

It was my turn to laugh. "Probably," I said.

"My mom is German. *Very* German."

"My favorite band is German," I said, happy to have something positive to contribute.

"Really?"

"Yep."

"What's it called?"

"Kraftwerk."

She frowned. "Never heard of it. What kind of music do these Germans of yours play?"

"German, I guess," I said with a smile.

She looked at me skeptically, apparently failing to see the humor in my response.

"It's electronic," I explained, wincing a little at how silly I sounded. "You know, with synthesizers and stuff. Yeah, if I had to pick one word for it, I would say electronic."

"Nice. Anyway, my mom is very proud of her heritage, so we all have German names."

What a thing, I thought. To *know* your mother. Where she's from, who she *is*, to have her pass that identity on to you.

"My sister is Trudi," Magda said. "It's short for Hiltrude, hence the Trudi. She's an artist. She did all the drawings in here."

"Wow," I said, looking at the sea-monster drawings again. "They're really good. Amazing, really. I can barely draw a stick person."

"Yeah, me neither."

Huzzah! Common ground!

"What *do* you like?" I asked, now a lot more comfortable. "Math?"

"No!" she laughed, shaking her head. "I hate math. I mean, I like the idea of it. I'm just not any good at it. I'm barely pulling a C in this. I like to read. And write. I want to be a writer someday."

Was it silly, in that moment, for me to imagine the two of us tucked away in a little cottage somewhere in the Bavarian Alps, filling our notebooks with our soon-to-be-famous novels? I needed some kind of ballast, something to keep me anchored to the ground. I opted to continue with the small talk.

"Is it just you and your sister?"

"No. I have a little brother, too. Sigi. Short for Siegfried."

"That I knew," I said. "Siegfried is my favorite hero. Well, favorite *Germanic* hero. Theseus is my favorite hero." I'm not sure why I felt the need to disclose that fact. I guess I just wanted to stop half-lying to her. She deserved better.

"Our Sigi's a hero too," she said, her voice quiet. "He's sick a lot." She screwed up her mouth for a few seconds, then turned her attention back to her algebra book, scribbling and chewing.

I considered asking more about her little brother, but decided it wasn't my business. Besides, it seemed to make her a little sad, which was the last thing I wanted to do.

Sticking with what was true, I said, "I like your name."

Of course, her name could have been Kreimhild and I still would have thought it beautiful.

She looked up at me and smiled. "Thanks. I like your name too."

We alternated between working and talking, Magda on the algebra she hated and me on the outline of a new plan. By the time her sister got off an hour later and Magda was forced (reluctantly, I like to think) to leave, it was like we had known each other forever. The pain I felt when she left signaled the return of the big hole of missing things. The little piece of paper in my pocket with her name and address helped, it was a start. As I made my way from the *Luftschlösser* back to the parking lot, I found the pain slowly diminishing, almost disappearing altogether, as thoughts of her poured into the space of her absence and filled it up.

I mouthed her name as I walked along, sounding out the syllables according to the German pronunciation: *Mawg-duh*. Magda. Magda. *Magdalena*. A perfect name for a perfect person. A name straight out of myth. A shield-maiden name, a Valkyrie name.

Repeating her name led to happy thoughts, thoughts which lifted me off of the pavement and carried me along. Dusk fell as I floated down the sidewalk back to the van. I felt restored. No, not restored. It was more than that. *I* was more. More than I had been before. Better. I was overflowing with optimism, with belief, once again up to whatever life decided to throw my way.

Which turned out to be, in this instance, Donald Coleman, shading his eyes with his hands and trying to see into the back of the van.

My first thought was to stay out of sight, wait until he went away. Then it occurred to me that he might start knocking on the window and wake up Gordon. I couldn't see that turning out to be a good thing. Dipping into the reserves of my newfound optimism, I took a deep breath and made for the van. From halfway across the street I called out, "Can I help you?"

Startled, Donald Coleman jerked back from the van and turned to look at me. He scratched his cheek and said, "Oh, hey, Sam. It's you."

"Yeah," I said. "It's me. Can I help you?"

He held his hands out, as if bestowing a blessing. "I tried following you," he said. "When you left. You were a little too quick for me. By the time I got down to the quad, you were gone."

He waited for me to say something, accepted my silence, then went on: "I knew it was futile, but I decided to look around for you anyway. I was about to give up when I saw this," he tilted his head in the direction of the van. "Which I recognized."

"Really?" I asked, not quite sure how someone who hadn't seen us for years could recognize our vehicle.

He nodded.

"How?"

"Well," he said. "It used to be mine."

"Oh." I didn't know what else to say.

Donald Coleman smiled. "Yeah. I sold it to your dad right after graduate school. For cheap, too. I have to admit, I'm kind of surprised to see what great shape it's in. It looks like it hasn't aged a day."

"Yeah, well, it's pretty much our home, so we take good care of it."

It was more than I should have said. Donald Coleman's face grew serious. His brow knit in concern, the lines of his forehead bunching into a V, like a stack of karate-chopped lumber. He scratched his chin, thinking.

"Sam. Where is your father?"

"I already told you that," I said, trying not to glance at the van where Gordon was sleeping even now. "He's at the hospital. At the Medical Center."

"That's right," he nodded. "You did tell me that. Can you take me there? Would it be possible for me to see him?"

I shook my head. "No, I don't think so. He's resting."

To my relief, Donald Coleman decided not to question me further on the subject. Talking about Gordon, thinking about him, brought back a little of the weight, the heaviness. It also made me a little bit angry.

"Why are you here?" I demanded.

He smiled weakly. "I wanted to apologize to you. For the way I acted earlier. I didn't mean to be so cold with you, it's just … you know, I hadn't thought about your dad or your mom—or you—for a long time and then there you were. It caught me by surprise. I'm sorry."

"It's okay," I said. "I guess it wasn't really fair of me to barge in on you like that."

"No, no, no," he said, holding his hands out again. "No, Sam. You didn't do anything wrong. Far from it."

We stood looking at each other for a moment.

"Look," he said. "I don't know what the trouble is, or how bad it is, but I'd like to help if I can."

I shook my head fiercely, not just as a way of refusing his offer, but also to push back the tears that came suddenly to my eyes.

"Thanks," I said. "But no. I don't know what you can do, really. I don't even know what the trouble *is*, so I don't know what kind of help we need. We only came here—I only brought us here—because I remembered you. I don't know why, but I did. I didn't even remember you right, and I don't know what I thought you would do, you're just the only person I could think of, the only person I know that Gordon knows. Besides my mother."

He sighed, staring hard at the ground between us. He looked at me again, searching my face for who-knows-what, his eyes sparkling fiercely.

"I'm breaking a promise here," he said. "But some promises aren't worth making, let alone keeping. I think maybe this is one of them."

He reached into his shirt pocket and pulled out a neon-yellow post-it note. "Take it," he said, holding it out to me. "It might be helpful to you."

I reached out and took the paper from him. Somehow knowing I wasn't quite prepared to read whatever was written on it, I stashed it quickly in my pocket.

He looked at me sympathetically. "I don't know what's going on, Sam. I think maybe you know a little more than you've told me—which is fair enough."

I shrugged.

He laughed softly. "All right. Call us even on that score. But listen to me. When you get it figured out, and if you decide you still want help, you know where to find me. Understand?"

I nodded.

I thought he was getting ready to tell me something more, something important, but he just extended his hand. I took it and shook it firmly.

"Okay then," he said.

"Okay then," I echoed. "Thank you."

Thank you, Uncle Don.

I watched him as he walked away, staring at the spot where he disappeared around the corner for a while, trying but failing to come up with a word to describe what I was feeling. I took the post-it note from my pocket and leaned against the side of the van. There, on the little square of paper, in a small, tidy script, Donald Coleman had written his name and address and phone number. Beneath that information, separated from it by a thumb's width of blank space were the following lines:

Janice Pembroke, Assoc. Professor of Anthropology,
California State University Chico
Home address: 78 Endicott Street, Chico.

I don't know how long I sat there, not moving, not breathing. I only know it took a long time for the words on the paper, for their *meaning*, to sink in, slowly penetrating the thick rind of a lifetime of not knowing. I didn't believe it at first, even though I was looking at it, even though it was right there in my hand. My mother's name. In my hand. When the reality of it hit home, I found I could only laugh; at how simple it was, how miraculous. How wonderful.

Whenever I have the chance, I like to sneak away to some secluded spot with my cigar box. Just to think about it, to wonder over its contents. Once certain I'm completely alone, I set the box in front of me and slip off the thick rubber band that keeps it securely closed. I wiggle my fingers in the air like a magician before his magic top hat, and open it up. I take the objects from it one by one, pondering each in turn before returning it to the box and stowing it away once again.

I have invented histories for each of the items, backstories to explain their presence in the box. I have no problem, for example, picturing her sitting at a candle-lit desk, the fountain pen in her hand as she dips it into a little glass ink pot, filling it up with blue-black ink and inscribing, with a beautiful, flowing script, her innermost thoughts and feelings in some secret journal. The oak twig, with its dark brown acorns (only one of which is still attached), is the souvenir of a solitary walk through some grassy meadow, or maybe a lazy fall afternoon spent beneath a giant tree in her childhood backyard. The coins allow me to retrace her various travels: England, Denmark, Peru, Turkey,

Japan. The corn cob pipe and the Soviet pin, I have decided, had been given to her by her father, my grandfather, emblems of his down-to-earth nature and political ideals, a torch passed from him to her and then on to me. The silver jack needs no explanation. It is the only thing from the box I use, its pointy ends burnished from a thousand snaps of my fingertips. My head nestled in the crook of my arm, my eyes level with the tabletop, I watch it spin, silently at first, whirring along magically, perfectly upright, waiting for the fleeting moment when it is perfectly poised, seemingly ready to float off the table, only to start oscillating a moment later, wobbling and teetering and coming to a stop.

The compass, I've decided, is not a regular compass, but one with a special property. I pull the battered lid open carefully, then watch the magnetic pointer come to life, wavering uncertainly before aligning itself with the earth's poles, the red tip never failing to line up with the squat N painted in blue on the rose. That N, however, does not stand for the cardinal direction North, but the truer north of my mother. Holding the compass in my outstretched palm, I like to imagine that no matter how far away she might be, my compass points straight to her.

The box and everything in it were hers, special objects filled with the magic of her presence, things she gave to Gordon to give to me. They were hers and now they're mine, because she wanted me to have them, because she wanted me to know that she was real, that I should never forget her. The fact that I didn't perfectly remember the exact circumstances in which it had been given to me didn't matter. What mattered is the fact that I had it. It was mine and it was real. There was no doubting it.

A giant woodpecker banged away at my tree, getting closer and closer to the spot where I lay, hidden and safe. No. It wasn't a woodpecker; it was a giant hand. The hand of an ogre, pounding on the weathered wood of the castle gate. I burrowed deeper into my nest of blankets, willing the obnoxious creature to go away. No such luck. The pounding continued, though the closer I rose toward consciousness the softer it became, until it was not so much a genuine pounding as a sharp knocking, like the sound of a knuckle tapping on a window.

On *my* window.

Tap, tap, tap.

I woke with a start, lurching violently into a seated position. The van was awash with sunlight, blasting its way through the thin curtains covering the side and rear windows. Someone was outside the van, knocking impatiently. A police officer. It had to be. A surge of panic spread instantly to every part of my body.

Tap, tap, tap.

I freed myself from the tangle of blankets and waited, but

there was nothing more. No more taps, no voice, no sound of any kind. Nothing.

I crawled to the back of the van on my hands and knees, careful to keep my head below the window. I pulled the corner of the curtain back and peeked out. It was Gordon.

I scrambled over to my sneakers and slipped them on, then popped open the rear doors and spilled out onto the parking lot.

"Good morning, Sam."

"Hey," I said, blinking against the bright morning sun.

He seemed pretty relaxed, standing there in the early morning light. His hands were thrust into the pockets of his khakis, his empty pipe wedged in the corner of his mouth. He seemed really quite fresh and, apart from his rumpled clothing, looked every inch himself.

It should have been strange, this encounter, but somehow it wasn't. The obvious questions—*What were we doing here? How did we get here? What happened over the past two days?*—didn't need to be asked. He knew. He knew what we were doing here and how we'd come to be here. Not the specifics, of course, but we both knew those didn't matter. We were here. It was now. That was all that mattered. That and what we were going to do next.

Gordon tapped non-existent ashes from his pipe with the butt of his palm, then inspected the bowl. In the quiet that followed, his face assumed one of the most complicated expressions I'd ever seen, equal parts pride, shame, gratitude, sadness.

"So," he said finally.

"So."

"What's the plan?"

For a second, I thought he was mocking me. Then I understood it was just an innocent expression.

"Plan?"

"For today. What do you want to do? Stay here?"

He gestured at the environs of Riverside with a sweep of his pipe.

A vision of Magda popped into my head, urging me to say, *Yes, Gordon. Let's stay. Let's live here for a while.* I tried not to think about how messed up it was that life had only allowed me to enjoy the bliss of meeting a girl I liked for all of five minutes before complicating everything again. The act of saying no was accompanied by actual physical pain, but there was nothing I could do about it. I didn't have a choice. There were more important things to do right now. Like driving north.

"No," I said. "We're not staying. But maybe we can come back. I like it here."

Picking up on my conflicting emotions, Gordon shot me a questioning look. When I said nothing further he simply nodded. "Sure. We can do that."

And that was it. Before you could say *boo*, we'd returned to our default positions, Gordon standing by the driver's side door, me at the passenger side. I waited for Gordon to unlock the doors.

"I need the keys, Sam," he called over the top of the van.

"Oh, yeah. Right."

I took the keys from my pocket and unlocked my door, then tossed them over the front of the van to Gordon. We climbed in and he started the engine.

"So."

"Yes?"

"Where to now?"

Gordon was genuinely offering me the opportunity to decide where we went from here, a rare honor. I mulled over various clever ways of answering, and decided to just come out with it.

"North," I said. "Chico."

His jaw tensed slightly, but otherwise Gordon made no visible response to my suggestion. He nodded and said, "Okay. Chico it is."

"Really?" I asked, somehow unwilling to believe it was going to be that easy. Gordon simply looked at me in a way that recommended I not push my luck too far.

"Do you know the way?"

My attempt to sound innocent was so overdone it only made the question even more ridiculous than it already was. Luckily, Gordon saw fit not to hit me with the withering look I deserved.

"I know about ten of them."

With a bemused shake of his head, he moved the driver's seat back and pulled out onto the empty street. I leaned around behind my seat and grabbed my notebook and pen from my backpack. I turned to the shortest list and crossed out the first entry: *Uncle Don*. My heart thudded in my chest as I risked a glance at the second: *Mom*. I closed the notebook and slipped it into the door panel.

Gordon made his way calmly to the interstate, merging onto the westbound side. We rolled down our windows, letting the still-clean mid-morning air come streaming in. I rested my forearm on the door, watching its forest of tiny golden hairs dance wildly in the wind.

Mom

"*She's a model and she's look-ing good, I'd like to take her home, that's un-der-stood.*"

I sang along with the detached German voice in an exaggeratedly mechanical version of my own, the blank look on my face betraying nothing of the giddiness I felt inside. Perched on the edge of my seat, I tapped out the moody synthesizer chords on the dashboard. "The Model" has never cracked my list of favorite songs. It's always struck me as a tad melancholy for a Kraftwerk song. Now it was right at the top, for no other reason than the fact that it contained the word *she*, my new favorite word, the world's best pronoun. I gazed ahead contentedly as we sped along the *autobahn*, thoughts of Magda mingling with daydreams of Janice Pembroke, my mother.

Gordon's right hand floated across the space between us and settled on my left forearm—letting me know I should probably give the air synth a rest—then returned it to its two o'clock position on the steering wheel. When I glanced over at the familiar profile of that grand, shaggy head, I couldn't help noticing the little creases tugging at the corner of his eye as he squinted in concentration at the road in front of him, the tight set of his mouth.

"Sorry," I said, understanding that it wouldn't do to push my luck.

An hour earlier, about twenty minutes out of Riverside, Gordon had merged on to the 10 westbound. His plan, as far as I could tell, was to head toward the coast—sixty miles on one of the busiest freeways in the state—before turning north and tackling the five-hundred miles to Chico. This choice of route, combined with the fact that he was puttering along in the slow lane, was enough to tell me that even though he'd consented to going to Chico, the trip would not be express. Amazingly enough, I didn't care; I didn't feel the slightest bit perturbed or impatient. Gordon could stall all he wanted, the most it would take to get to Chico was a couple of days. Which was okay with me. I'd waited my whole life to meet my mother; two more days were not going to kill me.

By way of compensating for his underhanded tactics, Gordon dipped his head toward the cassette crate, a gesture meant to indicate that I could pick the soundtrack for the first leg of our trip.

"Anything?" I asked.

"Anything you want."

Not one to look a gift horse in the mouth, I dug out *Trans-Europe Express* and popped it into the deck. When the tape had played through both sides, I replaced it with *The Man Machine*. The Vanagon seemed pleased with my selections, and purred happily under Gordon's light foot.

Apart from the shiny, spacey sounds of Kraftwerk, the drive passed in total silence. Nothing remarkable in that. We often go an entire day without saying anything to each other. Gordon, of course, has many types of silence. There's a silence that accompanies the pondering of some obscure intellectual matter, a silence that serves as an antidote for the general racket of everyday life, a silence that means he's simply following the twists and turns of his mind for the pure pleasure of it. There's also a silence for processing, for problem solving. That was the kind of silence that enveloped him now. He was working something over in his mind, turning it this way and that like a Rubik's Cube. He wouldn't stop—and he certainly wouldn't speak—until he'd completely solved it, until he'd restored all of the problem's sides to order.

I typically have only one kind of silence, the silence of daydreaming. On this occasion, however, my silence seemed almost drug-induced. The euphoria over recent events ran so deep my body felt like a chemical factory. But the source of my happiness was not a drug. It was love. Then again, maybe love is a drug. Who knows? If it is, then I have no qualms about admitting myself addicted. I was on a double dose and it was the best thing I'd ever felt.

"*... I want to meet her again.*"

"The Model" had come to an end. There were two more songs left on *The Man Machine*. Anticipating the end, I leaned over the crate and retrieved the empty case, grabbing the next tape—*Computer World*—at the same time. I didn't get as far as playing it; Gordon solved his puzzle in the middle of "Neon Lights." Without warning, he reached over and turned the stereo off. His eyes glued to the road in front of him, he cleared his throat and said, as if talking to the windshield, "There are some things we need to talk about."

Gordon poked the buttons on his door panel, rolling our windows up halfway, shutting out just enough wind to allow for our voices to be heard. The little muscles in his jaw fluttered, and his head nodded from side to side ever so slightly; signs of an internal dialogue. Whatever conversation we were about to have, he was going to have it with himself first.

A wave of nervous anticipation rippled through me. I sat and waited, not exactly eager to hear what he had to say. I would have preferred to daydream and listen to music.

Gordon took in a number of deep breaths, exhaling each one sharply, like someone working up the nerve to plunge into a pool of ice-cold water. He swallowed hard and nodded to himself, as if to confirm that he was indeed ready to begin. Without taking his eyes off the road, he said, "First of all, I can't tell you how sorry I am."

"It's okay Gordon, you don't—"

His right hand shot out into the space between us, cutting me off. "No Sam," he said firmly. "Please. Let me do this. I know where your heart is, believe me. I know your first impulse is to let me off the hook. It's your nature, making light of heavy things. I've taken advantage of that nature long enough. So just listen to what I have to say and think about it, and don't be in a hurry to brush it all under the rug and put a happy face on it, okay?"

"Okay."

"Good. I am sorry Sam, truly sorry, for all of this. I never intended for any of this to happen, having such a burden fall on you is the last thing I could ever want, believe me. I'm not apologizing for something I've done. I hope you'll understand it's not a question of doing. I'm sorry about what's *happening*, that it's happening to you. It's hard enough for me, let me tell you, so I can only imagine what you're going through. I just want you to understand that I'm sorry. For all of it."

Fighting back the urge to say, *it's okay, really, it's no big deal*, I shrugged and said, "I understand."

Gordon's forehead bunched up in thought, his lips forming silent words. He returned to his internal debate. After a while, the usual honey-like tone of his voice thin and brittle, he whispered, "I'm sick, Sam. Very sick."

I'd taken the butterflies in my stomach as proof that I was sufficiently apprehensive—that is to say, *prepared*—for anything he might say. Hearing the words *very sick*, I realized I was not. It wasn't just the words that caught me out. There was something in the sound of his voice, something I'd never heard before, a kind of defeated weariness mixed with fear. The butterflies swarmed into a cloud, then contracted, squeezing my intestines. I was torn in two, part of me wanting to know—*needing* to know—what was going on, the other not wanting to hear another word.

Gordon scratched the beard on his cheek.

"I have a ... *condition*. Something called 'dementia.' Do you know what that is?"

With a shake of my head I admitted that I did not.

"It's a word that's been around for a long time," he said, his voice still quiet but now a bit steadier. "For most of that time it's been synonymous with various forms of madness, some temporary, some permanent. These days it's essentially a medical term, a diagnosis, one that refers to the impairment of cognitive function."

"Impairment of *what*?"

"Cognitive function. Thought and behavior, basically. Dementia affects the way a person's brain works, makes it hard for them to behave normally. It's not so much a thing in itself," he continued, taking a deep breath, "as a collection of symptoms."

Just like that, he'd slipped into teaching mode, his words carefully chosen, his voice once again measured and calm. He shot a quick glance in my direction to see that I was still with him, then continued his monologue: "*Symptoms* are the noticeable effects of a disease, typically the direct result of damage to particular parts of the body, disrupting their function. The symptoms of dementia, the functions it disrupts, include language, memory, personality, motor function and so on."

And so on? Only one word managed to separate itself from this bewildering flow and sink its hook into my consciousness: *disease.*

As in Donald Coleman's office, I had the experience of being submerged. I could feel the sound of Gordon's voice growing more and more distant. The contracted cloud of butterflies became a block of cement. I sank through the passenger seat, dragged down by my own heaviness to the dark, airless depths. With each of Gordon's words I descended further, eventually landing on the ocean floor with a soft thud. I've come across the word *abyss* any number of times, one of those words I always kind of skated over, never bothering to ponder or understand it. I understood it now. I was in an abyss. I *was* an abyss.

Gordon's voice made its way to me from far above, drifting slowly down like the remains of dead sea creatures to the ocean floor. I tried to listen to the words, but found I could not understand them: "... through the presence of some underlying pathology," I heard a muffled voice say.

I fought my way—part of me did, anyway—back to the surface.

"Pathology?" Even though the word had come out my mouth, the sound of it reached my ears like a distant echo.

Gordon, now in full lecture mode, didn't seem to notice that I wasn't really there, that I was in fact far under water.

"Damage," he replied shortly, seemingly irritated at having to use such a simple word. "Dementia causes damage, Sam. To the brain."

A lifetime's rapport with language, with the easy give and take of words and the things they referred to, deserted me. I was unable to comprehend complete sentences. Only individual words made any sense, and though I understood each of them well enough on its own—*disease ... damage ... brain*—I could not connect them in a meaningful way.

Mistaking my confused silence for riveted attention, Gordon skipped along: "When it comes to brain pathology, the damaged tissue is referred to as a *lesion*. Lesions can result from trauma caused by an external source, such as a concussion—a brain contusion—from a fall or car accident or some other blow to the head, or something penetrating the skull and entering the brain, like a bullet or a piece of shrapnel. They can also result from something internal, organic, produced inside the body itself. This is what happens with neuro-degenerative diseases, Alzheimer's for instance, where the damage is done by amalgamations of peptides—senile plaques—and neurofibrillary tangles. These plaque and fibrous formations attach to brain tissue, destroying neurons and synapses and leading to atrophy of the frontal cortex, the parietal lobe, the cingulate—"

The onslaught of words had reduced me to a kind of witless automaton, a wind-up being capable only of repeating words in the form of questions.

"Parietal lobe?" I heard it ask.

"A big piece of the cerebral cortex," Gordon told it. "Right back here." With his right index finger, he pointed to a spot on top of his head, near the back. "It plays a big role in perception and sensation, integrates sensory data, and a whole bunch of other things."

The automaton nodded its head, as if it understood what it was hearing.

"Basically," he went on, "healthy brain tissue is replaced—*displaced*—by unhealthy tissue. And wherever this happens, the function performed by that part of the brain is impaired. Or lost."

"Lost?"

"Eventually," Gordon said, nodding ruefully. "Let's say an area that controls the ability to maintain focus and attention is damaged. That damage might cause the person suffering it to phase in and out of alertness. They might seem totally normal one minute, the next, they're virtually catatonic. It's called 'fluctuating cognition' and it's a primary symptom of certain kinds of dementia."

Fluctuating cognition. Something about that term restored the use of language to me. It was the phrase Dr. Moser had used. More than that, it was a phrase I understood. I knew it intimately. It perfectly described the last year or so of Gordon's life. With a jarring suddenness, I realized he was talking about something real. The weight holding me disappeared. I rose steadily upward, back to the surface of things, rejoining the body that sat in my seat. My mind racing, I thought back to my encounter with Dr. Moser. He *knew* what was wrong with Gordon, just by looking at him. I remembered him rattling off a bunch of names at one point. Names, I now realized, for different types of dementia.

"What type is it?" I asked.

"Type?"

"Yeah. What type of dementia do you have?"

Gordon shot me a puzzled glance, surprised, perhaps, by my sudden forcefulness. "DLB."

"Which is?"

"Dementia with Lewy Bodies."

Louie Bawdy. Another one of Dr. Moser's phrases.

"How did you get it?"

"Protein deposits—globs of unorganized matter—form in the brain," he said with an odd shrug. "Wherever these globs of stuff form, the brain cells in that area die off. When enough of the brain cells in a given area die off, well, I've already told you what happens then."

"I don't mean, *what causes it*," I said, surprised at the edge in my voice. "I mean, how did you get it?"

Gordon shook his head.

"I don't know, Sam. Nobody knows."

The weary tone that accompanied his initial admission returned.

"It's not something you *catch*, like the flu, or the chickenpox. And you don't get it from doing something unhealthy, like smoking or drinking or eating lead paint. You don't *get* it, Sam. It just happens to you."

"Oh."

It was all I could say. I never doubted that something was wrong with Gordon, attacking his mind, weakening his spirit. But I had assumed his affliction was something of his own making, something mental, psychological. It's not that I thought he was faking it. I thought it was just a state of mind—something under his control at some level—not a disease. It would go away when he was ready for it to go away. All I'd done this past year, basically, was take the wheel for a bit, steer the van until Gordon decided it was over. It never once occurred to me that the problem might be something physical, something *in* his brain. This wasn't some temporary weakness of Gordon's mind, or his spirit, or his soul. It was a disease, a form of matter, attacking his brain. Eating it. My pulse thundered in my ears. For the first time since this all began, I was scared. Truly scared.

"It's not very common for this to happen to someone my age," Gordon said quietly. "It's rather rare, in fact. Usually, it happens to people older than me. A lot older."

The muscles in his jaw worked, his hands tightened on the steering wheel, turning his knuckles white. Then he relaxed, sighing softly and shaking his head.

"I'm sorry," he whispered again. "I should have said something, I should never have let things get like this."

This time, I did not have to resist the urge to say, *it's okay*. I found that I was angry. I have no idea where it came from, I wasn't the one with dementia, after all, Gordon was. If anything, he should have been angry, while I should have been reassuring and helpful. But I wasn't helpful. I was angry. And the fact that I was angry when I didn't want to be only made me angrier.

"How do you know all this?" I demanded.

He shrugged.

"I've had my suspicions."

"*Suspicions?*"

"I've been looking into it for a while. I've figured out a few things."

"Figured out?"

"I've been studying the issue, Sam."

Studying the issue? What did that mean? What was he trying to say?

"For how long?"

"For a while now."

I stared at him accusingly. "You *knew?*"

"No, Sam," he said patiently. "I didn't know. Not at first. I had my suspicions, but I didn't know."

"But now you know?"

"Yeah. I'm pretty sure."

He sighed and scratched his beard, hard enough that I could hear the scraping of his whiskers above the engine's mechanical drone.

"And you didn't think you should share your knowledge with me?"

"I wasn't sure, Sam," he said, his voice an uncertain whisper. "I'm wasn't sure."

I pinched the skin of my forearm, hard, as if a little physical pain might divert the anger that was about to spill over. It worked, but not in the way I intended. I stared at the bright red mark on my arm, watching it slowly fade away, along with my anger.

"Okay," I said, "So what do you do for it?"

"Do?"

"What's the cure, how do you make it go away?"

Gordon closed his eyes for a full three seconds, then opened them. "It doesn't go away," he said.

"What do you mean?"

"There's no cure, Sam."

Gordon poked the controls again, rolling the windows halfway down, letting the wind back into the van and signaling that the conversation was over.

So much for anger. It would have been nice to hold onto mine a little longer—really, I would have enjoyed it—but as quickly as it had bubbled up it was gone, replaced by a looming fear.

The van returned to silence. Well, not the van. The engine rumbled, the wind roared through the half-open windows, the tapes rattled in the orange crate. The van was as loud as ever. It was Gordon and I who had returned to silence.

His silence, at least, was understandable. We'd reached Los Angeles, and he needed to pay attention to where he was going. His brow knit in concentration as he navigated the congested downtown maze of freeways and six-lane "boulevards." As usual, he seemed totally absorbed by the road in front of him. His large hands held the wheel at ten and two, ropey muscles standing out on his lean, hairy forearms. The wind whipped his hair about his head, and the edges of his beard fluttered in the turbulence. He weaved his way through the confusing tangle of on-ramps and off-ramps and cloverleafs calmly, eventually merging onto Highway 101 north, where he promptly returned to the slow lane, taking up his former snail's pace once again.

I would have liked nothing more than to sink into a deep, untroubled sleep, but there was no chance of that. My mind was spinning like a demonic jack, careening this way and that, wobbling ever more wildly as it spun but refusing to fall over or even slow down. Gordon hurt me, in a way I didn't understand, and I was afraid. Afraid of his disease, afraid of the idea that he could actually die, afraid of what else he hadn't told me, afraid that we'd never make it to Chico.

Just to give myself something to do, I took the worn, floppy California road map from the glove box. I unfolded it gingerly, careful as always not to tear it. Once I had it spread out in front of me, I crawled into it like a weary shipwreck survivor hauling himself onto a life raft.

I let my eyes wander slowly over the creased and weathered paper, devouring every detail: the jagged line of the northern coast, where towering cliffs met the sea; the puckered wrinkles of the Sierras; the irregular circles and ovals of lakes and reservoirs; the veiny blue of the north/south interstates. I traced every possible route to Chico, committing them all to memory. I measured the distance separating me from my mother: the length of my hand. She was that close. And yet, she wasn't. Chico was still five hundred miles away, even by the shortest route. Impatience crept up on me and I cursed the giant, elongated state of California. Why I couldn't live in Delaware or Rhode Island, someplace where an hour took you from one end of the state to the other?

At two o'clock, we made it to Ventura and the coast. Gordon exited 101 and pulled into town, stopping at the first gas station he saw. After filling the tank, he drove to a downtown supermarket, where we picked up a couple deli sandwiches, some potato salad, and two bottles of seltzer. We left the van in the parking lot and walked the few blocks from town to the beach. We made our way to the end of the public pier and sat on a wooden bench to eat our lunch. A gentle ocean breeze softened the hard summer sun, and though the wood of the bench was old and splintery, it gave off a pleasant warmth.

We watched the pelicans as we ate, gliding along in perfect formation just above the sparkling blue skin of the Pacific.

Halfway through my sandwich, I found eating tiresome, a kind of unwanted work I didn't have the energy for. Reluctantly swallowing the food in my mouth, I covered what was left of the sandwich in its foil-paper wrapper and dropped it into the paper bag. In the space of a few hours, my belief that things were looking up had disappeared, evaporating to the point where I was defeated by a sandwich. I tried to fathom the implication of Gordon's confession, but only grew more confused. Grasping for something positive—anything would do, even a simple happy thought—I imagined him sensing my mood and coming to my rescue, leading me out of my dilemma, as he had done so many times before, with a mysterious but edifying dialogue. If he knew what I was feeling, though, he didn't show it. He just sat there, eating his sandwich, his gaze locked on the distant horizon, his slow, thoughtful chewing punctuated by occasional swigs of seltzer.

Gordon finished his lunch and we walked back to the van. The temperature had risen to the point where the day was officially sweltering, and climbing into the van was like climbing into an oven. Still, heat or no, I was glad to be rolling again.

Instead of getting back onto 101, however, Gordon drove inland. I tried not to let this change of course bother me. At least the heat did not seem to be affecting him. He was still fully himself, as far as I could tell. He sat relaxed in his seat, totally in control. He seemed strangely light-hearted, and even started in on one of his whistling improvisations, the kind where he takes two different annoying songs and fuses them into an even more annoying hybrid. In this instance, "Tannenbaum" and "O Canada."

Half an hour later, on a tree-lined avenue in the town of Ojai, he pulled the van over and parked beneath the partial shade of a row of Sycamores. This sudden stop made me nervous. Were we about to have another *conversation*? Was he stalling? Was he starting to feel unwell?

"What's up?" I asked cautiously.

Picking up on my apprehension, Gordon smiled reassuringly. "Nothing's up, Sam. Just something I wanted you to see."

"Oh, okay. What?"

"Just a place. A library. One of my favorites. Don't worry, you'll love it."

A library. How long had it been since I last enjoyed the peace and security of a library's four walls? Days? Weeks? I couldn't remember exactly. It seemed a lifetime ago. To spend some time in a library, to experience even an hour of *home*, was exactly what I needed. Excited at the prospect, I hopped hurriedly from the van. Gordon and I crossed the broad, sun-soaked avenue to a small, L-shaped stucco building with terra-cotta roof tiles. A central courtyard, shaded by a large walnut tree, was nestled in the crook of the L. A small wooden sign was fixed to a low post near the edge of the building, depicting a youth in silhouette with a book on his knees, seated atop the words: *Ojai Library*. We passed through an opening in the low stucco wall surrounding the library and strolled casually across the shady courtyard, enjoying the little oasis of cool air.

We did not need to see the library hours to know it was closed. The entrance, a wall of glass with a glass door set in it, revealed an empty, unlit interior. I walked up to the transparent barrier, pressed my face against it, and peered inside. Gordon was right to love the place. A vaulted ceiling, supported by a system of dark wooden beams, made the library seem taller on the inside than it was on the outside. Beautiful opaque-glass globes hung from the beams, no doubt bathing the room in soft light when it was open. The main reading room was open and airy, with low tables and chairs and tidy stacks of books arranged with plenty of space between them, the walls lined with dark, book-filled shelves. A large, wooden courtesy desk with a couple computer terminals stood off to the right, flanked by two antique oak catalogue cabinets, the kind that always had drawers filled with well-thumbed, Dewey-decimalled index cards.

The inch of glass separating me from those cabinets might as well have been a foot of concrete. I couldn't shake the suspicion that I would never set foot in a library again. Like Moses on Mt. Nebo, I would be allowed to see my Promised Land but not enter it. Separated from that quiet reading room, with its inviting stillness, its promise of new words and worlds, I felt a new and deep sense of loss. For reasons I couldn't possibly understand, I had been banished from my only home. There was something threatening in this loss of home, a shift away from the stable world of the past toward one that was unknown and vaguely sinister, one where I would find only closed doors and empty libraries. I didn't feel angry or cheated, though. I felt empty, deflated. It was just another component of the chaos and flux overrunning my world, just one more thing I had no choice but to accept.

In the glass, I could see a reflection of Gordon shake its head in disappointment and turn to leave. I lingered on for a bit, sitting on a raised concrete planter in the courtyard, listening to the chatter of songbirds and the sound of traffic on the street beyond, letting my own disappointment dwindle down to nothing before trudging back to the van.

It was three o'clock. We were still almost four-hundred-fifty miles from Chico. Half a day had only brought us seventy-five miles closer to our goal, to *my* goal. None of which seemed to bother Gordon, who wasted no time launching back into his piercing rendition of "O Tannenbaum."

•

From Ojai, Gordon took Route 33 north, which wound its way up the Transverse Range through the Los Padres National Forest. The road twisted and turned as it rose, practically folding back on itself in some places in order to offer a reasonable grade. The cloudless sky was a brilliant blue, the strong afternoon sun an intense yellow-white. The air beyond the van's bubble of noise was perfectly still, and the parched hills rising up on either side of the road seemed to be holding their breath, like sentient tinderboxes terrified at the approach of humans and their flames.

Luckily for the forest, the road was pretty much deserted. Thirty-five miles on from Ojai, at the summit of Pine Mountain, we still hadn't seen another car. Not a single fire starter in sight. It was just the two of us. We were, as always, completely alone.

For the first time in my life, I felt the full force of our isolation. I felt insignificant and unknown and scared. I found myself wishing desperately for the presence of other people, even if they were just strangers in passing cars. Pretending to be occupied by the view outside my window—the same wallpaper of chaparral and scrub oak and Coulter pine I'd seen a million times—I wondered why I'd always thought our solitude was such a good thing. And then I understood that it had to do with fear. Fear of other people and what they would think of us, fear that we were just two oddballs doing everything wrong, fear of confronting the possibility that the lives other people led were actually better than ours. Fear of the truth, basically. Fear, I realized, I had inherited from Gordon.

Misplaced fear, I thought. The library, for example. It was not a stronghold, a sign of our uniqueness. It was a cave for cowering, a place to hide from reality. Maybe exile wouldn't be such a bad thing; maybe it would be better to be forced into confronting things head-on. And other people, how wrong have I been on that? Yesterday alone I met three people, two who were helpful when they didn't have to be, and one who was beautiful, wonderful. How I wished I were sitting in that café again, across the table from Magda with her cup of tea and her algebra and her wandering eye! Thinking about her, about driving *away* from the place where she was, only added to the feelings of hurt and helplessness that had been growing all day.

Something cracked then. I actually *heard* the crack. It was unmistakable, a simultaneous combination of every possible kind of crack: fissure, splinter, fracture, fault. At first I didn't understand exactly what had caused it, whether it was something inside of me or something in the world or something between the world and me. I looked at Gordon again, his face as close to expressionless as it is possible for a face to get, and realized that it was us. A split had formed between us. We were no longer in unspoken agreement, we were not of one mind, we were not, as we had always been, two peas in a pod. There was a distance between us, a cold and dark space, flowing with dark thoughts. My hurt turned to anger—anger at Gordon—and I resolved that from now on things were going be different. I didn't care if our life had to change completely for that to happen. I only knew that things could not stay the way they'd always been.

The road straightened out as we descended from the summit. Gordon threw the engine into neutral and we coasted most of the way to the valley below. My head was swimming with things I wanted to ask him, things I really wanted to know, things I needed to know. Things I *deserved* to know. I tried to read him like a sentence in a book, gauge his current state of being by his expression and posture and the angle of his head, but couldn't.

As before, my anger dissolved as quickly as it had flared

up. I found that as much as I wanted to, I couldn't bring myself to blame Gordon. He has a disease, after all. Something is destroying his brain. Destroying who he is, *ruining* everything he is. He has responded to this fact by doing nothing, changing nothing, going on as he always has, as if things would magically stay just as they'd always been. But so have I. It's as much my fault as his.

We hit the bottom of the grade, rolling quietly but with a fair amount speed onto the valley floor with its dusty and deserted network of farm roads. Gordon let the road soak up most of our momentum, then stepped on the clutch and slipped the engine into gear. It was not exactly happy at being called back into duty, responding with a whine before accepting its fate and roaring back to life.

Consulting the map tattooed on my brain, I calculated the remaining distance to Chico. Three-hundred-fifty miles, probably more. More than we could do in a day, anyway, especially at the speed Gordon was driving. But it wasn't even five yet, there was still plenty of time left in this day, and I figured if I just left him to it he could easily knock off another hundred miles.

I looked out at the barren, dried-up nothingness of Kern County. The mountains and forests were behind us, replaced by an endless flat expanse of alfalfa farms and fallow fields of hardened dirt and dried-up grass. It didn't offer much for the eye, and I soon found myself following the rhythmic rise and fall of the telephone wires as they raced from pole to pole. I hummed along silently with the peaking and valleying of the wires, the rhythm of it gradually hypnotizing me, quieting the hornet's nest of thoughts buzzing in my head and lolling me into a kind of a mindless stupor. Sleep was only half a step behind. I welcomed it gladly, my eyes practically slamming shut.

I woke in the worst way possible. Disoriented, my limbs heavy with a dull pain, my head encased in a bubble of mild panic; it felt like I was being yanked from sleep by the hand of an angry giant. Slumped against the half-closed window, I forced my leaden eyelids open. The landscape outside was a golden-brown blur, the sky a puzzling rose color. A globe of warm saliva fell from my open mouth and splashed on my forearm. A low-pitched whine, like the sound of a frightened beehive, harmonized periodically with the roar of the engine. Bleary-eyed, I sat up unsteadily and looked about the van. The sun shone dully in the upper corner of Gordon's window, much lower in the sky than it should have been. Confused, I looked at the dashboard clock: six ten. My foggy brain not yet up to performing even the most basic of mathematical tasks, I struggled to grasp the significance of those numbers.

In need of an anchor for my wayward consciousness, I looked over at Gordon, his familiar profile silhouetted against the big, yellow-orange sun. Rendered as a black form, his outline was like a kind of writing, a letter or a word that could be read. I knew from the shape of that form that something was wrong, that I was looking at a misspelled word. The head was too far forward on the neck, the shoulders too rounded off, the hands on the steering wheel too bent.

Just as it became clear that Gordon was on his way to a dark place, I understood the implication of the time: I'd been asleep for almost two hours. What had happened during those two hours was anyone's guess. We were no longer on Route 33, that much was certain. The road we were on was narrower, for one thing, and the telephone wires had disappeared. I tried to situate our present location on the map in my head, but it was pointless. There were no landmarks of any kind, no route markers, no buildings, no crossroads. We were in the epicenter of the middle of nowhere.

The road approached a dry gully and I noticed with relief that a sign had been planted at the foot of the overpass. I rolled my window down the rest of the way and practically stuck my head out of the van, eager not to miss this clue: SANTA YNEZ RIVER. It wasn't much of a river, just a wide, dry bed, filled with coyote brush and scrub sage and large, dirt-caked stones, but it *was* a place.

I took the map from the glove box and held it close to my face, scanning outward from Maricopa until I found the Santa Ynez, indicated on the map by the faintest gray squiggle. As far as I could figure it, Gordon had turned west onto Route 58 not long after I fell asleep, then left 58 sometime later, turning north on what was basically a farm road. If I was right, all we needed to do was keep heading north until we hit Route 41, then head east for a bit until we reached I-5, where we could rest and spend the night. If everything went well, we'd make it to I-5 by seven thirty, before it got dark. From there it was pretty much a three hundred mile straight shot to Chico, which we could easily cover the next day.

The strange hive sound returned, interrupting my plotting. I realized it was Gordon talking, in the same sorrowful voice he'd used when he cornered that woman in the shopping mall parking lot.

"Fields of pure color," he muttered sadly, shaking his head as if to rid it of something troubling.

I looked at him intently.

"It was here," he continued. "Right here. I'm sure of it."

"What was here, Gordon?"

He turned and looked at me. His eyes looked *at* mine but not *into* them, looked at *a* face, but not mine. He puzzled over me for a long time, longer than was safe. The van began drifting toward the side of the road and I reached over to straighten the wheel. Gordon swatted my hand away, then turned his attention back to driving, correcting our veer just as the van reached the shoulder.

A mile later he started in again. "Where, where, where?" he implored of no one in particular.

"Where *what*, Gordon? What are you looking for?"

"Flowers," he said, as if it should have been obvious. "Acres and acres of flowers."

"Flowers?"

"As far as the eye could see. Stunning, really. Beautiful. Stripes and bands and squares and rectangles of color—red, yellow, orange, violet, lavender, pink, blue, white—an ocean of color stretching off to the horizon with a precise, geometric beauty."

"Oh."

He frowned. His head bobbed, and he sank a little further.

"It was here," he mumbled, confused. "It was here. Now it's not here. It's not here, but I need it to be here."

"Why?"

"I wanted him to see it."

"Wanted *who* to see it?"

"Kai. He would love to see it, I wanted him to see it."

Kai. I tried not to be jealous. I knew there was no Kai. Kai just a phantom of Gordon's muddled brain. But I was tired of him stealing concern that should have been directed at me.

"Who is Kai, Gordon?" I prodded. "Is it me?"

No answer. Just the slightest shake of the head, so slight anyone but me would have missed it. That's all I got. His frown deepened during this admission, his eyes tunneling into the road ahead of him. His hands on the wheel were two bony knobs, white from the pressure of his grip.

"I'll tell you what," I said, rubbing my face wearily. "How about if I drive for a while? That way you don't have to worry about the road and can keep a lookout for the flowers."

"Okay."

A few miles after taking the wheel, I finally came to a junction, a sideways T with a signpost informing me that we were on Bitterwater Road. Another one of life's ham-fisted jokes, I suppose. The junction offered me one option, a right turn onto Brown Material Road, another joke. While I was eighty percent sure that staying on Bitterwater Road would eventually take us to Route 41, I had no idea where the right turn would lead. For whatever reason, I took it anyway.

Two miles along Brown Material, my risk-taking was rewarded by the reappearance of things and people, in the form of fence posts and barbed wire and derelict ranches with collapsing barns and a line of slow-moving farm vehicles. The presence of other people heading in the same direction as us was reassuring, but also frustrating. Five minutes earlier, we had the road to ourselves; now we were stuck in the middle of some kind of hayseed rush hour. We crawled along behind a flatbed loaded with produce crates, an eighteen-wheeler that was wider than our lane, a truck full of foul-smelling chickens, and, just in front of us, a pickup with plywood guardrails and a bed filled with goats. Though the sun behind us was inching ever closer toward the horizon, it was still really warm out. The van, no longer refreshed by the wind of speed, filled with hot air and farm smells. It was excruciating, affecting both Gordon and me. I thought about pulling out into the other lane and passing them all with one sustained burst of speed, but I didn't quite have the confidence for such a maneuver.

The goats in the back of the pickup stood bunched together, huddled shoulder to shoulder in the middle of the bed. All except for one: a small gray and white billy goat, which kept turning round and round in tight, agitated circles, seemingly losing his mind. Gordon seemed to take a cue from the goat. He began fidgeting in his seat, and out of the corner of my eye I could see his left hand come to life in his lap, the thumb rapidly working the tips of his fingers, one after the other, in time with the whirling goat. It was not a good sign.

Sure enough, he began mumbling to himself. "No! No! No!" he moaned. "Where are they taking me? No! What for? Why?" He repeated his questions over and over, pleading and braying until he sounded like a goat himself.

He was gone again. I knew it was coming from the moment I woke up, but even so I wasn't ready for it. Partly because I was still a little irritated about Kai, partly because I was just so tired of it all, and even though I knew it wouldn't help things in the least, I lashed out instead of staying calm.

"Stop it, Gordon!" I snapped. "No one's doing anything to you! You're fine!"

The silence that followed did not mean he'd taken my reprimand to heart, only that it had caused him to burrow deeper into himself, speeding up the usual rate of collapse. His left hand passed rapidly from fingertip rubbing to fist clenching before hardening into a kind of frozen, curled-up claw. Tremors shook the claw in his lap, and his chin began sliding toward his chest. He was sinking like a stone.

He went on mumble-moaning in a barely-audible whimper. Two words eventually emerged from his incomprehensible babble. Two words, which he repeated over and over.

"Not. Now."

Not now. The words poured from his trembling lips in a steady stream, until they became one word, pressing against my chest, piercing my innermost being. *Notnow.* I began repeating it too, silently. We were praying, I realized, each in our own way, each for our own thing.

I knew in my bones I wasn't up for this. *Notnow*, I implored. *Go away. Stop happening.*

I heard a soft hissing, like that of a startled snake or an open steam valve. I saw a dark spot appear in Gordon's crotch and spread rapidly down his right leg. He didn't move an inch, didn't show the slightest indication that he was aware of or cared about the fact that he was peeing on himself. He just sat there in his seat, peeing away.

Notnow, notnow, notnow.

And then, it just slipped out, I couldn't help it: "Fuck, Gordon! Fuck!"

He looked across at me, his face the picture of bewilderment. He turned his head this way and that, as if searching for this Gordon fellow who'd upset me so. Only gradually did he become aware of what had happened. He looked down at his lap, recoiling from the sight, his face contorting into a grimace of disgust. He buried his face in his frozen, gnarled hands. I watched him grow smaller, collapsing rapidly into himself like a dying star. Shaking his head in shame, he wailed and moaned.

"I'm sorry," he said. "I'm sorry, I'm so sorry."

Cursing at my loss of control, I slowed down and pulled the van onto the dusty shoulder. I got out and ran around to the passenger door, worried that Gordon might try to let himself out and fall into the empty irrigation ditch at the side of the road before I got there. Luckily, he stayed in his seat, inert. I opened the door and reached up to him, putting my hand gently on his shoulder.

"It's okay, Gordon," I said softly. "It's okay. C'mon, let's just get ourselves cleaned up. Then we'll find somewhere to rest, all right?"

He managed to nod his slumping head, his mouth agape. "Let's not blame Gordon," he implored. "It's not his fault."

Whatever the thing is in humans that lets us do the exact opposite of what we want came to my rescue, and I managed to smile instead of crying. "No harm no foul," I assured, holding my arms up in a conciliatory gesture. "Really, it's no big deal."

I helped him climb unsteadily from his seat, using all of my strength to keep him from tottering over, then guided him to the back of the van, his right claw clutching the fabric of my shirt for support. I opened the rear doors and sat him down on the fender while I scrambled inside and retrieved his last pair of clean pants. I soaked a hand cloth in melted ice water from the cooler, then wrung it out and handed it up to him so he could wash himself. I grabbed a towel and dampened another cloth to use on the seat, then scooted out of the van, placing the clean pants beside him.

"Go ahead and change, Gor ... Go ahead and change. I'll be right back."

I cleaned the seat as best as I could, given the circumstances. The urine had already started to ripen in the dusty heat, the smell of it was almost overpowering. I tried to be robotic about it, clearing my mind of everything but the task at hand.

When I'd gotten the seat as clean as I could, I folded the dry towel into a square and laid it on the seat. I went to check on Gordon, only to find him still sitting there with his things held limply in front of him—pants in one hand, wash cloth in the other—as if he had no idea what to do with them.

Notnow.

Gordon looked at me meekly. He was utterly helpless. I could probably have accepted him in any other form, even the delusional, mean-spirited conspiracy theorist. The one version I was not equipped to handle, I realized, was the version of him dependent on me, completely and totally dependent. That's completely *unfair*, not at all how things are supposed to be. He's the father and I'm the son. *He's* supposed to be taking care of *me*. His helplessness made me feel helpless too, in addition to the frustration and the desperation and the anger. I was on the verge of disintegrating, drifting apart into a million pieces.

Somehow, I remained intact. A lifetime's training in the harder thing wasn't going to let me off so easily. The situation *was* unfair, but that didn't change what had to be done. We were in the middle of nowhere, Gordon was soiled and sad and out of it, he needed help getting cleaned up and dressed, and the only one to help him do that was me. *The soul is therefore but an empty word …*

Lost Hills, California. I stood alone at the edge of the Pilot Travel Center's ocean-sized parking lot. No more than fifty yards away, cars and trucks barreled up and down Interstate 5, the turbulence of their passage sending clouds of roadside dust into the air, where it swirled maniacally before settling down in miniature drifts alongside the glass and plastic debris that littered the parking lot. The interstate, a vast swath of asphalt disappearing into the northern and southern horizons, cut a perfectly straight line through the nothingness, carrying real people to and from their business in the real world.

How different that straight line was compared to the way we did things. Meandering endlessly, always sticking to deserted back roads, puttering up and down wiggly mountain passes, waiting out the day in libraries, sleeping in out of the way places, avoiding the light. We were like the beetles that live in dead trees, chewing their way through the soft, smooth wood beneath the bark. The intricate markings they leave behind might look meaningful enough—the lost alphabet of an ancient civilization, or messages written in an alien script—but they're actually nothing more than the random by-product of blind, pointless tunneling. What were our travels, then, our *wanderings*, if not equally pointless doodles? How was our life, *my* life, any different than the lives of those bugs, munching blindly along in the dark and the damp, with no greater goal than the next mouthful of pulp? Was there any more meaning to be found in the pattern of our wandering? No. A cat's cradle, a length of string woven between our hands, back and forth and over and under until it had run out, then untied and started again. It occurred to me that just like those beetles, our lives were also conducted in a region of darkness, beneath the surface of the real world, a level below the place of straight lines where real people lived their real lives in the bright light of normalcy. For the first time in my life, I just wanted to be like those people, to move about in the open, in broad daylight, along the rational grid laid out by society, shuttled along to my home and school and shopping mall and soccer game.

I stood at the edge of that sorry parking lot, with its little dunes of sand and broken glass, and sighed. A longer and louder sigh than I would have thought it possible for a person to sigh. *Tomorrow*, I told myself. Tomorrow we'll be joining them. But I still had some work to do tonight if tomorrow was going to have any chance of being the tomorrow I wanted it to be. I turned away from the interstate and walked back toward the van, just in time to see the giant pink-orange sun, no doubt as exhausted by the day as I was, disappear in the west.

Five miles down the road from Gordon's accident, Brown Material Road ran into Route 46, where it ended. I took 46 east, passing through the appropriately named Lost Hills, with its handful of boarded-up storefronts and forest of lonely-looking oil derricks, and ended up here, a giant truck stop straddling I-5. We were thirty-five miles further south on I-5 than we would have been if I'd stuck to the original plan of taking Route 41, but considering that the needle on the fuel gauge had fallen to the left of the E by the time I pulled into the Travel Center, that was probably a stroke of luck.

The Vanagon was a bubble of heat in the slowly cooling evening, its engine still sighing wearily from the day's labors. Gordon lay fast asleep in the back, dead to the world, blissfully ignorant of all the damage he'd left in his wake. It probably would have made more sense to leave the van parked where it was and settle down for the night, but I wanted to fill up the gas tank now, so that tomorrow I could start driving as soon as I woke. I slipped quietly into the driver's seat and started the engine, which shuddered reluctantly back to life. I steered the van over to the brightly lit pumps, pulling up next to the one furthest from the mini-mart and the station attendant. I took Gordon's wallet from its nook in the door panel and opened it, hoping it would contain at least enough cash to fill up the tank. No such luck. It was completely empty. Not so much as a dollar bill.

My shoulders slumped dejectedly. I closed my eyes and listened to the electric buzz of the fluorescent lights for a while. Then I opened them again and stared off into the dark beyond the pumps. It was inevitable, really. The moment I'd long dreaded was finally here. We were out of cash and fuel, Gordon was practically comatose, the only option was his ATM card and I didn't have the slightest idea what his PIN was.

Summoning what was left of my will, I made a quick list of possible options. The way I saw it, there were three: 1) Wake Gordon now and try to get the number out of him; 2) Try to figure out the PIN for myself; 3) Wait until morning and hope things would be better then.

Waking Gordon was not really an option. It would only

make a dire situation worse, and there was no way of knowing who, or what, I would be waking. As for the second option, I've watched Gordon type his PIN on fuel pump and ATM keypads plenty of times, but never paid attention to *what* he typed. For some reason, I was certain it was six digits long, which didn't necessarily make the option any better. I don't know much about cryptography, but I'm pretty sure the odds of correctly guessing a six digit code are pretty small. The third option clearly made the most sense. Even so, it was the one I found least attractive. I was tired of waiting, tired of not doing. I went with my gut and option number two.

Taking a deep breath, I slipped the card from the wallet and walked around to the pump. I read the instructions on the sticker over the credit card slot: INSERT CARD AND REMOVE QUICKLY. I inserted the card in the direction indicated by the little picture next to the slot, then pulled it out. A message popped up on the dull gray screen: PLEASE ENTER PIN.

Realizing that I wasn't quite ready to do this, I pressed the CANCEL button. I stood there, thinking, debating. I didn't know how many tries it would take before I guessed the number correctly, but I wasn't going to get it on the first try. How many incorrect guesses could I enter at the pump before the attendant came out, assuming I was trying to rip him off with a stolen card? Probably not very many. Glancing over at the mini-mart, I noticed a sign reading *ATM Inside*. Better to try my luck inside, I thought.

I left the van at the pump and walked into the mini-mart. The attendant at the counter, a weaselly-looking guy in a tank top, with dark hair and a pencil mustache, was busy reading a magazine and didn't seem to notice me as I entered. I found the ATM at the end of the first aisle, sandwiched between a display of bottled water and racks of free newspapers. I sauntered over to it like it was an old friend. I took Gordon's card from my pocket. The longer I stared at the card, the more I began to believe I could figure it out. This was my father, after all. I just had to think the way he thought. Hadn't I been doing that my whole life?

The first thing I decided was that the number wouldn't be random. Gordon would have chosen something with personal significance. All I had to do was think of all the possible series of six numbers with meaning for Gordon, and enter them until I hit on the right one. Birthdays were the obvious candidates; two digits each for the month, day and year. The more I thought about it, the more I became convinced that it had to be a birthday. And there were only two birthdays that could possibly matter to Gordon: mine and his. It had to be. Feeling slightly euphoric at having figured it out so quickly, I inserted the card into the slot, typed in Gordon's birthdate, and waited for further instructions. The machine clicked and chirped for a couple seconds, then displayed the following message: INCORRECT PASSWORD. PLEASE RE-ENTER. I typed in Gordon's birthday once more, slowly this time, making sure I hit the correct keys. Same message. *Okay*, I thought. *Not Gordon's birthday then. It has to be mine.* I entered my six-digit birthdate and waited. Once again, the incorrect password message flashed up on the screen. I re-entered my dates. This time, I read the following: INCORRECT PASSWORD. YOUR CARD HAS BEEN RETAINED FOR SECURITY PURPOSES. PLEASE CONTACT YOUR BANK FOR FURTHER ASSISTANCE.

No! No! No!

I poked the CANCEL button repeatedly, but nothing happened. I pressed it again and held it down, still nothing. I hit the other keys, one after the other, as if one of them might be a magic do-over button, but nothing changed. The machine had swallowed Gordon's card and wasn't going to give it back. I stared at the message in utter disbelief. Then it disappeared from the screen, replaced by the same welcome message it had displayed when I started.

Gordon's card was gone.

I felt a surge of blind panic. Blood pounded at my temples and my ears started ringing, drowning out all other sound. I looked over my shoulder, scanning the mini-mart. It was completely empty apart from the cashier, still absorbed in his magazine. I thought of asking him for help, but quickly decided against it. Now was not the time or the place to turn to others. A sound, somewhere between a whimper and a strangled laugh, crawled out from the back of my throat. Out of pure frustration, I banged on the machine with my fist.

That got the cashier's attention. Getting up from his stool, he leaned forward over the counter and squinted at me. "Hey there," he called out, his voice disconcertingly high-pitched. "Little man. That's not a toy, right? Not a toy. Why don't you go back outside? I'm sure Mommy's looking for you."

Fuck you, you weasel, I thought. *What do you know about it?* I turned away from the machine and walked quickly to the exit, returning the man's stare long as I could. I shuddered involuntarily as I walked past the counter and out the door. Risking a quick glance over my shoulder, I could see the attendant walking down the aisle toward the ATM.

The ringing returned as I walked back to the van, growing louder with every step. Nothing else could be heard. Not a single sound from the outside world was audible against the clamor inside my head. I thought maybe I was going deaf. And why not? Why shouldn't I be? What reason did I have to expect anything better from life?

By the time I made it back to the van, however, the ringing had subsided, and the world's noises were making their way back into my consciousness: the hum of the fluorescent lights bleaching the station, the ocean-like sound of cars and trucks speeding along the interstate, the lively conversation of crickets scattered throughout the dark. I leaned against the back of the van and let the sound wash over me. What had I been thinking? What combination of bad judgment and wishful thinking made me believe that was actually going to work?

Instead of being put in its proper place, however, my thinking grew even more wishful. Maybe, I told myself, Gordon had another card, a spare he kept just for emergencies. In his backpack. Maybe he's even got a bunch of cash in there.

Spurred on by my new hunch, I opened the rear doors and climbed into the van, crawling past Gordon's sleeping form until I came to his backpack. I grabbed it by one of the shoulder straps and pulled it towards me. Considering how full it was, I was surprised by how light it felt. I almost fell over backward, so great was the difference between how heavy it looked and how light it actually was. Steadying myself, I scrambled back to the rear of the van and hopped outside.

What I was about to do was not something to be done lightly. Gordon and I live our lives right under each other's nose. We're used to it. Still, everyone needs a little privacy, a space that belongs only to them, things that are theirs alone. Our backpacks represent this space. In a way, they are like our bedrooms. Whatever we keep in them is for our own eyes only. Gordon stays out of mine and I stay out of his. I've often wondered what special things he keeps in his; I've even made lists about it. But actually looking inside is something I've never considered. If we have one taboo, one law that can never be broken, trespassing into the private space of the other's backpack is it.

Leaning against the side of the van, I prepared to cross that boundary. I took hold of the zipper, then hesitated, losing my resolve. This wasn't right. I didn't want to do it. But I had no choice. Gordon had created this situation, not me, and there was no other option. It had to be done. Despite a sudden foreboding, a certainty that I did not want to know what was in the backpack, I pressed on. Taking a deep breath, I unzipped the main compartment and peered inside.

It was filled with empty plastic grocery bags.

I sat on my knees in the back of the van, pulling plastic bags from Gordon's backpack. There must have been a hundred of them. White ones and tan ones and black ones, all wadded up and stuffed inside. The entire pack, every compartment, was filled with them. I pulled them out, one by one at first and then by the handful, until the pack was completely empty. No mementos, no official documents, no prized possessions, no reserve cash, no emergency bankcards. Whatever personal belongings it might once have held were long gone, discarded to make room for what the broken, demented Gordon considered more important: wads of plastic trash.

I read once, in an article on Tsunamis in *National Geographic*, about how, before the arrival of the actual wave, all the water along the shore is sucked rapidly out to sea, creating a super low tide, an instant, silent emptiness, a kind of vacuum that only increases the violence and destruction of the wave itself. I experienced that phenomenon now, looking into Gordon's empty backpack. I could feel everything that I was, everything I had always been, being pulled out of me and receding out to the beyond of some endless gray ocean. Everything was quiet. I did not breathe and as far as I could tell my heart was not beating. For a moment, brief and yet somehow endless, I was nothing, a pure and total emptiness. And then the wave crashed down on top of me, a tidal wave of utter frustration, a Tsunami of rage. I did not fight the arrival of the wave; I welcomed it, even though it seemed to me I would not survive it.

The backpack clutched in one hand, I jumped back into the van.

"Gordon!" I called angrily, taking his sleeping form by the shoulders and shaking him. "Gordon, wake up! Goddamn—" I stopped short, momentarily thrown off by the fact that he was already awake. He stared at me blankly.

Recovering, I held the backpack up for him to see, then chucked it at him.

"Where is your stuff, Gordon?" I demanded.

His head tottered slightly, his expression still blank.

"No way!" I yelled. "You're not getting off this time! Where is your stuff?"

"Stuff?" he asked absently.

"Yes, Gordon. Your *stuff*. The stuff in your backpack. Your fucking stuff. What did you do with it?"

Although I wouldn't have thought it possible, the look on his face became even more blank.

"I don't have any stuff," he said quietly.

In my entire life, I can't remember ever even *disliking* Gordon. Now, standing there looking at his blank face, listening to his stupid words, I hated him, I truly hated him, a feeling only made worse by the fact that I simultaneously hated myself for hating him. My frustration was total. I felt powerless, unable to control anything. Not even, it seemed, my own body. I watched my hand ball itself up into a fist and smack me repeatedly in the forehead.

I might have beaten myself senseless if Gordon hadn't reached out and stayed my arm. "No," he said simply, a strange authority in his voice. "Don't do that."

I stopped and looked at him. His face had assumed an expression of concern, sadness. There was a brief glimmer of understanding and awareness, which quickly faded out. One look into his eyes was enough to tell me Gordon wasn't in there, just the thing he'd become. I came back to myself a little. Ignoring the dull throb in the middle of my forehead, I nodded at him, even managed the hint of a smile. Taking in a couple of deep breaths, I let go of the fact that Gordon had thrown away the only things that might have been important to him—and possibly to me—and focused on our immediate problem.

"Look, Gordon." I said, trying to make my voice as reassuring as possible. "We're in sort of a pickle here."

"Oh?" he pouted, like a child who's just been told there are no more cookies. "Well, that's not good, is it?"

"No, Gordon. It's not."

It was too much. I found myself struggling to hold back the tears. During the silence that accompanied that struggle, Gordon tapped the side of his nose with his forefinger. He turned to me and said, "What kind of pickle?"

I rubbed my face and sighed.

"Well, basically, it's getting late and we're out of gas. More importantly, we're out of money. We don't have two dimes to—"

Raising his finger, Gordon interrupted.

"Ah-ah-ah!" he admonished brightly. "Not to worry. I have a bank card."

"Right," I said. "That's another part of the pickle. It looks like you threw out your card with the rest of your stuff."

I told myself this little white lie was a necessary thing, since it was a lot easier than trying to explain to Gordon what had actually happened to his card. The childish frown returned. He looked at the empty backpack lying on his lap, then at me, then back at the backpack, his confusion growing.

"I don't have any stuff," he repeated, shaking his head.

"Not any more," I said.

I didn't mean for it to sound so mean, so accusing, but that's the way it came out. I felt a twinge of guilt as I watched him cave in on himself.

"I'm sorry," he said.

What a world! I couldn't just be mad at my father for screwing everything up. No, I had to feel confused and remorseful about it at the same time. With a weary sigh, I looked out the rear of the van and stared at the front of the mini-mart. A lonely ice machine guarded one side of the entrance, a pyramid of blue wiper fluid bottles the other. The dirty windows were so plastered with hand-painted advertisements—for cigarettes and snack pies and ice cold beer—that it was almost impossible to see in or out. For a long time I just sat there, breathing slowly and deeply, trying to build up my resolve. When I turned my attention back to Gordon, he was staring at me intently.

"I don't know who you are," he said, his voice a caricature of reassurance. "But you have my sympathy. I'd like to be of assistance, if I may. If you don't mind."

I looked at him, saying nothing. I waited.

"Now," he said, patting his torso as if searching for something. "If I could only find my wallet, I would be happy to lend you some money, however much is required to see you through this little crisis of yours."

"Your wallet is empty, Gordon," I said. "There's no money in it."

He frowned again, though somehow I could tell this time he was more disappointed with me than with himself. "You oughtn't be such a killjoy, young man," he said accusingly.

"I'm only trying to help. But, never fear, my boy. Luck favors the prepared, as they say."

With a surprising sureness of movement, he leaned over and took hold of the cassette crate, dragging it toward him and hoisting it effortlessly onto his lap. He carefully removed the upper layers of punk and Kraftwerk tapes, then walked through the bottom layer of overdub stock with his index and middle fingers. I could tell he was enjoying himself. His finger-legs came to a stop over one of the tapes. He pulled the case from its spot and offered it to me.

"An empty vessel makes the most noise," he said cryptically.

I took the case from him and looked at the cover: Shadowfax. I turned the case over in my hand and then looked at Gordon, not really sure where all of this was going.

"Go on then," he said impatiently, poking his finger at the tape. "Open it up."

Popping the case open with my thumb, I was stunned to discover that it did not contain a cassette tape, but a stack of bills, folded neatly in half and wedged into the lid.

"A penny saved is a penny earned, don't you know," Gordon sang, tapping the side of his nose again.

I took the money from the case and counted it. Fifteen twenty-dollar bills.

"Will that be enough, young man?" he asked helpfully.

"Yeah," I said, nodding. "This will do it."

"Excellent. There's more where that came from." He dipped his hand back into the crate and pulled out three more cases. Fleetwood Mac, Poco, April Wine. Each of them was equally stuffed with twenty-dollar bills.

"A place for everything and everything in its place," he said with a wink, clearly quite pleased with himself. He winked again, then, after returning the crate to its customary spot, sat upright in his seat, eyes forward, hands folded on his lap, waiting.

Unsure what to make of this reversal of fortune, I decided not to question it. "Stay put, okay? I'm going to fill up the tank and get us something to eat."

I put the half the money in my pocket and looked again at the mini-mart. I didn't really feel like dealing with that attendant again, but what was he, compared to everything else that had happened that day? I hopped out of the van and walked back to the store.

Once again, the attendant did not bother to notice me. I walked right up to the cluttered, messy counter and waited for him to look up from his magazine, trying to bolster my confidence by focusing on his sorry excuse for a mustache. Eventually, tired of being ignored, I cleared my throat.

He finally looked at me, an irritated expression on his face. He made a point of puffing himself up, as if to make it clear how much bigger than me he was.

"Can I help you?" he asked in his high-pitched voice. He could not have sounded less helpful.

"Gas please," I said.

"Right," he laughed. "Got some money from Mommy, huh little man?"

Strangely enough, I wasn't insulted. In fact, I decided to hit him with the truth, see how he liked that.

"I don't have a mother," I said. "I'm with my father, who is very sick. He's probably going to die. We're driving to Chico. I just want to buy some gas, and maybe some food."

Everything about the man changed. His expression softened, and he shrank back down to his normal size. Dipping his head in apology, he said, "I'm sorry to hear that kid. I didn't mean anything. I was just joking with you."

"It's okay," I replied.

"Right. Cash or credit?"

"Cash," I said.

"Right," he said again. "Cash it is. What pump?"

"Hmm? Oh, I'm not sure, I didn't look. I'll go check."

"No, no. That's all right." He looked out at the Vanagon, the only vehicle in an empty sea of pumps. "Pump twenty-one," he said, nodding to himself. "Full tank?"

"Uh, yeah."

"Okay." He tapped something onto the screen in front of him. "Go ahead and fill it up. You can come back and pay when you're all done."

"Really? It works like that?"

"It does tonight," he answered with a wink.

"Thanks."

"No problem, chief."

I looked over my shoulder at the ATM. "And that machine," I added. "It ate my father's card."

I walked quickly back to pump twenty-one, where Gordon was engaged in an animated conversation with himself. I filled up the tank and went back inside to pay.

The attendant was no longer behind the counter. I grabbed a quart of orange juice, a loaf of white bread, and a small jar of peanut butter, then walked back over to the counter and waited for him to return. A series of computerized beeps sounded from behind me, followed by a loud snapping sound. I turned to see the attendant crawling out from behind the ATM. He pushed it back against the wall and walked up the aisle, disappearing through a door to my left. He reappeared behind the counter few seconds later. He smiled at me and held out his hand, three plastic bankcards fanned in his fingers.

"One of these your dad's?"

I stared at him in disbelief for a second, and took Gordon's card.

"Holy shit." I said. "Sorry. I mean, Wow! Thanks!"

"No problem. I mean, I'm not really supposed to do that.

And that thing—" with his chin he indicated the ATM, which was still beeping every few seconds. "That thing won't work until we get the service guy in here to re-set it, but that don't really matter."

I thanked him again and paid for the gas and the food. He started to put my stuff in a plastic bag, but I held up a hand to stop him. "That's all right," I said. "I don't need any bags. I'll just carry this stuff out."

"Suit yourself," he said.

I gathered the things up in my arms and turned to leave.

"Hang on," the attendant said, reaching beneath his counter. His hand re-emerged two seconds later holding a package of Hostess Sno-Balls, which he placed on top of the pile in my arms. "On the house," he said.

Unable to think of anything to say, I just smiled. He smiled back. I turned to leave then stopped. I looked over my shoulder at my new friend. "I was wondering."

"Yeah?"

"Can I ask a huge favor?"

"Name it."

"Would it be okay if we stayed in your parking lot until morning?"

The Pilot Travel Center parking lot turned out to be a kind of labyrinth, a maze of smaller lots and service roads. When I finally solved it and made my way onto the interstate, it was heading south, away from Chico. With a bewildered shake of my head, I drove to the next cloverleaf, eight miles further down, and turned around. We were northbound at last.

I could feel the difference almost immediately. Something had changed. Everything felt lighter, smoother, *easier.* No more deserted farm roads, no more sudden shortcuts, no more *off the beaten path.* Normal. That was it. For the first time in my life, we were moving along with everyone else, in a straight line, on a highway designed to get people from one real, well-known place to another. No more curlicues up and down and all across the state, no more pointless circles like beetles beneath the bark. Just drive in a straight line. It was that simple.

For the first time in days, maybe weeks, a feeling of complete calm filled the van. Gordon was sound asleep in the seat next to me, and although he occasionally twitched or moaned, he didn't seem to be in any sort of distress. The traffic around me was light but fast-moving. My usual tactic of driving at or below the speed limit so as to avoid standing out would have had the opposite effect, so I soon found myself cruising along at seventy-five miles per hour, faster than I'd ever driven before. I was nervous about pushing the Vanagon too hard, but it didn't seem bothered by the effort. In fact, it seemed almost happy about it, the engine emitting a contented hum.

Despite the monotonous landscape—endless fields of alfalfa and lettuce and dry, furrowed dirt broken only by the occasional ramshackle farm or solitary black oak—the time passed quickly, the miles falling away one by one. My head was swimming with lists. Lists of the things I would say to my mother when I saw her; lists of things we would do once we were reunited; lists of things we would do to take care of Gordon. I even found myself composing a list of possible opening lines for the letter I was going to write Magda once everything had been sorted out. Before long, these lists turned into waking dreams, little movies playing in my head, each with a happy beginning, middle, and end.

Two hours on from Lost Hills and we were a hundred and twenty miles closer to Chico. My body crackled with a strange kind of energy. At first, I thought it was a form of nervousness, or maybe a new level of fatigue, but then I realized it was just excitement, the thrill of anticipation. I felt completely and totally alive, just like I used to before Gordon got sick, only now it was not because things had somehow been restored to the way they were, but because they were going to change. It was ironic, I guess. For these past many months, my only thought had been finding the way back to our previous life. Now it was the prospect of starting a new one that drove me forward.

Two hundred miles to go. Brimming with confidence, I felt capable of anything: deep understanding, prodigious feats of strength, math; I even drove one-handed for a while.

Los Banos, Newman, Patterson, Tracy. Gas in Manteca. Stockton, Lodi, Elk Grove. We passed one cow town after another, each one bringing us that much closer to Chico. *Computer World* was playing at low volume, and the Vanagon chomped happily at the bit despite the steadily rising morning heat. I was happy, too. We'd be there in less than two hours.

I felt the first twinges of fatigue as we neared the outskirts of Sacramento. I didn't sleep much the night before. Gordon was up hallucinating well into the night, lying next to me and conversing with himself and Kai and a host of other visitors all the while. I tried to stay awake as long as I could, but ended up falling asleep to the sound of his mumbling. I woke with a start at the first light of morning, relieved to discover that he was still there, sleeping soundly. I willed myself to wake him too. He was amenable to a breakfast of peanut-butter sandwiches and orange juice, and I was able to coax him into the passenger seat with the promise of a fluffy pink Sno-Ball. We were on the road before eight; according to my calculations, that meant we'd make it to Chico by two.

I could hardly believe it. I would end the day in the presence of my mother. I tried to stay calm at the thought of it, but it wasn't easy. My thoughts turned once again into daydreams, happy visions of a life to come, interrupted by the occasional snort from a still-sleeping Gordon. I implored the gods not to let him wake. It would make things a lot easier for me if he just slept for the rest of the trip.

Sacramento, it turns out, is the center of its own web of busy highways, kind of like a smaller version of Los Angeles. Having spent the previous day driving through so much emptiness, it was a little unsettling to find myself trapped in heavy late-morning traffic. Suddenly unable to visualize the map, I realized, with a growing sense of panic, that I had no idea where I was going. I was just about to stay on I-5 when I heard Gordon say, "You're going to miss it."

Startled, I turned to look at him. He pointed through the windshield to the next off-ramp, only a couple hundred yards ahead. "You want to take 99," he said. "Right here."

That's right, I remembered suddenly. Route 99 north; that was the one, the road that would take us the rest of the way, right into Chico itself. And I had almost missed it. Who knows how far I would have gone before I realized my mistake?

"Thanks," I said, without really meaning it. Instead of feeling grateful, I was actually irritated at Gordon's last-second rescue. I wanted him to go back to sleep, where there was less chance of him wrecking things. And of course I was still angry with him. More than angry, actually. I was *done*. Done with this life he'd concocted, done with his way of doing things. Done with him. He was no Kvasir, no wise and noble hermit, source of knowledge and understanding, architect of my education and wellbeing. He was simply a small, selfish man, one who had sabotaged my life, denying me a normal childhood so he could play keep-away with his past.

I reached over to the tape deck and turned the volume up, hoping to make it clear that I was not in the mood for conversation. He seemed to take the hint, sitting meekly in his seat, watching the parched farmland flow past his window.

The tape played through side A, then auto-switched to side B. When side B had played through in its turn and switched once again to A, Gordon leaned forward and turned the deck off.

"What happened, Sam?" he asked.

"What do you mean?"

"Yesterday. What happened?"

"Nothing."

"*Nothing?*"

"Nothing important," I said, not bothering to hide my irritation. "It was no big deal."

He nodded. "I see. Even so, maybe I'd like to know what happened."

"Yesterday happened!" I retorted. "That's what! *It* happened, and *it* was yesterday. So it doesn't really matter anymore, does it?"

"It might be important for me to know, Sam," he said softly. "That's all."

"You don't *need* to know," I said through clenched teeth. "You don't *deserve* to know!"

He stared at me for a second, stung by my words, then returned to his silent contemplation of plum orchards and alfalfa fields.

Keen to eliminate any silence that Gordon might see as an invitation to talk again, I turned the stereo back on. I ejected *Computer World*, reached down into the crate and retrieved the empty case. I slipped the cassette inside and returned it to its slot, grabbing the one next to it without bothering to look. *Ralf and Florian*. Perfect. Of all the Kraftwerk tapes, it was the one Gordon hated the most. Recorded in 1973, its primitive electronics and simple, almost silly melodies really got under his skin. Personally, I loved it. Listening to it always made me feel simple and happy. Trying to keep both hands on the steering wheel while removing the tape, I fumbled the case and dropped it to the floor. Keeping my eyes on the road in front of me, I leaned down to my right and felt for the case.

"Let me get that," Gordon offered, leaning over and reaching for the case, taking hold of it at the same moment as me.

"I got it!" I snapped, snatching the case away from him and placing it in my lap. "I don't need your help, Gordon. Just leave me alone, okay?"

I put the tape in the deck and hit PLAY, turning the volume up as loud as I liked. Gordon shook his head but did not object.

I plunged right into the stream of brightly colored music, thinking to let the happy current of electronic marimbas and cymbals, of brass triangles and handclaps, carry me off to some other place. I didn't manage to escape completely, but the music did take the edge off of my anger. By the time the tape reached the fourth track—"Tanzmuzik"—I'd managed to return to a relative state of calm.

Knowing the song was one of my favorites, Gordon let it play to the end before reaching over and turning the deck off. He'd reached his limits, apparently. I drove on and said nothing. Hoping against hope that he would not start in again, I focused hard on the distant horizon, at the illusion of water shimmering there, always wavering just out of reach.

Eventually, I heard him scratching at his beard, one of those gestures that heralds the announcement of *something important.*

"Look, Sam," he began. "I'm sorry. I truly am. You have every right to be upset, to be angry with me. I'd be surprised, shocked, if you weren't. But I understand how you feel. I honestly do."

The tone of his voice was so genuinely apologetic, so full of regret and a kind of tired sadness that I didn't bother to object or cut him off. I gave him the slightest of nods, to let him know I was listening, and waited.

"This isn't about yesterday," he went on. "You're right: whatever happened, happened, and there's not a whole lot that can done about it now. But ... whatever it was, whatever you had to do, I'm sorry, and thank you."

I shrugged a half-hearted *you're welcome.*

"Sam. I don't know exactly what you're planning, but I think I have a pretty good idea. I know what you want to happen, what you hope is going happen. But—"

"Don't waste your time, Gordon," I interrupted. "It's going to happen and you can't do anything to stop it. Not any more. Nothing's going to keep it from happening."

"I wasn't talking about trying to stop you, Sam."

"That's big of you."

He laughed under his breath. "I just don't think you know what you're getting yourself into."

"I see. So actually, you *are* trying to stop me."

"No, that's not what I meant."

"You can't stop it," I warned again. "It's happening. And when it does ... when it does, things are going to be different."

He was quiet then, presumably considering which tactic he should switch to in order to get his way. Eventually, he said, "Before you do this—and believe me, I'm *not* trying to talk you out of it—before you do this, there are some things you should know."

"Oh really?"

"Yes, really."

"Such as?"

"Such as, why things are the way they are, between your mother and me. Why things are the way they are for you and me."

It's ridiculous, really, the way life works. I've waited my whole life for this conversation, for Gordon to open up and communicate even the slightest bit of the past. Now here he was, clearly prepared to tell me everything, and all I wanted was for was for him to stop talking, to shut up and go back to sleep and leave me alone. It was just like at the campground a few days ago (*had it really only been a few days?*), when Gordon started to open up over our game of catch. Maybe I'd been wrong all along. Maybe, despite all my hoping and prodding and fantasizing over the years, the truth was I didn't want to know. No, that's not true. I *did*. I wanted to hear what he was going to say more than anything. It's just, I didn't want to hear it right then. I wanted to hear it on my terms, not his, I wanted him to tell because I asked him to tell me, not because he was hoping to throw a wrench in my plans.

"No," I said flatly.

"Sorry?"

"No, Gordon. I don't want to hear it. I don't want to hear or know about any of it."

"You don't—"

"I don't care," I lied.

"Sam, just listen. You should know ... you need to know—"

"*What?* What do I need to know? Why does it suddenly matter, after all these years? Why, *now?* Why is me knowing suddenly so important? What are you up to, Gordon?"

"I'm not up to anything, Sam."

"Right. What are you afraid of then?"

"Not what you think," he replied quietly.

"Just drop it, okay?"

"Sam, I understand—"

"*Shut up!*" I yelled.

I glanced at him. Predictably enough, his only response to my outburst was an arched eyebrow.

"Sorry," I said quickly, more out of reflex than sincerity. "I didn't mean that."

"It's all right, I got it. You don't want to know. I could just go ahead and tell you anyway, but I'm not going to do that. You're going to do what you're going to do. I'm only saying, make sure you think it through."

The anger I'd only just managed to get under control resurfaced in an instant.

"*Think it through? Think it through?* Are you serious? Do you think I haven't thought about this every day of my life? Do you honestly think I've thought about anything other than *this?*"

I wasn't myself; I was angry. I like to think it was my anger that led me to ask the next question.

"*Actually*," I said. "There is one thing I'd like to know about, one thing I really want you to tell me. Do you know what it is?"

"No, Sam. I don't."

"What I'd like to *know*, Gordon, is this: Who is Kai?"

He looked at me cautiously, a worried expression on his face. Clearly, my question had caught him by surprise, thrown him off balance.

"Kai?"

"Yes Gordon, *Kai*. Who is Kai?"

"How do you know that name?" he asked.

"How do I know Kai? Are you kidding? You talk about *Kai* all the time. You talk *to* Kai all the time."

It would have been enough to just leave it at that, I could tell by Gordon's expression that the damage had been done. But I found myself unable to stop, unable to resist delivering just one more blow. With unmistakable meanness, I continued: "In the middle of the night, in broad daylight, whenever you're *out of it*. When your mind is off who-knows-where. All that seems to matter to you is Kai. So that's it, that's all I want to know: What's so important about Kai?"

I didn't get an answer, but I don't think I was looking for one. It wasn't really a question of finding out about Kai. I just wanted Gordon—not the broken part of Gordon, the *diseased* part of Gordon—but the actual, good old Gordon, the one who was looking at me now, to know that the only thing separating him from oblivion was me, that he was dependent on *me*.

I could feel him shrinking in the seat next to me, losing volume, slowly collapsing in on himself. It wasn't the fact that I knew about Kai that affected him. It was the implication of what I'd said, the undeniable reality of what had been going on for the past year, the awareness of having lost himself. When I turned to look again, it was not at the father I'd always idolized. It was at a broken man, slumped in his seat, staring absently at the passing landscape.

I regretted saying what I'd said, of course, the very moment I said it. But not as much as I thought I would. Not as much as I would have a year ago, or a month ago, or even three days ago. But this wasn't about the past. It wasn't even about the present. It was about the future. About tomorrow. About a whole string of tomorrows, where everything would be different. And tomorrow would begin today, as soon as I'd crossed the insignificant blob of time and space separating me from my mother.

It was all farms and orchards as far as Yuba City. After that, nothing but dry, golden hills and parched riverbeds as we began climbing out of the valley. It was one o'clock and easily ninety out. I'd replaced *Ralf and Florian* with *Radio-Activity*, and I grooved along to songs full of cello-esque synthesizers, walkie-talkie vocals and amplified Geiger counters, my brain waves in perfect sync with the music.

Gordon, meanwhile, retreated further into his shell. He hadn't moved since turning away from me to stare out the window. I couldn't tell if he was lost in a private world of thought or just absent. He fell asleep for a few minutes just after we passed through Yuba City, then woke again. He chewed at the inside of his lower lip and rubbed the tips of his fingers together, always an indication that he was heading south.

Then, on a sign just outside Oroville, I read: CHICO 23 MI.

My heart thumped in my chest. My palms were sweating and my stomach groaned nervously. Ignoring the fact that Gordon's agitation was growing the closer we got to Chico, I turned up the music. My music. My mother's music. The music that lived inside us both, connecting us at the most basic level. The music that proved I was more than just a product of Gordon; I was part someone else, too. It was like a kind of psychic radar, pouring out in waves from the van, locating my mother and bouncing back to me, guiding me along, pulling me closer and closer to my goal.

Before I really understood what was happening, I found myself driving through the heart of the town itself. I took the exit for downtown Chico, pulling off 99 and turning onto First Avenue.

I'd made it. I was here.

I had no idea where Endicott Street was, of course, but honestly, finding directions to my mother's house would be child's play after everything it had taken to get to this point. I drove along slowly, in a bit of a daze. For a main thoroughfare, First Avenue was not busy, quite sleepy actually. Small, leafy trees lined the wide uneven sidewalks and filled the yards, shading houses that were all a little different from each other, cottages and bungalows and stucco boxes and even a few weathered Victorians. I followed the signs toward the university, thinking it might be the best place to ask for directions.

I cast a glance at Gordon's hands, clenched in his lap. Not a great sign, of course, but not yet an emergency. They were not shaking, he was not clenching and unclenching them, he was not muttering under his breath or talking to people who weren't there. He was simply doing what any person might do when they were tense or nervous.

And why wouldn't he be nervous? He must have known where we were, must have recognized it. They'd lived here together, I was certain of it. It's the only possible explanation for why we'd never come anywhere near here before.

The campus finally came into view. Gordon shook his head. "No," he said under his breath.

"What?"

"No," he repeated, though I had the feeling he wasn't so much talking to me as trying to ward off some malignant force visible only to him. His right leg bounced rapidly up and down. He pounded his fist against the top of his thigh, then reached over to the stereo and hit the eject button with his knuckle, snatching the cassette the instant it popped out of the slot.

"Enough, already!" he said, his voice thick with hatred. "Enough with the bleeps and the bloops and the fucking robots!"

Holding the cassette upside down, he pinched the bottom of it and pulled, unraveling a length of tape from the housing. He yanked out another length of tape, then, with a little jerk of his wrist, threw the cassette right out the open window and into the street.

"Gordon!" I shouted. "What the hell are you *doing?!*"

Instead of answering my question, he folded his arms across his chest and sat silently in his seat, looking straight ahead through the windshield.

I was more exasperated than angry. My first impulse was to pull the van over, retrieve the tape and try to fix it. It was my tape, after all; I wasn't about to let him start wrecking *my* stuff. Then I realized it didn't really matter. My mother would almost certainly have this album in her own music collection, along with all the other Kraftwerk albums and any number of electronic bands I'd never even heard about. Not only that, it wouldn't be on some stupid, outdated technology like a cassette tape, but on a CD or a computer file or something. I decided to shrug off Gordon's childish attempt to hurt me, letting the tape lie where it landed, and drove on.

"Whatever, Gordon," I said, glaring at him and giving him a disapproving shake of the head. I put the incident quickly behind me, and went back to looking instead for someone who could give me directions.

I asked the first person I saw, a student crossing in front of the van while we sat at a four-way stop sign. Pausing in the middle of the crosswalk, he furrowed his brow and thought, looking around sheepishly before shrugging and saying, "Sorry dude, I don't know."

I thanked him anyway and drove on. The heat must have been keeping people inside, because there seemed to be no one about. Then it occurred to me: Gordon might know. Not might, *must*. He had to know.

"Gordon!"

He turned and looked at me, his face a blank.

"What?"

"Where is Endicott Street?"

I could only imagine what kind of creaturely ruse he was devising in order to avoid answering my question. So I was surprised to hear him say, "Up there." He pointed through the window with a thrust of his chin. "Straight ahead. Two blocks, then turn right."

I nodded and drove on, too stunned to say anything. The Vanagon must have driven itself, since my whole body was suddenly overrun with tiny vibrations and I couldn't feel anything; not my hands on the wheel, not my butt in the seat, not my foot on the gas pedal. I came to the intersection of First and Endicott. I rounded the corner, then rolled along slowly, scanning each and every house number until I came, at long last, to the one I was looking for. I pulled to a stop across the street and cut the engine. I drew a deep breath and looked at the house, drinking it all in. 78 Endicott Street. My mother's house.

It wasn't a big house, but it wasn't small either. It was somewhere in between, sort of like a large bungalow, set back from the street on a large, shady lot filled with fruit trees and manicured bushes and little islands of colorful flowers. The wood siding was painted blue-gray, the window and roof trim in cream and faded red. A concrete path ran straight from the sidewalk to the house, cutting through a small crabgrass lawn to an open, wrap-around porch. A broad wooden door, painted in the same faded red as the windows, was set front and center, framed on either side by two large windows. A single large pane of frosted glass was set in the upper half of the door.

It was a nice house. A beautiful house. Tidy. Symmetrical. I liked it immediately. I imagined a version of me growing up here: a small child tottering happily around the yard, a growing boy sequestered in a tree fort in the giant linden on one side of the house, the current me skipping out the front door and down the porch, heading off to the local high school, a homemade lunch tucked carefully inside a backpack full of books.

In every way, this place was my Ithaca.

Well, not in *every* way. For one thing, it's not really possible to return to a home that was never yours. For another, I suppose I'm more like Telemachus then Odysseus, and his journey paled in comparison to that of his father. But if you imagine a version of the Odyssey where Telemachus meets up with his father and accompanies him on his ten-year journey home, or one where he spends his youth searching for news of his mother rather than his father, then you'll understand how I felt.

Gordon felt differently. If anything, this was the opposite of Ithaca for him, the place he was forever avoiding returning to. He refused to cast even the slightest glance at the house, pretending to find the opposite side of the street far more interesting. I could practically smell the turmoil inside of him.

I reached behind his chair and grabbed my backpack. I took a couple deep breaths to steady myself, then pushed down on the lever and opened my door. I slid out of my seat to the ground, slinging my backpack onto my shoulders. It was a wonderful moment, planting my feet on the soil of my new home for the first time.

"I'm not coming with you," Gordon growled, his attention still fixed on the view outside his window.

"Perfect," I replied. "That's great. I don't want you to come anyway."

It was the truth. What could he possibly bring to this reunion but disaster, what else could he do but ruin it?

He did not respond at first. Then, in his best Dr. Zaius voice, he said, "Don't look for it, Taylor. You might not like what you find."

"Not now, Gordon."

I couldn't tell if he was on the way to that other place, or just playing some kind of game. Either way, I didn't need him sabotaging the moment I'd waited for my whole life. What I needed was for him to stay put. I should not have left him, I knew it in my heart, but I was so tired of the burden of him. I wanted to be free of it, even for a few minutes. Just thinking about it made me angry. I scowled at him.

"Stay here Gordon," I commanded. I closed the door, leaving him alone with his thoughts, whatever they might be.

I took a deep breath and walked across the street toward the house. I made it as far as the sidewalk before I hesitated, suddenly filled with doubt. What if she wasn't home? What if she was away on vacation, or on a sabbatical? What if she had a new family, and they were all inside? What if she no longer lived here, in this house, or even this town?

No. That wasn't going to be the case. Somehow, despite the less-than-enjoyable lessons life had been teaching me lately, I knew this would be different. I was not walking into disappointment.

She would be here.

I climbed the concrete steps up to the porch and stood before the front door. The frosted glass was too opaque to see through, and the windows on either side of it were hung with gauzy curtain, so I couldn't make out anything inside. I looked for a doorbell, but didn't find one. I raised my hand and knocked on the door softly. So softly, in fact, that it barely made a sound. I knocked again, hard enough to be heard this time, and waited.

Nothing.

I knocked once more, this time rapping my knuckles on the glass. A couple seconds later, I heard movement inside, the faint sound of shoes walking across a wooden floor. I saw a shadow moving behind the glass, growing larger as it approached. A finger pulled one of the curtains aside, enough for the person inside to see out, but not enough for me to see in.

There was a click, the doorknob turned. The door opened about ten inches, and stopped. I stared dumbly at the face that appeared in the narrow opening, a face I'd imagined and re-imagined ten thousand times. A face I'd painstakingly constructed from hopes, dreams, art books, movies, from the endless examination of my own features. Now that it was right in front of me, however, I found myself unable to focus on it. The color of her eyes, the shape of her mouth, the tone of her skin, whether or not her earlobes were detached, all of the little details that were so essential to my portrait of her escaped me. I was able to comprehend only that her hair was brown and straight and shoulder length, that it was tucked behind large-ish ears (*like mine!*), that it framed an oval-shaped face.

My mute bewilderment had no end, forcing the face to ask, "Yes? Can I help you?"

"Um, yes," I said tentatively, beyond nervous. "Hi. Um, I'm looking for Janice Pembroke?"

She looked at intently me for a second, as if considering how to answer, then said warily, "I'm Janice."

Janice. Her. Mom.

"It's me," I said, breathless. "Sam."

The expression that crossed her then face was not, as I expected, one of surprise or amazement. It wasn't even an expression really. It was more like a shadow, the kind cast by a single small cloud on an otherwise bright sunny day. A shadow of what, I couldn't really say, for as quickly as it had come it was gone. Most likely, I had just imagined it. I mean, I was barely able to focus on her face; how could I expect to read it?

"I know who you are."

"Oh." It sounded stupid, like something a dumb fourteen-year-old would say. But it was all I could manage.

"What are you doing here?"

I was confused. Of all the versions of this conversation I'd played out in my head, none of them started off like this. Instead of making the obvious reply—*It's me, Sam. Your son.*

I'm here, I'm back, I'm ready for you to be in my life, for me to be in yours—I simply said, "I've been looking for you."

She nodded. "Of course."

Of course?

The silence that followed was long and awkward. I wish I could say it wasn't, but it was. I thought back to my meeting with Donald Coleman. That hadn't gotten off to a very good start either. Then, like now, I'd simply appeared out of thin air, popping in completely unannounced. My mother was no doubt just as shocked as he had been. Her neutral response was just her way of processing the initial surprise. I had been preparing for this moment for a long time, I was ready for it. But it must have been a jolt to her. She needed time to catch up to the situation. And the best way to do that, I decided, was by sticking to facts.

"You're my mother," I said.

Her eyes creased, the corners of her mouth turned up. A smile.

"I am your mother," she replied. "And you've been looking for me. And now you've found me."

"Um, yeah. That's right."

"Anything else?"

"I'm sorry?"

"Never mind," she said, shaking her head. "How did you get here?"

"I drove."

"You drove?"

"Um, yeah." I could feel my face turning red. "I drive sometimes. Quite a bit, actually. I mean, I'm not old enough to have a license, but—"

"I know how old you are."

Of course.

"Where are you *driving* from?"

"Riverside."

She nodded in mild surprise. "I see. Is that where you live?"

"No."

"Mmm-hmm. Where *do* you live?"

Something in her tone made me suspect she already knew the answer to that question.

I shrugged.

"Nowhere?"

"It's complicated," I said, surprised at how defensive I sounded.

"I'm sure it is."

Things were not supposed to be going like this. It was all wrong. Clearly, we were both a little bit unprepared for this encounter. That it had gotten off to an awkward start was probably to be expected. We just needed to accept that it was happening and move on to the next stage.

"May I come inside?" I asked politely.

The pause that followed was longer than I would have liked, but didn't dampen the thrill I felt when she stepped aside—when *my mother stepped aside*—and with a simple gesture of her hand invited me into her house.

Into *our* house.

I stepped through the doorway into a large, shaded entry. The air inside was cool, making me realize just how hot it was outside. Apart from the dark wood floors and white-painted walls, I didn't have much of a chance to take note of interior details, as my mother guided me quickly into an adjacent room.

I took advantage of the opportunity to observe her more closely as she led the way, even if it was only from behind. She wore a button-down white-collared shirt, untucked, the sleeves folded neatly up to her elbows. It reminded me of one of Gordon's shirts, but the material was much nicer. It was softer, and flowed in a way that made me think it had been made just for her. Her dark blue linen pants were also loose and flowing, reaching down to just above her ankles. Her leather-strap sandals were simple, but also kind of elegant, their hard soles slapping softly on the floor as she walked. Her arms and feet were tanned, her skin color close to mine. I could now see that her shoulder-length light brown hair was streaked here and there with gray. I could tell, even through her loose-fitting clothes, that she wasn't lean and stringy like Gordon. But she wasn't heavy or soft either. Just normal, I guess. She walked lightly and gracefully.

The room she led me to was spacious and comfortable. The floor was the same dark wood as the entry, though a large blue rug mostly covered it. A long couch, more like a bench with cushions and pillows, was built into the far wall, spanning from one large, curtained window to the other. Two wood and leather chairs—one with arms, the other without—sat directly across from the bench. The space between the chairs and bench was taken up by a large, low coffee table, made of the same dark wood as everything else, its surface bare except for a couple vases of dried flowers. A clean, unused fireplace was set into the far wall, the red brick hearth and façade trimmed with a border of blue ceramic tiles. The dark wood mantle was lined with small framed photographs, mostly of a dog. A German Shepherd by the looks of it, though I couldn't be certain from where I stood. There were no books or other objects I would have expected in the home of a Professor of Anthropology, but I figured those things would be in another room, probably in her study. The house was old, but it felt solid and well made. I had that sense that everything, the house, the moldings, the furniture, the carpets and fabrics, were all part of an organic whole, designed at the same time by the same person. I liked it a lot. I felt comfortable and strangely at peace in it.

"I like your ... I like the house," I said.

"Craftsman," she replied absently.

"Oh, right. How old is it?"

"1920."

"Wow," I said, a little too earnestly.

I let my backpack slide from my shoulder and made for the cushioned bench.

"No. Not there." She motioned to the smaller of the two chairs. "Here. Please."

"Oh. Sorry."

I walked over to the chair and lowered myself into it carefully. I sat upright with the best posture I could muster, backpack on the floor between my feet. She climbed into the larger chair, pulling her right leg up onto it while letting her left dangle over the side. Turning her body slightly to the left so that she was facing me directly, she looked at me with a steady, even gaze.

I couldn't think of a single thing to say. I was so overwhelmed by the fact that I was actually sitting in front of her that it didn't even occur to me to *say* something. I looked into her face eagerly, ready to find the answers to so many questions there. Strange as it might sound, I was still having trouble focusing on her face. Apart from her ears—specifically, her earlobes, which were like mine, I found it impossible to distinguish individual features. It might have had something to do with the fact that I was searching for so many things in it all at once, but I found her face resisting my ability to comprehend. It was beautiful, in a way. That much I knew. It's just, I couldn't say what it was that made it beautiful. The only explanation for it I could come up with was something like balance. I couldn't separate out individual features, I told myself, because none of them stood out from the others. Nothing was too big or too small, or oddly shaped, or weird looking. Everything fit together perfectly. Something about her merged so perfectly with the images of statues and paintings that I had always imagined her onto that I couldn't quite yet sort out the real her. Still, even though we had just met, and despite our admittedly rocky start, I felt at home in her presence. At ease. Safe. Welcome. The way I felt in a new book.

"So," she said, apparently tired of waiting for me to begin. "You've come all the way from Riverside."

I nodded. "Yes."

Little changes in her expression finally allowed me to focus on the different features of her face, like the tiny creases that formed in the corners of her eyes when she narrowed them; sort of like wrinkles, only softer. I waited expectantly for the corners of her mouth to crease as well, for her lips to form the same subtle knowing smile as Gordon's, but they did not. She kept them firmly pressed in a perfectly straight line.

"Why?"

The abruptness of her question caught me a little off guard. Never mind that the answer was obvious, just as it had been when she first answered the door: *It's me, Sam. Your son. I'm here. At long last, I'm here. To be with you, to be together, to make up for lost time, to have the life we're supposed to have.*

"To see you," I said instead, my voice sounding puzzled even to my own ears.

She nodded, holding me in her steady, even gaze for a few seconds. "Why now?"

I have to admit that I found her tone odd. It sounded more like an accusation than a question. I considered the many different ways I could answer her question, deciding to go with the one that felt the most truthful. "Until a few days ago I didn't know where to find you."

Her expression seemed to soften a little. Enough, anyway, to tell me she understood the full implication of that sentence, just as I'd hoped and knew she would. Her eyes—blue eyes, I now saw, not gray like mine—sparkled mischievously. "And you've been looking for me for a long time, have you?"

"Well, I've always thought about it."

"I see. Thinking about looking but not looking."

"No," I admitted. "Not actively."

"Not actively," she repeated, laughing to herself under her breath. "So, when did you begin to *actively* look for me?"

"I don't know," I shrugged. "A couple of weeks ago, I guess."

"And what happened a couple of weeks ago that caused you

to stop thinking about looking and start looking actively?"

I couldn't tell if she was scolding me or just playing with me. "Gordon," I said.

She tensed visibly at the mention of his name.

"*Gordon?*"

"My father. He's out—"

"I *know* who he is."

"I'm sorry. Obviously. Yeah."

She didn't seem to hear me. She looked out one of the windows, her eyebrows (not bushy like mine, but sparse) pulled into a puzzled frown, merging above the bridge of her nose (small and straight like mine, but somehow different). Her lips moved, as if forming silent words. She laughed to herself again, shaking her head and muttering, "Calls him Gordon."

I frowned too, realizing I was just a little bit out to sea. Apparently, getting a conversation to follow the direction you wanted required some sort of special skill, one that I lacked. Once again, the one actually taking place was unfolding quite differently than the one I'd rehearsed in my head.

But I was learning, at least. What I had to do was just step up and take the initiative, get things back on track, then nudge the conversation in the direction I wanted it to go. What we needed, I thought, was to establish our connection, the genetic similarity that practically guaranteed our affinity. I thought of the Kraftwerk tapes. The tapes that Gordon held on to because they were hers, the tapes that were now mine, mine because the music on them was perfectly matched to the way my brain was wired. Wiring I shared with her.

I cleared my throat. "So," I began nonchalantly. "What are your musical tastes?"

She shifted her gaze from the window to me.

"I'm sorry?"

"What kind of music do you like?" I said. "You know, what

are you into? Pop? Classical? *Electronica*, maybe?"

Her frown returned and she tilted her head slightly. Not in the way that Gordon and I do, in order to show thoughtful consideration of something, but in an entirely different way. It felt like an accusation, as if she were putting the blame for her confusion squarely on my shoulders.

"I don't really listen to music," she said.

"I don't understand."

"There's nothing to understand," she said defensively. "I don't really listen to music. I mean, obviously, I *listen* to music. Everybody does. It's just that it doesn't particularly matter to me what it is."

"Not even German minimalist techno?" I asked, utterly perplexed.

"No, not even that. Whatever it is."

Considering the way she was looking at me, I was pretty sure she saw right through my tactics.

"Look, Samuel."

"Sam," I said with a smile, ignoring the fact that my name didn't exactly roll off her tongue. "Call me Sam."

"Look, *Sam*," she said, not finding the shorter version of my name any easier than the full one. "Before this goes any further, there are some things you should know, things that will help you understand your ... your *situation*. Things your father should have told you by now but probably hasn't. Almost certainly hasn't."

I nodded eagerly. This was more like it. I leaned back into the chair, ready for discovery.

"Gordon and I—your father and I—met a long time ago, when we were in college. In graduate school. Six months after we met, we moved in together. A year later, we married in a civil ceremony. Quietly, discreetly. Just the two of us and a Justice of the Peace. His parents had both passed away when he was a teenager—" my jaw dropped visibly at *that* revelation "—and my parents, well, we didn't exactly get along. We took our PhDs the same year. Then we moved here and started working."

I felt a little thrill at that disclosure. It confirmed what I'd always known. "Right. Gordon was a professor too?"

"No," she replied, shaking her head. "No, he wasn't. I was lucky enough get a position in the Anthropology department straight out of graduate school. Sort of unheard of, really. Certainly not the kind of opportunity you pass up. I took the job and we moved up here, even though there was little chance of a position for him."

She paused, looking again through the window, her gaze far away.

"It was unfair, to be honest. He was better than me, in some ways, so great at communicating, at conveying the essence of something."

Great at communicating. I had to shake my head at that one.

"He would have made a great teacher, if he could've just got there, but he didn't have it in him to play the game. It's all he wanted to do, really. Just teach. He didn't want anything to do with the rest of it; the departmental politics, the conferences, the scramble for notoriety. But the timing just wasn't right in his case. There wasn't a whole lot of opportunity in his field. He interviewed at a couple of obscure schools, smaller and even more out of the way than this one. He'd come back, tell me things went well, they liked him but couldn't offer him a position, which I'm pretty sure is not true. There's no way schools like that would pass up the chance to get someone like him. I can only think that he turned them all down. Truth is, he wasn't going to leave, wasn't going to separate from me just to suit his own career goals, not even temporarily. He wasn't ambitious—he didn't have an ambitious bone in his body—he just wanted to apply his talents in a way that people, students, might benefit from. After a couple of years, things changed, I could have gotten him something here, it wouldn't have been a problem. Universities have ways of making things work for spouses who are both academics. Of course, he wouldn't hear of it. He put his own career on hold, waited for something to open up, here at State or one of the nearby Communities, anything. He even applied to Oroville High School. They had no idea what to make of him: *over-qualified* or some other bullshit. I'm sure they didn't think he would be committed, didn't think he'd stay. Which shows how little they knew him. He did a little writing for a friend of mine and a few other places, but it was pointless. There was no real satisfaction in it for him, no sense of earning his keep. Not that he needed to, we got along just fine on my salary. A little goes a long way up here and I make more than a little. Anyway, nothing ever came up. One day I came home to find that he'd taken a job with campus operations and that was that."

"Operations?"

"The Plant," she said. "The physical upkeep of the campus. Maintaining things, repairing them, cleaning up—"

"Cleaning up? What do you mean? Like a—"

"Janitor? Yeah, basically. That's what he did, what he chose to do." She waved the thought of it away with her hand. "He applied himself to his job, got good at it, *great* at it, never told anyone he worked with about his PhD, never let anyone know how god-damned smart he was."

I was finding it a little difficult to keep up, the information was pouring in so fast. It was already over my head, I was drowning in it.

"His PhD?" I whispered. "What was it in?"

"Philosophy," she said absently. "Philosophy of science, materialism, cognition."

I nodded. *Philosophy.* I turned the word over and over in my mind, marveling at it like a rare shell found on a distant seashore.

She went back to staring out of the window, her nose scrunched up as if the memories she was revisiting had a bad smell to them.

"I worried about him at first," she went on. "It had to be killing him. It would have killed me, that's for certain. But he never complained, not once. Somehow, he made it work."

"What happened then?"

"What happened?" she echoed, still staring out into the yard. "Nothing happened. Everything was great, actually. Perfect almost. He accepted it, I accepted it, we made it work. We couldn't have been happier."

She was silent for a while then, and I was too. It was amazing, really. I'd just learned more about her and Gordon in two minutes than I had in a whole lifetime. I needed time to process all it, but I wasn't going to get it.

"Then there was you."

I was too busy struggling to understand what that comment might mean to be worried about it. "Pardon?"

"You've never heard any of this before, have you?"

I shook my head. "No. Gordon doesn't really talk about the past."

"Not a word? About any of it? About me? About *us*?"

"Nothing."

She laughed. A strange laugh, one that sounded simultaneously incredulous and unsurprised.

"Incredible," she said, a sharp edge creeping into her voice. "He breaks the agreement that mattered and honors the one that didn't."

I understood nothing of what was happening.

"*Agreement?*"

She tilted her head to one side and regarded me, her expression softening.

No, that wasn't it, not at all.

Her expression *didn't* soften. Quite the opposite. If anything, it hardened. Only then did I realize that from the moment I told her who I was, she hadn't really looked at me, didn't actually seem interested in me, wasn't searching my face with a hunger for details, the way I studied hers. She'd been going on the whole time as if she were alone, as if I wasn't even there, like an actor in a one-person show. Well, she was looking at me now, and not with fondness. She was appraising me, weighing me against something else. Judging me, as if trying to decide whether or not I deserved more of the story, whether I was worthy of her time. I couldn't shake the sudden suspicion that I'd somehow walked into a trap; one I'd set for myself. In my own eagerness, I hadn't bothered to notice that maybe she was less than happy about me being there. My palms were sweating profusely. I felt the familiar rabbit heartbeat begin pounding away in my chest.

"Yes. We had an agreement," she said, her voice measured. "Your father and I. *Gordon* and I. A belief we shared from the beginning of our relationship, one that was essential to who we were."

Thump, thump, thump.

I was Rabbit, the prey, too afraid to move, unable to pull itself away from the predator's path.

"We agreed that we would never start a family, that we would never have children."

Thump, thump, thump.

"Oh," Rabbit-me said meekly.

"Yeah. *Oh.*"

I actually laughed, so bewildered was I at life's ability to confound me, to produce anything but what I wanted. In order to keep that laugh from turning into tears, I had to focus my entire being on the simple things, like breathing. As if from far away I heard Rabbit ask: "And that was the 'agreement that mattered'?"

Instead of answering me, she simply resumed her cold appraisal, her head tipped to one side in that way that was not Gordon's. She said nothing.

Something in me, a little piece of Gordon, I think, came forward, concerned over what it considered to be a line of faulty reasoning.

"I don't understand. You said Gordon broke your agreement. But it sounds to me like the kind of agreement ... like the kind of thing two people have to *agree* to break. I mean, how can you have a child—how could you have me—if both of you didn't agree to it? If *you* didn't agree to it?"

It was an honest question, one I hoped didn't sound like an accusation. The last thing I wanted to do was upset or anger her. She didn't seem angry, just kind of tired. Her shoulders sagged a little and she closed her eyes.

"Fine," she said, apparently conceding my point. "But that doesn't change the fact that the only reason I had you was because your father wanted it, because of the pressure he put on me to—"

Something about that didn't sound right to me. "Gordon pressured you to break your agreement?" I interrupted.

That question did seem to bother her.

"No," she said, scowling slightly. "Not directly, not in a way someone like you—someone *your age*—would understand."

She composed herself, gracing me with a thin smile. "It's complicated. You have to understand him, what he's like."

Understand him. I decided to let that one pass.

"The thing about him was, he never compromised, on anything. It wasn't that he was difficult, that he refused to compromise. It's more like the possibility of it just never occurred to him, didn't exist for him. He did things the way he knew they should be done, end of story. It was all so natural, the way he thought about things, the way he did things, it always seemed like he did the right thing, even if it wasn't always easy, even if there were consequences for him."

"The harder thing," I murmured.

She snorted softly. "Is that what he calls it?" She shook her head slowly, turning the idea over in her mind.

"The truth is," she continued, "he never complained about what had happened, the fact that he'd sacrificed his aspirations for us, for me. He never seemed to resent me, or the fact that things had worked out perfectly for me. He just quietly accepted the situation for what it was—what he *thought* it was. He did his job, better than it needed to be done, to him that was just the way you did things. It was a trap really. On the one hand, he hadn't compromised us, our marriage, putting aside his own goals so that we wouldn't have to be apart. On the other, he'd actually compromised everything about himself, on an individual level. What he was, what he needed. The compromise was so complete, so deep, he got lost in it."

I struggled to make sense of what she was saying. I had a thousand questions to ask her, but I held them all back. I decided to let her go on, even though I had no idea where she would end up, even though I knew I didn't really want to hear it.

"So, no. He did not pressure me. In fact, he only brought the idea up once. He backtracked immediately of course, made it sound like he was just joking. But it was all he needed to do and he knew it. *He* might have accepted the situation for what it was. *He* might have been at peace with it. But *I* felt incredibly guilty about it, just as he knew I would. And that guilt weakened me. I felt like I owed it to him, like I owed him something. So I gave in, and we got pregnant. With you."

A shiver ran through her then, at the memory of things she clearly hadn't spoken of—hadn't *thought* of—for a long time. She was shaking slightly as she stared out the window, looking into the past.

"It was obvious right away that it was what he truly wanted. From the moment he found out, all during the pregnancy, when you were born, he was happier than I'd ever seen him."

"And you?" The question came out on its own. It probably would have been better not to ask it, but I couldn't hold it back.

She looked at me, staring so hard into my eyes that I had to look down at my knees.

"Me? *I* regretted it almost immediately. The thought that doing the very thing we'd agreed not to do made him so happy, gave him something he needed, something he couldn't get from me, I resented that."

She paused, frowning and biting at her lip.

"That resentment, and the feeling that I'd made a terrible mistake, grew with time, right along with you. You came and nothing changed. There was a brief moment, in the afterglow of the days just after you were born, when I thought I could do it, when I was able to share in his happiness."

A brief moment. My rapidly evolving understanding of life now leaned towards it being a kind of giant, invisible hand, one that enjoys closing itself around people's internal organs. At that moment it seemed to be having fun with my stomach. I breathed with difficulty, through an open mouth.

"But it didn't last," she went on. "As soon as the possibility that the whole thing might somehow actually work opened up, it closed again, the glow faded, and I knew I couldn't do it."

The whole thing. Couldn't do it.

"I kept waiting, hoping, thinking that I just needed time, maybe I would grow into it. Months went by, a year, and I didn't feel any differently. It was awful, hating myself for not being able to feel like I wanted you, my own child. But I didn't. It was a fact, a cold, hard, undeniable fact. It was the truth and there was no way around it. The fact that he—your father, Gordon—was happy as a clam only made things worse. It was like some kind of switch flipped on in him when you came along. He changed from the person I knew, the person I loved, the person who loved me, into something different. He was a father, and that was all that mattered to him. Nothing else. The sudden difference in us—him with his happiness, his contentment, me with my anger and resentment—put a gap between us, one that couldn't be closed."

I did not want to ask the next question, knew I didn't want to hear the answer, but I wasn't able to stop it.

"What happened then?" I whispered.

Her answer was simple and final: "It didn't work."

Didn't work.

Out to sea again, Rabbit adrift in a little wooden box, nothing but gray foamy waves as far as the eye could see.

In military history books, there are always situations when a famous general has to withdraw from the field of battle, to accept that he has been temporarily beaten, in order to save what remains. Living to fight another day: It's how famous generals got to be famous. This was *my* moment. I had barged into the fray, unprepared for any outcome except the one I had dreamed up in my head. It was no longer a question of getting things back on track. I needed to withdraw while I still had the chance. Apologize for appearing out-of-the-blue, excuse myself, let the reality of it sink in, give her some time to process it, ask only that she allow me to come back, maybe tomorrow, maybe next week.

But that's not what I did. Instead, I heard Rabbit venture timidly, "What was the *other* agreement? The one that didn't matter?"

She glared openly at me. At some level, I understood that I had opened old wounds, brought back memories she didn't want to think about, painful things she hadn't thought about for a long time. That I had done it unwittingly, innocently, didn't change the fact that I'd done it.

"Our agreement about you," she said coolly. "The agreement that Gordon would leave, with you, that you were *his*. That he could take you wherever he wanted, raise you as he saw fit. That he was never to bring you here, to see me, that it would be best if he never spoke to you about me at all, that you didn't need to know."

"And that agreement didn't matter?" I barely heard my own question, so loud was the roaring in my ears.

She shook her head.

"Not the last part. All I really wanted from him was a promise that he would keep you away from me, that he would raise you in such a way that you wouldn't bother to come looking for me."

My insides fluttered wildly, painfully, as if something trapped in my body was desperate to find a way out.

"What did Gordon get out if it?" Rabbit asked.

"Money."

"Money?"

"Yes, *money*. One thousand dollars a month, wired automatically to his bank account until you reach the age of eighteen. A thousand dollars a month, for your material needs and my peace of mind."

Half of me sat there staring blankly at her, trying to make sense of what she was saying. The other half was thinking about Gordon, sitting in the sweltering van, clutching desperately to his disintegrating world like a beggar to the brim of his hat. I was hit by a full understanding of the scope of what he'd done, what it had cost him to be my father.

And there he was, out in the van, losing his very being.

"I don't understand," I said. "You're my mother."

"No, I'm not. I'm sorry. I'm sure you probably don't believe that, but it's true. I could sit here for hours trying to explain it to you, exactly why I feel the way I do, why I've *always* felt the way I do, but it won't change anything for either of us, it won't make a difference. I gave birth to you, but I'm not your mother. I have never been your mother. I understand that you must hate me for saying that, must wonder how I can possibly say it, but it's the truth. I'm sorry, I don't know what else to say, except I never wanted to be sitting here doing this."

"Right." I said, nodding vacantly. "That's what the thousand dollars a month is for."

I thought she might get mad at that, tell me off, but she just smiled at me instead. A weak smile, admittedly, but still a smile. A half-hearted attempt to keep an uncomfortable situation from getting worse.

My mind buzzed frantically during the long, awkward silence that followed, turning its useless circles once again, desperately searching for some miracle that would fix this mess. I realized I had one last card to play, one final appeal to make. Leaning back in my chair, I reached into my backpack and pulled out the cigar box. I held it out in the space between us.

"What about this? Why would you give this to me, why would you want me to have this, if I wasn't supposed to think about you, if I wasn't supposed to search for you?"

She recoiled slightly, a puzzled expression on her face. She shook her head as if to say, *I don't know what that is.*

I opened the box and took out the compass. I held it out for her to see.

"You wanted me to have this. Why? Why would you give this to me if you didn't want me to think about you, if you didn't want me to find you?"

"I don't know what you're talking about," she said. "That is not mine, it didn't come from me. I've never seen any of that stuff before."

How could life possibly be like this? How did people get through it, how did they manage to deal with it long enough to get old? Oh, to go back in time, to the moment before I rang her doorbell, before I knew where she lived, before any of this started. Back to when it was just Gordon and me, when the world was *my* world. Sitting in a library reading, hiking somewhere, driving through a mountain pass, innocent and happy, not knowing anything, not wanting to know anything.

The expression on my face must have been pretty awful, because she finally looked at me with something like sympathy. She leaned in toward me. "Are you okay?"

I closed my hand over the compass and waved it in front of me in an effort to indicate that I was fine. Even though I wasn't fine; I was suffocating. I needed to get out of there and into the open, where I could breathe again. But Rabbit wasn't finished. "Who is Kai?" it whispered.

In an instant, the look of sympathy fell from her face. Her eyes left mine and went automatically to the fireplace, to the framed photographs on the mantel.

"How do you know about Kai?" she demanded.

I shrugged, as if to say, *how does anyone know about anything?*

Her eyes fixed on the mantel, she said, "Kai was our dog. Not just any dog. Kai was special, very special, something you wouldn't—" She spun around to face me, her eyes full of rage. "Gordon and Kai and me. We were *already* a family, you see. That's how it was, that's what made us happy. And that's how we agreed things were supposed to stay. Just the *three* of us. But you came, and things were hard, on all of us."

She was shaking a little, and her voice trembled. "One day

Kai … it was nothing, just a scratch, a tiny little scratch. An accident. Gordon—*your father*—and Kai went for a drive. They were gone all afternoon, and when he came back—" she had to whisper it, "when he came back, he was alone."

Well, at least the disaster was complete. Kai, the specter haunting Gordon's noble, crumbling mind, the symbol of his regret, was a dog.

A fucking dog.

For whatever strange reason—I don't think I'll ever really understand why—I smiled.

I wanted away, to be anywhere but there, but Rabbit had one final question. With a kind of serene calm that comes from surrendering to the chopping block, it asked: "Do you regret it?"

I was fully prepared for the *yes* or the *no*; either answer would do. But neither came. She said nothing. She didn't move, she didn't breathe. She just stared at me, boring into me with those piercing blue eyes for what seemed an eternity. And then her face, her full face, snapped into focus, and I could see that I'd been right to imagine it as the face of a Greek goddess all these years. It *was* beautiful, but also terrible, stern and cold and full of anger.

Finally, she moved. Standing up from her chair, she loomed over me. "Things were perfect here," the terrible, beautiful goddess thundered. "Our life together was perfect. That life fell apart and I was left here, alone, with no one. There was no one else, no one but me to put my life back together, back the way I liked it. And I did, a long time ago. And now you're here all over again and it's not going to happen, I'm not going to let it happen again, and you need to leave! Now! Please."

I need to leave.

Even before she hurled those words at me I was already thinking it, I wanted only to be out of there. One hand still clutching the compass, I shoved the cigar box into the backpack with the other and zipped it up. I stood up unsteadily and slung it onto my back. There was a sound of crashing waves in my ears and everything was dark, except for a narrow path of light leading to the door. I mumbled an absurd "Thank you" and shuffled with single-minded purpose toward the door, drawn to it like one of those near-death people to their portal of light. It opened as if by magic when I reached it, though I knew this was just Janice Pembroke opening it for me in order to speed up my departure. I'm not sure if we said goodbye to each other or not. I only know that I thought it odd, as I floated across the threshold, passing from the dark interior to the white-hot shimmer of a summer afternoon, that she hadn't once asked how Gordon was.

I stood on the porch with my back to the door. The hot air wrapped itself around me eagerly, as if excited at my return. It was absolutely still outside, absolutely quiet, there was no sound apart from the soft click of the door as it closed behind me. Like Lot on the plain of Jordan, I resisted the temptation to turn around, to look over my shoulder. I'll never know whether she stood behind the door for a while, looking out at me through the curtain, or whether she just went back to whatever she was doing before I arrived. I was not surprised to find that I didn't care one way or the other. I was too numb to care. I walked carefully to the edge of the porch, like a nervous hiker hugging a narrow path on the side of a cliff. I sat down tentatively, my feet perched on the bottom step, backpack wedged between my knees.

A single bird called out, whistling the same note over and over. It was soon joined by others, chirping and whistling and chattering all at once, as if the most important thing in life, the only thing that mattered, was talking. Not listening, never listening, just talking, shouting, constantly and as loudly as possible. Thousands of insects answered the call, adding their buzzing and clicking and metallic screeching to the chorus. There were a few seconds where it actually sounded like music, like some kind of natural symphony, before descending rapidly into an oppressive, continuous drone, a song of heat and hopelessness, pressing in on me from all sides.

Nothing about what had just happened seemed real; the house at my back, the woman inside it who was supposed to be my mother, the impossible-to-comprehend history that had been related to me. None of it was real. Maybe it was just a little too much for me to process properly, maybe it had all happened too quickly, maybe I was in some kind of shock, but I could hardly remember anything of what had just taken place, could not call a single concrete detail to mind, even though it had happened (*hadn't it?*) just minutes, seconds ago.

I realized that it didn't seem real because it wasn't real. Not in any way that mattered. Sure, the house was real. I was sitting on its porch after all. But it wasn't real for me; it wasn't my reality. Little by little, I understood, I had convinced myself that the life Gordon and I lived, the road we traveled, was somehow less real than that of so-called normal people, sold myself on the idea that the world I'd always lived in, the only reality I'd ever known, the one that had always been good enough for me, was not as real as the stuff going on around me, stuff I'd never really cared about. Just because things in my world—in our world—had gotten a little tough, just because I started doubting, I decided it needed to be abandoned, exchanged for a better one where everything hard would be taken care of, where *someone else* would take care of it. But that wasn't the way things really were; that's not how our reality worked. In our world, there was no one else to fix things. Was that really so bad? So we had to take care of things ourselves, so what? It was a fact, why run away from it? I was almost able to convince myself that the disaster I'd just experienced didn't really happen. Not to me. It happened to a *version* of me, one I'd dreamed up, one that wasn't real.

What about the real me then, the one sitting on the porch beneath the afternoon sun, listening to nature screaming its head off? Well, that me—the real me—was having the strange sensation of floating and sinking at the same time.

I was getting pretty used to the sinking. I'd been doing a lot of it lately, after all. But the floating was something new. I imagined myself as a completely hollow object, like a melon that's had its insides scooped out but is still whole on the outside. I was hollow, but I wasn't *empty*. It was almost like part of me—the part that was most truly me—was trapped inside another part of me, the scooped-out melon of my body.

And then I understood that what people call the soul, that strange thing that is not a thing, does indeed exist. It turns out that the soul is not some other thing, something different from the body and existing apart from it. It's not part of the body either, not a product of it like breath or saliva or even thought. I don't know how to explain it, but it was pretty clear to me that even though body and soul are not two different things, they're not exactly one and the same thing either. The soul is the part of us that knows what life is supposed to be: a rising, a floating, a joy. The rub is reality, the thing people make of the world with their choices and decisions. Reality keeps life from being what it's meant to be, turns it into something else; into a kind of strangling thing, a lead balloon that traps the soul and sinks it.

Which is what happened to me.

I sank.

Determined by the choices of others—choices older and more powerful than me—I sank right through the porch, through the earth on which it was built, through the murk. I drifted slowly down, into the dark. I gave in completely, I did not fight against the sinking in any way, did nothing at all to speed up or delay the moment when my feet would come to rest on the prehistoric sea bed far below.

I had no way of telling up from down, no real sense of the passage of time, so I can't say exactly when it was that I stopped sinking and began rising, how long it took me to pop up onto the surface of things again, into myself, body and soul, sitting on the porch. I only know that at some point I became aware of something tugging me upward by the hand, something light and sharp. It was almost like the buoyancy of another soul had been added to my own. It wasn't much, just enough for me to rise, to float, to feel a speck of joy. Which was enough.

I opened my eyes. The birds and insects had finished their piece and everything was once again quiet. A lone sparrow was sizing me up from the low-hanging branch of a small juniper a few feet away, trying to decide whether or not to make a dash for a seed lying on the ground halfway between us. Guessing correctly that I posed no real threat, it hopped forward quickly, picked up the seed, shelled it, ate the nut inside and flew off to another bush. I smiled at it, a little jealous. I looked down at my balled up hand, curious to see what it was that had pulled me back. I opened my hand and there, sitting in the middle of my palm, was the compass.

My compass, the one Gordon gave me. Just like everything else in the box, it turns out. Just like everything else in my life. In an instant, I understood everything he had done, and why he had done it. Because it had to be done. The harder thing. Which, I now understood, was not always the better thing, or the right thing, or even the smarter thing.

I understood, too, that the harder thing doesn't always have to be so hard, that it's a lot easier if two people do it together. Which is how things will have to be for Gordon and me from now on. For whatever time we have left together, we'll do the harder thing together. It's the only way, really. There's just too much we have to do, too much we have to figure out. We have to do it together, as partners. *Together.*

What more does anyone need from life, what more can anyone hope for? The basic necessities obviously; food, clothing, shelter. Safety, I think. A sense of security, knowing someone has your back. To be known, understood, accepted for who you are. For someone to see and acknowledge the things you do and remember them. A witness, I guess. I've always had all that, I still have it. Now it's time for me to become it.

I leaned forward and opened the backpack, slipping the compass into the cigar box. Pushing the box to one side, I took out my pen and my notebook, flipping through it until I came to the shortest list. I uncapped the pen and, with a single firm line, crossed out the word *Mom*. I thought about tearing the page out, crumpling it up and maybe eating it, but decided to leave it right where it was. I turned to the next page, which was blank, and started on a new list: *Things To Do*. The harder thing takes planning, after all. I chewed on the end of my pen for a moment, and wrote: *Return to Riverside,* followed by, *See Dr. Moser* and, *Learn to like tea. Go to school. Prepare for the future.* I chewed on the pen a little more, then wrote, *Let Gordon know he's loved. Every day.* It was all I could think of for the time being. Which was fine.

I stowed the notebook and pen away. I stood up straight and tall, wanting to seem resolute in case anyone happened to be watching. Slipping my backpack onto my shoulders, I skipped lightly off the porch and made my way to the van, taking the longer route down the paved walkway instead of cutting across the lawn. I could not help picturing Gordon making the same walk, all those years ago, a small child in his arms. Down the walk and across the street to the van, strapping me into a child seat and driving off into a life full of unknowns, nothing to guide him but the strength of his mind and his love for his son.

For the first time in a long time, I felt like a kid. Not like a child, but like the fourteen-year-old I am, good at some things, not so good at others. A kind of Odysseus after all. Like him, I had returned at the end of a long ordeal. Not to my family, to my kingdom, but to myself. I felt free and light, giddy almost. The smile produced by that giddiness was still on my face when I got back to the van and found it empty.

Gordon was gone.

It was like the review for a surreal Broadway musical: I laughed, I cried, I gurgled. I pounded my fist into my palm, then into my forehead. I stood next to the van, arms rigid against my sides, hands clenched as tightly as possible. I tilted my head back as far as it would go, staring angrily into the endless blue. I opened my mouth, preparing to scream my lungs out, to let loose a primal howl, a challenge to the gods that would purge all the frustration and hurt and anger that had built up over the course of my so-called short life.

But nothing came.

No deafening roar, no beastly bellow, no cry of fury. Just me standing there like an idiot, mouth open to the sky, gasping like a goldfish that's flopped out of its bowl. I managed only a defeated sigh, the air leaving my lungs not in a mad angry rush but with a sorry whimper.

I lowered my head, closing my eyes tight and pressing my thumbs against the lids, more angry with myself then anything, unable to shake the feeling that this time I'd lost him for good. The heat, the time of day, the emotional impact of being here, in this place, the fact that he was already starting to slip when I went into the house. What did I think was going to happen?

The pressure against my eyes gave rise to a kind of alternate universe, one filled with wavering fields of little red stars, dense clouds of blue and green gas, distant swirling galaxies of the purest white. For a moment, I had the happy illusion of traveling through this other universe. Not in a ship or spacesuit or anything like that. Just me, the innermost part of me, impervious to the cold and the radiation and the lack of oxygen, cruising along wherever I wanted, at whatever speed I wanted. I would have happily lost myself in that place, stayed there forever. If it existed. But it didn't, it wasn't real. It was an illusion, one that only seemed to be there because I happened to be standing in the middle of the street, pressing my thumbs into my eyeballs. The voice of Charlton Heston rang in my ears, taunting me: *There is only one reality left.*

Reluctantly, I open my eyes. The busy, brightly colored universe beneath my eyelids carries on for a few seconds, and then fades away, unable to compete with the stronger, harsher light of the real world.

That world returns at its own leisurely pace, the way all smug, powerful things do, locking slowly but inevitably back into focus. When it does, I find myself laughing: there is Gordon, walking down the street toward me. Gordon, with his great salt-and-pepper lion's head, striding along in his trusty work boots and his last clean pair of khakis and his last clean white-collared shirt.

The man who is like a world. My father.

He doesn't see me at first; he's busy tinkering with something. As he gets closer, I can see that it's the cassette he so recently chucked out the window. He's holding it in the palm of his left hand while winding the loose tape back into it with the pinkie of his right. He's still working at it, completely absorbed in the task, when he reaches the van. When he does look up, he doesn't seem the least bit surprised to see me standing in front of him. He pauses, searching my face intently, no doubt reading the entire story of my *joyous reunion* there. He shakes his head sorrowfully, but says nothing. He finishes winding the tape, then holds it out to me like a peace offering.

"I'm sorry, Sam."

"It's okay, Gordon," I shrug. "It's just a piece of plastic."

"I'm not talking about the tape, Sam. I'm talking about all of it. I'm sorry for ... for everything. I'm tired of saying it, of *having* to say it, but it's true. I'm sorry for what I've done, the way I've done it, the decisions I've made. It's all been so unfair to you. I know that, I've always known it, I just ... in the beginning I was so focused on just taking care of you, on keeping our heads above water, I ... I was so unprepared for what happened, I mean, I never really thought she'd actually stick to her guns. I was so caught out, so unprepared at first that it was just a question of getting on, day by day, there was no time to sort and plan and then the day-by-day become the-way-things-were and I just let things stay like that because it was easier, somehow. It was a routine, a way of life."

I can't help smiling at him.

"I don't know what's fair and what's not, Gordon. I really don't. As for easier ... I kind of have to disagree with you on that. The thing is, I don't regret a single day of my life. Well, except for today, maybe. But it can't be like that anymore. We can't do it the way we've always done it. You can't do it anymore, and I can't do it for you, that's obvious. We have to do the rest differently. We have to do it together. Right?"

Instead of replying, he throws his arms around me, pulling me in close to him, holding me tight. I do the same to him. I don't want it to end, it can go on forever, as far as I'm concerned. It's all I need. All anyone needs. He lets go, places his hands on my shoulders, holds me at arm's length. There is sadness in his eyes, and regret, but also pride. And hope, I think.

"How about I drive for a while?" he suggests with a smile.

"Are you okay?" I ask. "I mean ... earlier ... you didn't seem so ... you didn't seem okay."

"I'm fine, Sam. I'm fine. I don't know what happened. It was uncanny, really. I felt myself going under, I could feel it happening, but something stopped it. Something pulled me back. I can't explain it. I'm fine."

"Okay," I say. "That would be great. You driving, I mean."

I reach into my pocket and pull out the keys, drop them into his palm, glad to be relieved of their weight.

We hop into the van and strap ourselves into our seats. Gordon puts the key in the ignition and starts the engine. Before he pulls away from the curb, I reach across and put a hand on his shoulder.

"Thank you, Gordon," I say quietly. "For *everything*."

He nods. A pool of water gathers in his right eye, sparkling like a liquid diamond before falling into his lap.

"Telegram Sam," he whispers, wiping his eye with his thumb and shaking his head, as if at the wonder of it.

I laugh at the sound of my old nickname, and he laughs too. We're still laughing, laughing just for the sake of laughing, laughing for no other reason than the pure joy of it, when he throws the van into gear and pulls into the street.

"Where to?" he asks.

"Riverside," I say, without moment's hesitation. "It's the best bet, I think. For both of us. We have people there. What do you think?"

"We have people?" He chews at the corner of his mouth for a second then nods. "I think you're right," he says sagely. "I think you might be right."

Instead of turning left on First Avenue and retracing our path through town, Gordon turns right. Whatever. The route is his call. I'm just happy to leave the driving and decision making to him. I slap the salvaged *Radio-Activity* cassette in the deck and push PLAY. There's no sound at first. Five seconds go by, ten, still nothing. Then, after fifteen seconds or so, sound can be heard through the speakers. Not Kraftwerk, though. Something different, something alien. Like a camel eating a lettuce sandwich. Underwater. It's not half bad, actually. But it's not Kraftwerk. I fast-forward the tape, checking the sound periodically, but pretty much everything seems to have been munched.

Gordon winces. "Jesus," he says. "Sorry about that."

I repeat my line about it being just a piece of plastic, tell him it's not a big deal. And it's not. I'm sure we can find another copy somewhere. Even if we don't, I've got five other Kraftwerk tapes to listen to.

Gordon winds his way through town, seemingly at random. I begin to wonder if he might have gotten himself lost when he pulls into the parking lot of a wrap/smoothie restaurant. He pulls a twenty from the Shadowfax case and disappears into the restaurant, while I continue my search and rescue operation on the tape.

The Kraftwerk tapes. That's one mystery solved at least: not my mother's tapes at all. Nothing but dupe fodder the whole time. Well, not the whole time. At some point, I took a shine to them, and Gordon let them become mine. Simple as that. The thought brings a smile to my face.

I'm still smiling when he returns, a purply-blue smoothie in each hand. He climbs back into the van and hands one to me, placing the other in the driver's side cup-cozy.

"Strawberry-Beet-Guava," he says proudly. "With wheatgrass and extract of ginger."

I nod skeptically before taking an exploratory tug on my straw. I let the strange combination slide over my tongue to the back of my throat and down my esophagus, find myself pleasantly surprised, instantly cool, calm, at peace.

A couple nifty shortcuts later and we're back on the interstate. Gordon soon has the Vanagon humming happily along in a way I can never quite manage. It's understandable. He's a better driver than me, of course. More than that, though, he just has a bond with this vehicle, a real symbiotic kind of thing.

A few miles beyond the Chico city limits, I come across an ungarbled stretch of tape. The last track on side B: "Ohm Sweet Ohm." Perfect. My favorite song on the whole album.

The tune unfolds in its measured, unhurried way, building gradually, gaining in momentum and rhythm and complexity as it goes along. Chico is a distant memory by the time it hits full stride, morphing from a collection of simplistic sounds and slow, plodding drumbeats into an upbeat, catchy, slightly corny tune. As if on cue, or maybe through some sort of father/son telepathy, our arms slip simultaneously out of our open windows, fingers pointed forward, hands slicing through the hot summer air like supersonic airplanes. I look over at Gordon, hot wind buffeting his beard and shaggy head of hair and the rolled-up shirt sleeve, his eyes focused in that familiar way on the road ahead. He bobs his head in time with the beat, and I can't help feeling that, maybe for the first time, he's genuinely enjoying this music. My music. And then I understand that, for the moment at least, I don't have to worry about the soul of this man.

How long will the moment last? Who knows? And what difference would knowing make? Take it from me, knowing the facts doesn't change who you really are, doesn't change what your soul already knows.

We are here and it is now.

*In memory of
John Chervinsky, Felisha Foster,
and Jim Allspaugh*